*Dedication*

*To Jim and Roxann, the best family anyone could ask for.*
*Your love and support means the world to me.*
*All my love.*

# A Matter of Choice

*by Laura Landon*

This is a work of fiction. Names, characters, places, and incidents either
are the product of the author's imagination or are used fictitiously. Any
resemblance to actual persons living or dead is entirely coincidental.

A MATTER OF CHOICE
Copyright © 2011 by Laura Landon
First print edition
ISBN 978-1-937216-09-2

Cover design by Prairie Muse utilizing selected photos from
© Seprimoris | © Malyugin | Dreamstime.com
www.prairiemuse.com

# Chapter 1

Joshua Camden, ninth Marquess of Montfort, saw her in the distance, and smiled.

Even though she stood with her back to him, his gut tightened when her fiery copper hair glistened. The unique coloring was like a magnet that drew him to her. She was truly a vision of loveliness: her small, lithe body waiting to be held, the smooth, creamy skin of her shoulders bared in anticipation of his touch, her long, graceful neck begging to be kissed.

She was almost hidden in the shadowy darkness off the stone pathway in a far off corner of the garden. There wasn't a doubt why she was here. Why she'd chosen this secluded spot for their rendezvous.

The clouds chose that exact moment to let the moonlight wash over her. His body reacted with alarming desperation and he hastened his steps.

He was glad she was so lost in thought she didn't hear him approach. He wanted to take her by surprise, to hold her willing body in his arms, touch her supple flesh in the palms of his hands, taste her lips. No matter what the *ton's* expectations were, he had no plans of marrying anytime soon. He'd take his pleasures where and when he wanted. And right now he wanted the willing widow, Lady Paxton. The message she'd sent him couldn't have been clearer. She was available. No strings attached. No strings expected. Exactly the way Joshua wanted it.

The moon slid behind a cloud, shielding the two of them in the shadows. It was perfect. In one swift movement, he stepped up behind her. He deftly wrapped one arm around her waist while the other hand skimmed her torso, over the smooth satin of her gown. When he felt the swell of her breast, he moved his fingers inward. He cupped one breast, letting its heaviness rest in the palm of his hand. Her gasp of surprise made him smile.

The feel of her was perfection.

With a sigh of satisfaction, he lowered his head and kissed her neck. The clean scent of lilacs and roses and other intoxicating smells he couldn't name wafted across his senses and he moaned in pleasure.

"You are even lovelier than I remembered," he muttered against her soft flesh. "I've been dreaming of this all night."

He felt the sharp intake of her breath, heard her cry of surprise, and felt her move within his grasp. He steadied her as she struggled and let his hands span her narrow waist. Then she twisted out of his arms to face him.

His mind barely had time to register that the woman he held was not Lady Paxton before her hand swung forward and connected with his cheek. The blow she delivered was hard enough to snap his head to the side. The shock of what he'd done calamitous enough to send his senses reeling.

❧

"Bloody hell," he muttered, staring at her in shocked disbelief. "You're not..."

"I most certainly...am...not!"

Lady Allison Townsend glared at the man who'd manhandled her with an anger so intense she saw red. Recognition dawned and she glared at the Marquess of Montfort as disgust oozed from every pore of her body. With her lips clamped tight and her fists anchored on her hips, she raised her shoulders in battle-ready preparedness. When she was sure she had Montfort's full attention, she countered his step backward and began to verbally flay him within an inch of his rakish hide.

"How dare you," she hissed, straightening her already ramrod stiff spine even further.

He lifted his hand and rubbed his jaw. She hoped she'd hurt him.

"My abject apologies, my lady. I thought you were...I mean, I thought—"

She listened to him stutter like a schoolboy desperate to invent an excuse for his behavior, then stop as if he realized he could hardly reveal the woman for whom she'd been mistaken.

"There is no point in making excuses, my lord. Your reputation as a rake and a scoundrel is widely known. Every female old enough to attend her first ball has been warned about you."

He arched his brows. "Really?"

If what he'd done flustered him at all, his embarrassment only lasted a moment. Then he smiled.

Her temper raged hotter when she saw the wicked grin on his face. "You are despicable," she hissed. "Is it normal for you to accost unsuspecting women and throw your unwelcome attentions upon them?"

He thought barely a moment. "To be honest, most women don't find my attentions unwelcome."

She sucked in a breath teeming with fury. Before her stood a perfect example of the kind of man she'd always detested. Men like the Marquess of Montfort were the reason she refused to marry, the reason she would never trust her heart again.

She gave him as cold a glare as possible in the darkness. To her frustration, he ignored her and struck a casual pose that caused her heart to beat faster. She hated that he was so handsome. Hated even more that the feel of his hands on her body caused her blood to boil. But most of all, she hated that his smile caused molten lava to seep through her veins.

She took a step backwards, stopping when the trunk of a large tree kept her from separating herself further from him. She pitied the poor women who were so weak that they succumbed to his charm and good looks.

"I admit," he continued, "that I made a mistake..."

He stepped closer and anchored his hand against the tree. He was close. Too close. She ducked beneath his outstretched arm, needing to put space between them.

"...and I offer my most sincere apology." He bowed most graciously.

She was almost ready to overlook what he'd done until he lifted his head. There was a broad smile on his face. A smile as alluring and confident as any she'd ever seen. A smile she was sure he'd used on countless women.

"But I cannot lie," he lifted her gloved hand in his, "and say I didn't enjoy myself. You are a very beautiful woman. But doubtless you've been told that numerous times."

Allison pulled her hand out of his grasp. "You are disgusting," she said with a renewed flare of her temper. "You are a rogue of the worst kind. So confident of your good looks and charm that you think every woman will submit to your overtures."

He shrugged his shoulders as if her rejection was inconsequential. "I don't usually have problems in that area," he admitted, his mouth widening to a breathtaking grin. "We all have to make use of the advantages with which we were born."

"How conceited. I'm sure you think your title and your looks are all you need to have every door opened to you. That with only those two attributes, every woman in London will clamor to be your wife."

His smile wavered. His eyebrows shot upward. "What makes you think I'm searching for a wife?"

Allison studied his features. A deep frown now covered his forehead. "Perhaps that's not your goal right at this moment, but the day will come when you will need an heir. A *legitimate* heir. Then you will look for a wife. And heaven help the poor, unsuspecting female who will be required to sacrifice her happiness when she marries you."

"I hate to disappoint you, my lady. But as to your first accusation, I have not made it a practice to leave illegitimate offspring scattered throughout England."

Allison had the good grace to feel her cheeks warm at his blunt words. She prayed he couldn't notice in the dark.

"As to the second, why are you so sure being married to me would be such a trial?"

"Because there isn't a woman alive who doesn't want to be proud to take her husband's name and walk through Society with her head held high."

"And you think that would be impossible for the woman who married me?"

"It would if that woman were naïve enough to let love and fidelity be important to her."

"Love?" He laughed. "Don't tell me you're one of those romantic ninnies who believes in love?"

Of course she wasn't, but she wasn't about to admit that to him.

He continued. "Name me one couple of the *ton* who married for love and remained in that unpleasant state for long."

She couldn't. And it made her even more furious that he knew she couldn't. "I suppose you consider fidelity just as impossible," she chided, her temper flaring.

He laughed. "Why would anyone eat the fruit from just one tree in an orchard when there are dozens of trees that offer delicacies just as enticing?"

Allison fisted her hands at her side to keep from striking him again. The Marquess of Montfort was proving to be everything she despised in a man.

"But don't feel too sorry for all the wives in London," he said. "A woman always gains far more from a marriage than does her husband."

His voice contained a great amount of confidence which infuriated her even more. She was suddenly incensed. "Oh, pray tell. What would a woman gain from marriage to you?"

"Everything. She would be well cared for, as well as clothed and housed extravagantly. And, she would eventually bear the title, Duchess of Ashbury."

Allison nearly choked. "What more could any woman desire?" She made sure her voice dripped with sarcasm.

"I somehow doubt you mean that as a compliment."

"I most certainly do not. Are fancy gowns and a title all you think a woman wants from a marriage?"

"Of course. Every woman I know is desperate to find a husband who will provide for her every need. Every female here tonight is evaluating this year's crop of eligible men, then ranking them according to their ability to provide for her." He looked at her with his brows arched. "Which I assume is why you're here tonight. Have you chosen the man who best fits your requirements?"

The breath caught in Allison's throat. His accusation made her feel a hypocrite, a fraud. And he infuriated her.

He raised his darks brows inquisitively. "Is that why you have come to such a secluded spot in Lady Cowpepper's garden? Is it possible you came out here to meet someone and I arrived first? That you were not nearly so virtuous as you'd like everyone to believe?"

Before she had time to think, her arm involuntarily swung through the air and slapped the Marquess of Montfort's face. Hard.

Then, she spun on her heel and walked back to the ballroom, holding her head high and her back straight. She prayed she would never set eyes on him again. She had without a doubt, just met the most repulsive man on earth —and perhaps broken her wrist as a reminder.

When she reached the house, she stepped across the threshold and into the crush of people gathered in the ballroom. She rubbed her aching wrist. She could not believe what she'd just done. She'd slapped him, the Marquess of Montfort. Not once but twice.

She pressed her hands over her mouth to stop the small cry that wanted to rush out. She'd never struck anyone in her entire life. Never even been tempted.

The first time she could surely justify. He had, after all, accosted her. Dared to touch her, to kiss her.

A whirlpool of something she'd never felt before swirled in the pit of her stomach when she remembered being held against him: the heat of his body, the strength of his chest and arms, his hands roaming over her, and his lips kissing her neck.

She fanned her face. She did not want the memory of his touch to affect her like it did. She refused to let his attentions have any meaning. Refused to admit that she'd been driven purely by the riotous emotions he set rampaging through her. That his touch had any bearing on what she'd done. But it had. And she hated herself for it. He'd left her with no choice but to slap him.

The second time, though. Oh, heavens. She'd let her temper get away from her. She'd become so angry she'd slapped him again.

Allison rubbed her wrist. Her stomach churned and she took several deep breaths to calm herself. Montfort was the most infuriating man she'd ever met.

Why was her brother forcing her to marry? She didn't need a man's name. She didn't want his—

"Lady Allison. There you are."

She looked up to find the Earl of Archbite standing before her. He'd shown a great deal of interest in her of late. And what was of even more importance, he affected her like the calming trickle of a lazy stream, the opposite of Lord Montfort's crashing waves against the rocks. Like a comforting presence able to soothe her tattered nerves, compared to Montfort's threats and turmoil. She relaxed and breathed a steady breath for the first time since Montfort had pulled her against his hard, immovable chest.

"The musicale is about to begin. Would you do me the honor of accompanying me?"

"I'd be delighted." She took control of her emotions and placed her hand upon Lord Archbite's outstretched arm.

By the time they entered Lady Cowpepper's elegant music room, most of the seats were filled, leaving them to sit toward the back. She didn't mind. For as much as she loved music, she didn't consider either of Lady Cowpepper's daughters more than passably talented.

She settled in her chair as Lady Francine, the oldest, began her first selection, a lovely Italian aria. When the song ended, Lord Archbite leaned closer to say something. Allison turned her head—and her breath caught.

The marquess stood with his shoulder propped casually against the door frame, his arms crossed over his broad chest, his gaze locked with hers.

His inordinate height separated him from the rest of the guests, and a whirlpool of raging emotions swirled out of control deep inside her. She chastised herself when she realized she couldn't pull her gaze from him.

A slow smile spread across his face and he graciously

lowered his head in acknowledgment. Such a subtle greeting. So unnerving. So confident. As if he relished the effect he knew he had on all women.

In a show of rebuke, she lifted her chin and turned her head. She wanted to wipe the smile from his face, and for a tiny fraction of a second, she was glad she'd slapped him. But she was also afraid. Never before had any man affected her as strongly as he had.

She averted her gaze, struggling for as long as possible to keep from looking back to the spot where he stood, forcing herself to concentrate on the musical performance. But a power she couldn't control pulled her gaze to where he stood. Fortunately, this time he wasn't watching her. His gaze was fixed on someone sitting on the other side of the room.

Without seeming obvious, she turned her head enough to see who'd captured Lord Montfort's interest. For some reason, the recognition galled her. He was focused intently on the recently widowed Lady Serena Paxton.

The striking redhead wore an emerald green gown with an indecently revealing décolletage. But more telling was the look on her face. It was obvious that she was extremely pleased with Lord Montfort's attentions.

When the overly polite applause for Lady Francine's vocal selection dwindled, Lady Darlene took her place at the piano to play one of Mozart's earlier works. Allison took advantage of the momentary lull to look again to where Montfort stood. With his eyes locked on Lady Paxton's, he briefly nodded his head, then without notice, left by the nearest side entrance.

Allison turned her gaze back to Lady Paxton. A few

moments later, the woman left the room by an exit on the other side.

Allison's cheeks flamed. One would have to be an imbecile not to know what the two intended. Or that Lady Paxton was the woman Montfort had come to that secluded spot in the garden to meet. The woman for whom he'd mistaken her.

Allison's opinion of him plummeted further, if that were possible. He was a womanizer and rake of the worst kind. She pitied the woman he eventually took as his wife. He would never change. Men with those leanings never did. His poor wife would never be able to walk through Society with her head high. Everyone would know of her husband's infidelities.

Lady Darlene's piano selection ended and Allison turned her attention back to Lord Archbite. If she had to marry—and she did if she wanted to keep her inheritance —he was worth her consideration.

He was handsome enough, yet not too handsome to attract every woman in Society. And if she were any judge, the puppy-dog look of adoration she detected in his gaze said he was more than mildly enamored of her.

With a heavy sigh, she realized she finally had at least one name for her list of possible marriage candidates.

The thought was not comforting in the least.

# Chapter 2

IT HAD BEEN TWO WEEKS since Joshua had last seen his father. Two weeks since their last confrontation. Joshua was foolish enough to think he'd have at least a month's respite before the next battle, but he'd run into his father at White's earlier in the day.

His father had never been able to tolerate him. Today was no different. In fact, today's battle had been more hostile than ever. His father's words filled with more bitterness and loathing. And not for the first time, Joshua realized that the growing hatred that consumed his father was unhealthy.

Joshua stood at the back of the Earl of Ploddingdale's ballroom and slowly nursed his second drink. He needed help forgetting the niggling fear that warned him the end result of his father's anger would be catastrophic.

The recurring focus of his tirade had again been that the wrong son would some day carry the Ashbury title. He never missed an opportunity to lay more blame at Joshua's feet for his brother Philip's death.

Joshua threw a swallow of liquor to the back of his throat. Bloody hell! Didn't he know Joshua would give anything to relive that day and be the one who'd died instead of Phillip?

Joshua replayed the confrontation from this afternoon. He wanted to reject the idea that his father had lost his grip on stability, but it was almost as if his desire to punish Joshua for Phillip's death consumed him to the point that he no longer had a firm hold on sanity.

Joshua refused to contemplate anything so drastic. The ramifications were too terrifying. Instead, he pushed all thought of his father to the back of his mind and concentrated again on the crush of guests crowding into the Earl of Ploddingdale's townhouse. Perhaps *she* would be here again tonight. Lady Allison Townsend.

He'd discovered her name after their unforgettable meeting in Lady Cowpepper's garden. For some reason he didn't understand, he couldn't erase her from his mind. What a spitfire the lady was.

Joshua cradled his glass of brandy while his gaze swept the room. He looked for her at every function he attended. He refused to consider why he was so fascinated with her. Perhaps the attraction was nothing more than curiosity over a woman brave enough, or foolish enough to slap him—twice.

He lifted the glass to take another drink, then stopped with his arm midway to his mouth. There she was. Ready to descend the stairs and make her introductions to their host and hostess.

A smile crossed his lips. She looked even lovelier this evening than she had the last time he'd seen her. The gown she wore tonight reminded him of the way she'd looked the night he'd mistaken her for Lady Paxton. The style showed off her full bodice and narrow waist to perfection.

He remembered how perfectly she'd fit in his arms and how heavily her breast had rested in the palm of his hand.

Her neck was bare again except for the exquisite necklace of glowing emeralds that matched her dark green gown. The lower half of his body tightened uncomfortably when he recalled his lips nuzzling her soft, delicate flesh. She was a challenge, far more complex than any other female he knew. But she was the last woman he would allow to trap him.

She was far too intelligent to manipulate, far too independent to control, and her tongue was far too sharp for his taste. It was obvious her expectations were high, and the man who married her would never be able to get by with even the smallest indiscretion. And because she was in attendance again tonight, rumors that she was serious in her attempt to find a husband were undoubtedly true.

The thought chilled his blood and sent a warning racing through him. Yet, for some reason he could not explain, she remained an enigma—an enigma with mysterious powers that drew him to her.

At every ball and social event held in the last two weeks, he'd approached her at least once a night to ask her to dance. He enjoyed seeing her shocked expression turn to anger. Just as he enjoyed every excuse she made as to why she couldn't oblige him: her dance card was filled; she was tired and preferred to sit this dance out; she'd injured her ankle on the last dance; she needed to speak with her brother; or the excuse she most commonly used, she'd promised this dance to Lord Archbite, who followed her around like a love-smitten puppy.

It was more than a game to Joshua now. Taunting her was his answer to ease the boredom that suffocated him each evening. He loved to see her cheeks flush when he approached her, but even more, he reveled in the fire that flashed from her eyes when she was forced to acknowledge him.

Hell, she was a fiery thing. But at least she hadn't slapped him again.

"On whom are you concentrating? Surely it can't be the unapproachable Lady Allison again?"

Joshua turned to find his closest friend, Lionel Fortright, Earl of Chardwell, standing next to him. The two had formed a bond in their youth that had deepened over the years. Joshua welcomed Chardwell's presence with his usual sense of relief, and smiled.

"She doesn't appear to be happy tonight. Can you tell?"

"Take care, my friend," Chardwell said, taking a glass from a passing footman's tray. "The rumor circulating is that she must marry before her twenty-fifth birthday or lose a dowry that is the envy of every female in London."

"Oh, I have no intention of being caught in *that* trap. But why do you think she hasn't married before now?" Joshua asked. "Has she made no attempt to find a husband until this Season?"

"Don't you remember? She was betrothed several years ago—to Viscount Bradley. The Earl of Puttingsworth killed him in a jealous rage after finding him in bed with his wife."

"Ah, yes. How could I have forgotten that scandal? It was talked about for most of that Season. No wonder..."

"No wonder what?"

"Oh, nothing." Joshua concentrated on Lady Allison and smiled. "Look, Chardwell. The pressures of selecting a suitable husband must be weighing on her."

"How can you know that?"

"Look at the frown on her pretty forehead and the way her lips press together." Joshua slowly sipped from his glass. "And see how she's fisting her hands at her side?"

Chardwell shook his head on a laugh. "I think you've spent too much time studying the lady if you notice such small details, Montfort."

"She's an interesting woman to study." He kept his gaze on her. He knew eventually she'd notice him. She always did. Their gazes somehow seemed drawn to each other. Then her cheeks would flush a vibrant, rosy hue and he would see another flash of fire in her eyes. Every nerve in his body tingled in anticipation.

"Are you going to ask her to dance again tonight?"

"Of course. The first waltz."

"Aren't you tired of being rejected?"

"I've become immune. Besides, I believe she's weakening to my charms."

"Weakening?" Chardwell laughed so loudly the couples standing close turned to stare.

Joshua gave his friend a sideways glance that contained more than a bit of humor.

"If anything," Chardwell continued, his voice much softer, "she's more resolved than ever to avoid you. She was barely polite when she refused you at the Codmore ball on Wednesday."

"I think she did not feel well." Joshua watched her make her way down the stairs behind her brother and his wife, the Earl and Countess of Hartley. "I wasn't the only one she refused."

"I noticed she didn't refuse Archbite *his* two dances."

Joshua didn't respond, but watched as she greeted their host and hostess, then stepped into the crush of people. "I seem to have lost her, Chardwell. Do you see her?"

"You'd best be careful, Montfort. She's become quite an obsession."

He looked at his friend in shock. "It's a game. I've never met a woman who took such an instant dislike to me. I'm used to unabashed adoration when I turn on my charm, not open hostility."

"I can imagine what a blow she is to your ego."

"Don't be ridiculous. I simply enjoy sparring with her. She's a challenge. Nothing more."

"I hope I won't have an opportunity to remind you of that on your wedding day."

"Bloody hell, man. You'll never see me take a trip down the aisle. Can you imagine the pleasure half of London would get from seeing me leg shackled? I would never give them such satisfaction."

"People who play with fire have been known to get burned. And rumor has it she's attending the nightly round of parties because her twenty-fifth birthday is approaching. If she intends to keep her inheritance, she will have to marry before that date."

"How interesting." He cast a glance over the crowd and found the lovely Lady Allison as she reached a gathering of ladies against the opposite side of the ballroom.

"Don't worry. I have no intention of falling into any woman's trap. Fortunately, she has already decided I won't do."

He took note of her fiery copper hair and deep emerald gown and his breath caught. He couldn't tear his gaze from her. Dear Lord, what a vision.

"If you'll excuse me, Chardwell," he said, handing his empty glass to a passing footman, "I think it is almost time for the orchestra to play a waltz."

He ignored Chardwell's hearty laugh and walked toward her. He kept his head high and wore a confident smile on his face. Her presence made having to be here almost enjoyable. He would miss her when their little game was over.

❧

The dull throbbing in Allison's head grew more intense with each passing minute. She knew exactly when it had started. The minute her brother David had summoned her to his study again this afternoon to discuss her progress in choosing a husband.

Less than four weeks remained until her twenty-fifth birthday.

She'd tried again to convince him to allow her to remain single. She'd tried to reason with him but he wouldn't listen to anything she said. She'd even promised she would remain in the country and not be a bother to anyone. But he'd refused to consider her suggestion. The more she argued that she didn't want to marry, the more adamant he became. And the angrier. He even repeated his threat to choose a husband for her if she didn't choose one herself in the next two weeks.

She fisted her hands. What was so terrible about a woman wanting to live her life without taking a husband?

Surely she wasn't the *only* woman in all of London who didn't want to marry.

She thought of the courage it took for her sisters to walk proudly at their husbands' sides, pretending it didn't matter that their husbands did not love them enough to be faithful. She could never be so brave.

Couldn't David understand that she could never face Society if it was common knowledge that her husband kept a mistress? Couldn't he understand her pride would never survive?

No, he couldn't. He'd been unsympathetic through every argument, which was why her attempts to plead a headache and stay home tonight met with his flat refusal. Now she'd have to put up with the noise, the laughter, the gossip...and the Marquess of Montfort's insistent demand to dance a waltz again tonight.

Her head pounded anew and she looked longingly at the open double doors that led onto the patio. She'd give anything to be able to hide in the dark until this evening was over. But that was impossible.

"Lady Allison."

She spun around. The Earl of Archbite stood beside her.

"I was hoping you would be here tonight."

She felt her cheeks warm. And her heart plummet. She hadn't seen him approach. Didn't want his attention—not tonight.

"Lord Archbite." She pasted a friendly smile on her face though she didn't feel at all like smiling. "How nice to see you."

"There's quite a crush tonight, isn't there?"

"Yes. Lady Ploddingdale's creativity is seldom surpassed." Allison took note of the footmen dressed in puce and lime green, and shuddered.

"Oh, yes," Archbite continued. "Tonight's affair is overflowing with color. Puts one in quite the festive mood, doesn't it?"

Allison forced a smile. Inside, she cringed. Could Lord Archbite be serious? She concluded that he was. *Ugh!* "Yes," she answered, because an answer seemed necessary. "It's very...festive."

She scanned the growing crowd as she listened to the music the orchestra played from the other side of the room. They were in the middle of a quadrille, and after the quadrille, they generally played a waltz. Her pulse raced and her blood pounded harder in her head. Perhaps tonight he would not bother her. Perhaps she'd set him down hard enough the last time that she'd convinced him she didn't intend to dance with him—ever.

The music ended and the dancers moved to find partners for the next set. She lifted her gaze to look around the room and her heart stuttered in her chest. He was coming toward her, his broad shoulders filling his handsomely tailored jacket to perfection, his expertly tied cravat glowing a brilliant white against his bronzed skin. The corners of his mouth lifted slightly. Then his gaze locked with hers and his lips parted to a wide-open smile.

From halfway across the room he graced her with a look so breathtaking it stole the air from her body. How dare he bother her again tonight. What more did she have to do to convince him she didn't want him anywhere near her?

Her temper simmered at a slow boil as she prepared to give him the set-down he deserved.

"…haven't forgotten. Have you?" Percy finished, pulling her back from her nightmare.

She shook her head. "I'm sorry. What did you say?"

"I wanted to remind you of Mother's musicale tomorrow night."

She tried to take a deep breath and find a reply to Percy's question but found it impossible. The Marquess of Montfort stood directly behind Percy.

He towered over poor Percy by almost a head, and his shoulders outstretched Percy's by nearly half a foot on either side. Percy looked more effeminate tonight than usual. Montfort more threatening.

So far, Percy hadn't noticed Montfort standing behind him. She prayed he wouldn't turn around. She feared Montfort might startle him.

"Your mother what?"

"Her musical. I want to make sure you plan to attend."

She forced a smile. "I wouldn't miss it for the world."

"Wonderful. Do you need transportation? I could send a carriage for you?"

Montfort rudely shook his head as if to prompt her refusal.

"Ah, no." She directed an angry glare in Montfort's direction. "Thank you, but that won't be necessary. My brother and his wife also plan to attend. I'll come with them."

Montfort gave her a nod, as if her answer met with his approval.

"I also wondered," Percy said hesitantly, "if you would

be available for callers tomorrow afternoon?"

Montfort lifted his brows and crossed his arms over his chest, as if he, too, were interested in her answer.

"If you are receiving, I would like to call on you."

Montfort's brows furrowed into a deep frown and he shook his head as if he expected her to heed his advice and refuse Lord Archbite's request to visit.

"I have no plans to go out," she answered. Regrettably, her words came out clipped and angry, and Percy looked at her in confusion. He hesitated with uncertainty before he continued.

"Perhaps then we could take a drive through the park?"

Montfort shook his head harder and Allison gritted her teeth in frustration.

"No! Yes! I would be delighted!"

Percy blinked twice when she growled out her answer and looked at her as if she'd taken leave of her senses. "Unless, of course, you'd prefer not to," he stammered. "Or it rains."

The tone of his voice was filled with trepidation. She knew her flare of temper confused and intimidated him.

"No, I'd love to." Her head pounded, her cheeks burned, her temper neared the boiling point. And the orchestra struck a waltz.

The Marquess of Montfort picked that moment to step out from behind Percy. "Lady Allison." He bowed graciously before her. "I believe this is my waltz."

"No!"

Several people standing nearby turned to look at her. Even Percy stared at her in wide-eyed astonishment. Only Montfort smiled.

"Please," he said, placing his hand over his heart. "I beg of you. Don't turn me away brokenhearted again."

In an uncharacteristic show of bravery, Percy lifted his shoulders and faced the dragon in her defense. "The lady made it quite clear that she doesn't want to dance with you."

Montfort's narrowed gaze drilled Percy and a cold chill washed over her.

Neither man moved a muscle.

The expression on Montfort's face darkened and she knew only raw determination kept Percy from shrinking away.

She held her breath. They looked like David and Goliath facing each other. Only Allison's David didn't have any special advantage on his side. Montfort didn't need any.

"I believe I was speaking to Lady Allison," Montfort responded, his tone soft and deadly. Allison heard the threat in his voice. Felt the danger.

Percy obviously didn't. He puffed his narrow shoulders. "And I believe I heard the lady say she did not want to dance with you."

A muscle at the side of Montfort's jaw twitched. This had gone far enough. Of course, she was not concerned for Montfort, but for Percy. She knew she had to stop the two adversaries before they caused a scene. Before Percy got hurt.

"I have changed my mind, Lord Archbite." She placed her hand on Percy's arm. "I did promise Lord Montfort this dance." She turned to Montfort. "I apologize, my lord. I forgot."

"Are you sure?" Percy asked. The look on his face told

her he would fight to the death for her.

"Yes, I'm sure."

With an angry scowl, Percy stepped back when Montfort extended his arm.

She hesitated, then placed her hand on Montfort's sleeve. She could feel Percy's glare as they made their way onto the dance floor.

"Why are you doing this?" she said under her breath when he pulled her toward him to begin their dance.

She couldn't remember ever being so angry. She had always been able to brush suitors off. Why was Montfort so different? He wasn't serious about courting her. He'd made that fact perfectly clear the first time they'd met.

"Doing what?" He stepped in perfect time to the lilting waltz, effortlessly gliding across the floor with her in his arms. He was an expert dancer. But she knew he would be. She pursed her lips in an angry pout.

"Don't play the fool, my lord. You know exactly what I mean. Pursuing me when I have made it more than clear that I want nothing whatsoever to do with you. Bothering me when I have repeatedly indicated I don't want you anywhere near."

"Is that what your refusals meant?" The look of innocence on his face was almost laughable.

"You know it is."

He executed another turn and held her even closer. She pulled away. "It's not proper to hold me so close. People will talk."

"People are already talking. Dancing with me is cause for people to talk." He arched an eyebrow, which gave him a dark, rakish look. "I have a reputation, you know."

She rolled her eyes heavenward. "Everyone knows your reputation. You've done nothing by your words or actions to quell the wild rumors and speculation that surround you."

"Is that admiration I hear in your voice?"

Allison nearly stumbled over her feet. "It most certainly is not. I find your actions reprehensible. And you have yet to answer my question. Why are you doing this?"

"If you must know, I have decided to save you." He pulled her closer. His arms held her securely as they moved across the dance floor and she felt…safe.

Her skin tingled where he touched her. The room seemed much warmer than before. "Save me from what?" She kept her voice low enough not to draw attention.

"From Lord Archbite, of course."

She came to a halt and tried to pull out of his arms. The marquess countered her actions by clamping his hand around her waist and leading her to the side of the dance floor. The minute they stepped through the open double doors and onto the flagstone terrace, she spun around to face him. "From Lord Archbite? How dare you!"

He escorted her to the secluded side of the patio where they could not be overheard. "It is quite obvious, Lady Allison, that you have come back into Society to find a husband."

She felt her cheeks blaze. She had a difficult time keeping her pointed gaze focused on him.

"There's no need to deny it. There's nothing unusual about a woman desperate to find a husband. You are, after all, not that young any more." He held up his hand when she started to say something. "We've already covered the advantages of love and marriage and know each other's viewpoints. I wish you every success in your endeavor. I have therefore decided to assist you."

"You pompous idiot." She clenched her teeth and struggled to hold her temper. "You arrogant—"

Montfort held up his hand to stop her words. "You almost have Archbite where you want him. Ready to take the fall. It is obvious to even the most disinterested observer that he is prepared to ask for your hand."

Allison knew what he said was true, but hearing the words out loud caused a sickening weight to churn in the pit of her stomach. "Lord Achbite's intentions are none of your concern."

"But they are. Surely you know the two of you are not the least suited?"

Allison's hands fisted at her side so tightly they ached. "Of all the—"

"Oh, really, Allie." He leaned casually against a corner pillar anchoring the balustrade and crossed his arms over his chest. For several uncomfortable seconds he stared at her with a serious look on his face.

He appeared even more the rake than before and her heart pounded harder in her breast. If she wasn't careful her temper would get the better of her. No one could infuriate her like he could.

"You're not a fool, my lady. Surely you've considered the drawbacks to marrying Archbite?"

"There are no drawbacks. Lord Archbite is sincere in his suit. He is wealthy beyond measure and would not marry me only for my dowry. And most of all, he doesn't have the reputation of a scoundrel. He's not famous for his mistresses, or for trying to seduce every female he meets."

"Are you referring to me?"

The amused glint in his eyes only made her angrier. "If the boot fits…"

He gave her a hearty laugh. "And how do you intend to compete with his mother."

"His mother? I'm not marrying his mother."

"But you are. The strings that connect the two are inseparable. Archbite has not made a move since he was out of nappies without first consulting dear Mama. He is not strong enough to begin now. Which leads us to another problem."

He lowered himself to the balustrade railing and sat. This put him at eye level with her, on an even field. Her courage surged with renewed vigor. "And that would be?" She anchored her fists on her hips.

"He is not strong enough to be your match. You would devour him within a week."

Allison could not hide her shock. "I do not need a husband who is strong."

"But you do. Or you will run over him at every turn and be unhappy for the rest of your life."

She stood speechless, her heart not sure how fast or slow to beat. "You must think very little of me," she said when she could again speak.

"On the contrary. I think quite highly of you. I recognize your strengths and know you wouldn't be content with a weak husband for even a day, let alone your entire life."

"I see you consider yourself an expert on the qualities that attract a man and a woman. How is it, sir, that you are not married? Can you recognize these characteristics in everyone but yourself?"

"I am not the one considering marriage. You are."

"Yes. But since I am not for one second considering marriage to *you*, I would appreciate it if you kept your opinions to yourself."

He pushed himself from the railing and towered over her, his legs anchored wide. "Very well, but first let me impart another piece of information before I leave you to your own demise. Lord Archbite is not all he seems."

"What do you mean by that?"

"Only that it would be to your advantage to make some inquiries before you connect yourself too deeply with him."

"Why are you doing this? Do you dislike him that much? Or is it me?"

"I do not dislike him at all." He shrugged, as if the warning he'd issued was inconsequential. As if omitting her last question would not be noticed. Her blood ran cold. Her temper erupted.

"You are disgusting."

A smile crossed his face. "I believe you've already mentioned that."

"Thank you for your concern. Now please leave me alone."

"You're angry."

"Angry?" she said, as if she could not believe that surprised him. "I have been bullied, insulted, and by association to you, been made the object of gossip. And you called me a fool."

"I didn't call you a fool. I said marrying Archbite would indeed be foolish."

Montfort placed a finger beneath her chin and lifted upward until her gaze locked with his. "He cannot release one portion of the passion you have hidden inside you. And you do not even know it is there."

"I don't have the faintest idea what you mean."

"I know. And you should."

Before she could react, he grasped her shoulders and pulled her close. She knew he intended to kiss her. Just as she knew she couldn't allow it. She would never be the same if she did.

She brought her hands up to push him away but it was no use. He was too strong. Too powerful. Too desirable.

His arms wrapped around her and his mouth pressed against hers.

The kiss was soft, gentle. Almost chaste. And she held herself still, locking every muscle, using every ounce of fortitude she possessed to close her mind to the heat swirling through her body.

"Don't fight me," he whispered. His lips brushed feathery kisses over her cheek and down the side of her face. "You need to know what you have to offer some very fortunate man."

Before she could make another attempt to escape his grasp, his mouth pressed more firmly against hers. His lips covered hers with a possessiveness that was inescapable. With amazing skill he moved over her, tasting her, drinking from her, and demanding something.

She had no idea what it was.

She swore she would not let his kisses affect her. Just as she swore she would not kiss him back. But when his mouth opened atop hers, she lost her battle.

Fiery passion swirled in the pit of her stomach when his tongue probed the crease of her lips, churning her insides with an uncontrollable yearning. Her heart pounded in her breast. Blood thundered in her head. And she clung to him as if he alone could keep her from falling, when it was his fault she could not stand.

She couldn't breathe, couldn't take in enough air to survive. So she opened her mouth and let him breathe with her, for her. And he deepened his kiss.

She moaned, the sound a desperate plea for more.

His tongue entered, searched, found, conquered.

She struggled one last time, then wrapped her arms around his neck and pulled him to her. His lips moved with an expertise that destroyed every effort to stop him. She held him closer, then yielded to his kisses and his touch.

His kisses continued for an eternity, each one more consuming than the last. When he finally lifted his mouth from hers, she sank against him like the weak, wanton woman he'd made her.

She couldn't move, didn't have the strength to stand on her own. She pressed her cheek against his chest and listened to his heart thunder inside his breast. It beat as violently as her own.

Eventually, deep inside a never-opened recess of her mind, a door opened and she realized the mistake she'd made.

The kiss they'd shared had not been simple and chaste as every other kiss she'd experienced before. But earthy and passionate. He'd opened a Pandora's Box of desires she didn't want to know were locked inside her. He'd changed everything she'd convinced herself she wanted.

If she must marry, as her brother insisted she do, then marriage to Lord Archbite was the only marriage she would consider. Because he demanded nothing. She felt nothing for him. Her emotions were safe with him. There was no risk to her heart.

With one passionate kiss, the Marquess of Montfort had ruined everything. He'd destroyed every illusion she'd constructed in her attempt to live a safe, emotionless life.

Damn him.

Damn him!

He cupped her cheeks in his hands and lifted her face. "See, my lady. You deserve more."

She twisted out of his arms and stepped away from him, her legs still unsteady beneath her. "How dare you. How dare you!"

Allison wanted to strike him. Her hands fisted tighter and moved involuntarily at her side.

He glanced down at her clenched fists. "I wouldn't if I were you. I rarely let a woman strike me once. I allowed it the other night because I deserved it. I will not tolerate it again."

Allison clamped her hands against her side, wishing for once she were a man and could answer his threat. He deserved her anger more tonight than before. He had no idea what he'd done.

She spun away from him and ran back into the house, not caring what anyone thought when they saw her fleeing for her life.

# *Chapter 3*

THE EARL OF ARCHBITE CALLED to escort her on a carriage ride that next afternoon as promised. The day was brilliantly clear without the hint of a rain cloud in the sky. A slight breeze, warm from the bright sunshine, washed over them as they made their way through Hyde Park. All in all, it was a picture perfect day.

But Allison hardly noticed. Instead, she spent the entire time watching over her shoulder, waiting for the Marquess of Montfort to ride up behind them and spoil it.

"Is something wrong?" The earl looked behind him to where she focused her gaze.

Allison jerked ahead, swearing she would not look back again. Swearing she would give Montfort the cut if he was foolish enough to bother them. "No. Nothing is wrong."

"It's just that you keep looking behind you as if you're expecting someone. Are you expecting someone?"

"Of course not. It's just such a wonderful day that I'm trying to absorb it all."

He gave her a warm smile and leaned back in the seat,

seeming very relaxed and content. Allison felt a sense of familiarity being with him too. The familiarity she felt when she was with … her brother.

That she'd just compared him to David disappointed her. She shoved the thought out of her mind as if it had never been born.

Chastising herself for her foolishness, she sat back against the leather cushion. She was determined to enjoy the rest of the ride. Determined *not* to remember the reason she'd gotten very little sleep last night. Or the turmoil that raged through her body since Montfort had so thoroughly kissed her. She would not allow herself to think of him.

"It really is a beautiful day." She moved her parasol further back on her shoulder so the sunshine could hit her face.

"Yes. But not nearly as beautiful as you."

The sincerity of his compliment took her by surprise and she gave him a sideways glance. The adoring look on his face bespoke the depth of his feelings. She lowered her gaze to her lap.

"Don't be embarrassed." He placed his gloved hand atop hers. "You *are* beautiful. Even more so with a blush to your cheeks. I cannot believe you are not already married."

"I never wanted to marry. Not after—"

"Don't, my lady." He lifted a finger to stop her. "What happened to Lord Bradley did not reflect on you in the least. I don't want you to ever think of his betrayal again."

Allison tried to put a smile on her face, but knew she came up short. Percy only patted her hand in a reassuring manner and focused on the path ahead. Allison took the opportunity to study him.

Lord Archbite was an only child. His father had been well up in years when he was born, then had died unexpectedly a few years later. He'd left Percy his wealth, his title, and a doting Mother who lived only for her son. This undoubtedly explained the close connection between the two.

Some saw his devotion to his mother as a weakness, but Allison did not. It was a quality she wasn't sure she understood, but it somehow comforted her. Surely that devotion, that faithfulness, would transfer to his wife after he married.

She should consider herself lucky he was interested in her. He was exactly the kind of man she wanted. Someone wealthy enough that her dowry was of no interest. Someone who did not have a reputation as a rake and scoundrel with a string of mistresses scattered throughout London. Someone who would honor his vows and be faithful to her.

Someone as different from Montfort as any man could be.

"I'm glad you have come back into Society. Glad you accepted my invitation this afternoon. It gives me hope."

"Hope?"

His gaze locked with hers. "Until now, a permanent arrangement of any kind did not interest me. You have changed my mind."

Allison's cheeks warmed and she knew it had nothing to do with the midday sun shining on her face.

Her heart beat faster and her breathing turned rapid and shallow. She knew what was coming next, what words he intended to say.

An overwhelming sense of panic washed over her. She suddenly realized she didn't want to hear what he was going to tell her.

He turned to face her, his heartfelt sincerity plain to see. "I cannot let another day pass before I tell you my feelings. You have captured my heart and I am convinced the sun rises and sets in you. Next to my mother, you are truly the most virtuous woman I know."

He cradled her free hand and pressed it to his chest.

A stronger tremor of panic raced through her. Why didn't his words thrill her? Why didn't her heart soar at his proclamation? Instead, she felt trapped. Uncomfortable. As if committing to anything right now would be a mistake.

"I've admired you forever. You are perfection itself, above reproach. Mother says a match between our two families would be advantageous to us both."

She couldn't breathe. Couldn't keep her heart from racing out of control. "Lord Archbite." She pulled her hand away from him. Her voice sounded barely more than a whisper that quivered with a timidity totally alien to her nature. What was wrong with her? "I am extremely flattered by your compliments, exaggerated though they may be. It would be a lie to pretend I am oblivious to your intentions. I am not. I appreciate your feelings. But …" She hesitated until she could find a way to say what she needed to say. "Please. I need time before you declare yourself."

The wounded look in Percy's eyes made her feel terrible.

"Of course. How rude of me to be so forward. This is hardly the time or the place for such a delicate discussion.

It was thoughtless of me not to realize you might not return my feelings with the same intensity."

"No. It's not that—"

He held up his hand to stop her protest. "Is there someone else, then?"

"No. Oh, no."

His features relaxed. "Perhaps you could give me an idea of how much time you require?"

"The end of the month," she said, trying to keep her voice level. "Just until the end of the month."

"Of course." His face opened to a wide grin. "That is only two weeks. Be assured that my feelings will not change in that short a time. Although it will seem like a lifetime to me, I can understand your need to consider such a monumental decision."

"Thank you." She forced her lips to relax enough to smile at him.

She'd avoided crossing an invisible line that would irrevocably connect her to Percy. The emotions that surged through her were indescribable. Relief. Reprieve.

Her breath caught. What was she doing? This was what she wanted, what she'd been after. She only had two more weeks to find a husband, so why had she stopped him from asking for her hand?

*Because you don't love him,* a loud voice screamed in her head.

*But I don't believe in love,* another voice countered. And she didn't. She was well acquainted with greed and lust. She'd seen it in her parents' marriage, and knew it was the basis for her three sisters' marriages. But she'd never seen a married couple who loved each other. Even David's affiliation with his wife remained a mystery. She wasn't sure if their relationship was based on love, or simply a fondness necessitated by the need to provide the next generation of Hartley heirs.

Perhaps there was such a thing as love. Perhaps in time she could learn to love the Earl of Archbite. But for now, she still had two weeks of freedom. Two weeks that she did not have to think about what her future held for her.

Two weeks to convince herself that her future was not as dismal as it seemed.

❧

The Earl of Archbite's townhouse was already a buzz of activity when Allison and her brother, David, and his wife, Lynette, arrived for the musicale. Percy's mother, the Countess of Archbite, met each of her guests with the same regal aplomb as befitted a queen. Percy stood next to her.

The guest list was never overly large for any function Lady Archbite hosted. Invitations were sent only to a select few. Which might be part of the reason the invitations were so coveted by all of Society.

Tonight was no different. Only the most elite of Society were here.

"Lord and Lady Hartley," Lady Archbite said, greeting David and Lynette. "I'm so honored you could attend."

"Thank you, Lady Archbite," David said. "It was kind of you to extend the invitation."

Allison saw a slight smile cross David's face. She wondered what her brother would say if he knew how close Lord Archbite had come to stating his intentions this afternoon.

He undoubtedly would be elated.

"Lord Hartley. Lady Hartley," Percy greeted, nodding politely to David and bowing over Lynette's hand.

The look on David's face remained friendly when he greeted Percy.

A sudden thought raced through her mind. She couldn't imagine the two of them as brothers-in-law. Once she married him—*if* she married him, Percy would be an odd mix in her otherwise handsome family. Allison pushed such a ridiculous thought from her mind.

"And Lady Allison," the countess said, forcing Allison's attention back to their hostess.

She curtsied. "Good evening, Lady Archbite. I am so looking forward to this evening. I hear you have commissioned the talented Mademoiselle Miranda Bochaut to sing selected arias from her favorite operas."

"Do you enjoy the opera?" the countess asked.

"Yes. David tells me I'm hopelessly addicted."

The countess smiled. "No one who enjoys the opera is ever hopeless. Perhaps there is something in particular you'd like to hear tonight. I could see if Mademoiselle Bochaut has it in her repertoire."

"Oh, no." Allison was embarrassed to be given such an honor. Her first thought was that the countess knew of her conversation with Percy this afternoon and was making every effort to smooth the way between them.

"I insist," the countess added.

David's expression changed. His eyes brightened with a glimmer of hopefulness, followed by a look she often saw when he was pleased. A flash of panic rose inside her.

Of course David would approve. Why shouldn't he?

"I am honored, Lady Archbite. Perhaps something from Saint-Saen's *Samson and Delilah*. It is new, and causing quit the stir. For the rest, I acquiesce to Mademoiselle Bochaut's discretion."

Lady Archbite nodded to a footman standing close by and he scooted off, presumably to relay the request to Mademoiselle Bochaut. Allison looked to Percy for some sort of answer, but found him gazing at her with undiluted adoration in his eyes.

He reached for her hand and held it to his lips far longer that usual. "Lady Allison. It would be my pleasure if you would allow me to escort you into the music room when it is time for the performance. I am sure you would enjoy seats closest to the front when Mademoiselle Bochaut sings your selection."

"How considerate." She smiled at Percy and was reminded of how attentive he was, how devoted. If she *had* to marry, weren't those the qualities she looked for in the man she would take as her husband?

She curtsied again, then walked with David and Lynette through the spacious rooms where a growing crowd gathered.

David didn't say anything as they wound their way through the guests but he seemed smugly content. She knew he hadn't wanted to come tonight, but was doing so to aid her in her search for a husband. The pleased look on his face indicated he'd decided his effort was worth it.

They entered the large ballroom and Allison looked around. Huge potted plants dotted the room against the outside walls, giving it a warmth not usually found in ballrooms. A dozen glistening chandeliers hung from the ceiling, each glowing with hundreds of candles. And in the center of the room there was a trickling fountain that splashed gently into a round pool. Several lighted marble pathways angled from the pool like the spokes of a wheel.

An occasional palm tree or flowering bush made the pathways seem like a walk through a real garden.

Toward the back, a small chamber orchestra played music. In the front, long banquet tables angled in the corners, laden with foods and drink of every kind. She made her excuses to David and Lynette, then walked to one of the tables.

It was daunting to realize that some day this house could be hers. Her mouth turned dry as cotton and she reached for a glass of punch sitting at the end of the table.

"Allow me," a low, darkly-rich voice said from behind her.

The breath left her body. She slowly turned to glare at the Marquess of Montfort. "What are you doing here?"

"I assume the same as you, my lady. Waiting to hear the beautiful Mademoiselle Miranda Bochaut sing."

"You don't even like music," she said, then turned hot from head to toe when the marquess released a full, booming laugh.

"See how little you know me? Actually, I'm quite fond of music. Especially the opera. You could say I am a patron. Mademoiselle Bochaut and I have been friends for years." He paused. "Close friends."

She caught his meaning immediately and the rakish gleam in his eyes set her teeth on edge. "You are—"

He held up his hand to stop her. "I know. You've mentioned this before. I do wish you'd alter your opinion of me. Your low regard pains me." He placed one hand over his heart.

"I doubt that's possible." She looked around the room, then glared at him like a soldier facing his enemy. "How did you get in?"

"I was invited."

He handed her a glass of champagne then reached behind her and lifted another glass from the table. His shoulder brushed against her, the heat from his body nearly setting her on fire. A shiver raced through her.

"I assure you. I had an invitation. Being the heir apparent to a dukedom does have its privileges."

She turned her back to him and focused on the other guests that conversed in small groups. She knew her action was blatantly rude, but didn't care. She wished Montfort would take her hint and leave her alone.

He didn't.

"Would you like to stroll through the gardens before the performance?" His voice was a husky whisper in her ear.

Her heart pounded in her breast and her stomach swirled as if someone had released a thousand butterflies inside her. She couldn't look into his midnight blue eyes without getting lost. The affect he had on her emotions terrified her.

Allison pasted a sweet smile on her face and turned back to him. "Lord Archbite suggested the same thing. I prefer to wait for him."

He arched a brow. "Then at least walk with me through the corridors. It will be much quieter."

He didn't give her a choice, but placed his arm beneath

her elbow and escorted her toward the door. Before she could escape him, they were strolling down the long, narrow gallery where all the ancestral Archbite portraits hung.

Mirrored candles glimmered on either side of each portrait that cast the room in muted brightness. It also accentuated Montfort's perfect features in a brilliant glow.

"They're not a particularly handsome lot, are they?" He stopped in front of one of the ugliest men she'd ever seen.

"The merit of a man is not determined by his looks."

"I suppose you're right," he answered, then turned again and walked further down the long aisle. "You aren't seriously considering dear old Percy, are you, Allison?"

"What I am considering, seriously or not, is none of your concern. And I don't recall giving you leave to call me by my Christian name."

He stopped. "I assumed the kiss we shared the other night was all the permission I needed."

"That was rude." Allison's cheeks burned like fire. She tried to pull her hand from Montfort's arm but he clamped his hand over hers and held her tighter.

"There's no need to take offense. It was just a kiss."

*Just a kiss!*

She tried to avert her gaze but he placed his finger beneath her chin and forced her to look into his face.

"A very enjoyable kiss, I might add."

Then he smiled.

His teeth glowed bright against his bronzed flesh. The two creases on either side of his mouth deepened, causing his handsome face to become even more breathtaking. Her stomach flipped.

His noble features—high cheekbones, square-cut jaw, deep cleft in his chin—combined to give him a rugged look. She considered it a sin for anyone to be so handsome. A sin for her body to react like it did. No wonder he was so sure of himself. His looks had no doubt gotten him anything he ever wanted.

"I'm sorry I missed you this afternoon."

She gave him a curious look.

"I took a turn through the Park, hoping to see you."

"You were hoping to *bother* me." She tried to keep from clenching her teeth. Even though she didn't look at him, she could feel the warmth from his smile.

"I assure you, I only wanted to see you. But I had business to attend to that took longer than I thought."

"I can imagine. You were no doubt in the middle of a game of cards that couldn't be interrupted. Or more likely visiting one of your many female friends. Perhaps even the renowned Mademoiselle Bochaut. A ride through Hyde Park would hardly be worth the interruption."

"You don't have a good impression of me, do you? I can't imagine what I've done to deserve it."

"The rumors surrounding you don't leave room for a good impression. Which brings me back to an earlier question. Why have you taken an interest in me?"

"Perhaps I find you fascinating."

"Fascinating in what regard? Surely not as a friend. Definitely not as a mistress. Perhaps as a sparring partner." She snapped her gaze to his face. "Are you looking for a wife? Is this your manner of courtship?"

"Bloody hell, no!"

She clutched her hand to her throat and breathed a sigh

of relief. "Thank heavens."

He laughed. "My grandfather was in his forties when he sired my father. I have no intention of producing an heir until I at least reach fifty."

"Then why won't you leave me alone?"

"I told you before. I don't want to see you make a mistake."

"I don't intend to make a mistake. The Earl of Archbite is an intelligent man who carries himself with a great deal of confidence and dignity. He happens to be one of the most sought after bachelors in Society."

"Then let one of the other unsuspecting London debutantes win such a prize."

"What a horrible thing to say."

"I am only suggesting that you proceed with caution. You have waited this long to marry. Surely a few more months won't make a difference."

His words stung. Little did he know if the choice were hers, she would wait a lifetime to marry. As it was, she had less than two weeks.

He clasped his hands behind his back and pretended to study one of the portraits on the wall. "Does Hartley know how far things have progressed between the two of you?"

Blood pounded in her head. "David? What does David have to do with this?"

"I was just wondering—"

She needed him to leave. Needed to be away from him. "I have had enough of your interference, Lord Montfort. Now, please. Leave me alone—"

"Lady Allison?" Percy's voice echoed from the other end of the long corridor. "Are you all right?"

Allison stepped toward Percy but Montfort's arm snaked around her waist, making escape impossible.

"Of course the lady's all right. She and I were just enjoying some time alone. You don't mind, do you, Archbite?"

"As a matter of fact, I do." Percy walked forward, then stopped when he reached them.

"That's unfortunate," Montfort said.

An uncomfortable silence stretched between them and she suddenly feared what might happen.

"I'd like to go back now."

Both men held out an arm for her to take. She looked from one arm to the other, then lifted her head and looked into their faces. A smile graced Montfort's face, a look of undeterred confidence in his eyes.

Allison hesitated, then placed her hand on Lord Archbite's arm and walked with him to the exit. Her knees shook and a heavy weight pressed against her chest.

As if she'd just made the biggest mistake of her life.

❧

Joshua leaned his fists against the cement balustrade on Lady Archbite's patio and let the cool evening air wash over him. He didn't know why the hell it should matter who Lady Allison married. But it did.

He couldn't imagine her with Archbite. Couldn't imagine her being brow beaten by Archbite's mother. And that's what her life would be like until the day the dowager countess died, if Allison wanted there to be any sort of peaceful existence between her husband and herself.

And that would be the least of her problems.

Joshua raked his fingers through his hair and breathed

in a deep breath.

"I see you needed a little fresh air and solitude, too, Montfort."

Joshua turned around to see Allison's brother, the Earl of Hartley walking toward him. "Yes. There's something about a crowd of people that makes me yearn to escape to the country."

"I know the feeling. I'll be glad when my wife tires of the endless round of balls and parties and suggests we visit our country estate for a while."

Hartley stood at Joshua's left and focused his gaze on Lady Archbite's perfectly manicured garden. "I still miss him, you know."

"Yes, I know," Joshua answered, knowing who Hartley meant.

"Philip and I arrived at school the same year. We were friends from the start. Good friends. I couldn't believe he was taken away from us so young. Has your father come to terms with his death yet?"

"No."

"Give him time."

Joshua sighed. "I'm afraid two lifetimes will not be enough for him to accept what happened that day. He will always need someone to blame."

"Perhaps that is his grief talking."

"Perhaps."

"The accident wasn't your fault, Montfort."

Joshua tried to push the nightmare that still haunted him from his mind, but it refused to leave him alone. Instead, he remembered Philip pushing his horse too fast over rough and uneven ground, Philip attempting to jump

A MATTER OF CHOICE

the hedge that was too high for an inexperienced horse and rider, Philip's horse refusing to make the jump, then... Philip's broken body on the ground.

"In part, Father is right in blaming me. If I hadn't dared Philip to race..."

"Then Philip might have tripped on the stairs and fallen to his death."

Joshua's breath caught.

"None of us have a say in when we will die, you know. You give yourself far too much credit if you think you could have prevented God's will from happening."

"It's too bad Father doesn't share your opinion. He constantly wishes our roles had been reversed."

"That is your father's loss. Perhaps he simply cannot see your good points." Hartley shifted his weight. "Philip saw them, though. He thought very highly of you, you know."

Joshua shot him a sideways glance with raised eyebrows.

Hartley laughed. "Yes, even though he knew about your fondness for drinking, gambling, and a willing female, he said that being irresponsible was your way of disguising your true character."

Joshua smiled. "I always did have him fooled."

"Philip was much too perceptive to be fooled. Even by you. We were both lucky to have known him."

With that, the earl turned and walked toward the house.

"Hartley."

Hartley stopped.

"This is none of my concern, and if I am overstepping my bounds, please ignore my next comments."

"Yes?"

"During the past few weeks I have had the pleasure of

becoming acquainted with your sister."

"And…"

"And I believe Lord Archbite has formed quite a fondness for her."

"This concerns you?"

"I know his breeding is impeccable and he seems the perfect match for Lady Allison, but…"

"Go on, Montfort."

"Lord Archbite keeps a house near Mayfair Park."

"That is hardly scandalous. Many men, single and otherwise keep a mistress. If that's what you're implying."

"Lord Archbite's friend is an artist, a painter. His name is Rafael."

Hartley stiffened. His hands fisted at his side. "You're sure?"

"I encourage you to confirm this yourself."

He ignored Hartley's vile oath and turned to brace his hand atop the balustrade.

"Thank you, Montfort. I appreciate your candor."

Joshua didn't answer, but lifted his chin to let the cool breeze hit his face once again. At least Allison would be saved from that scandal.

❧

Allison sat in the lavish music room totally absorbed by the glorious sounds coming from the magnificent Mademoiselle Miranda Bochaut. Each note, each word, each melodic phrase was a benediction, a prayer to heaven. Her rich mezzo soprano voice filled the room with unhindered clarity and grace, her unequaled talent clearly a gift from above. Never before had Allison heard anything so beautiful.

Never before had she seen a woman more beautiful.

The singer couldn't be more than twenty-four or twenty-five, gracefully tall, with a figure as fragile as a china doll's. Her hair was the color of spun gold, which she wore up loose on the top of her head. Shimmering tendrils cascaded down to her shoulders, framing a face so lovely it could have belonged to an angel. Her cheeks held a faint blush, her lips a deep rose, her eyes the clearest blue Allison had ever seen.

And every note she sang, every word from her mouth flowed as if inspired by some unseen spirit. But it was not the angels to whom she sang. It was to the darkly clothed, handsome man leaning casually against the outer wall at the back of the room. Her gaze rested on him, the depth of her adoration a tribute to him. Her exposed emotions a declaration of devotion that was intended for the Marquess of Montfort.

Allison had requested a selection from *Samson and Delilah* without having heard the music. She knew the opera had caused some controversy, knew the words were stirring—even provocative—but she hadn't been prepared for the passion in the aria Mademoiselle Bochaut chose.

Every beautiful tone hinted at something private shared by two lovers. Each word a caress, each delicate note a kiss, each breath an intimate touch. And they were meant for him alone.

Tears flowed unabashedly down Allison's cheeks. She told herself the reason was because she'd never heard anything so beautiful, had never been moved so by such a heaven-sent voice. But she wasn't sure that was the reason.

She fought the ache that pressed against her breast. She didn't know why the look the beautiful singer shared with the Marquess of Montfort should affect her. Why their relationship with each other should bother her one way or the other. She only knew she'd never hurt like this before in her life.

## *Chapter 4*

Joshua took the stairs to his father's townhouse two at a time and stormed through the burgundy double doors the Duke of Ashbury's long-time butler, Higgins, held open.

"Where is he!" Joshua marched across the marble-floored entryway with Higgins following at a pace faster than Joshua had ever seen him shuffle.

"His Grace is in his study, my lord. But I don't believe he wishes to be disturbed."

"I'll just bet he doesn't." Joshua tossed Higgins his hat and cloak without breaking stride.

The butler's granite facial expression did not change. It was the same frozen look of regal indifference he'd worn for the twenty odd years Joshua had known him.

Without waiting for Higgins to catch up with him, he headed toward the study.

"Do you wish to be announced, my lord?"

"No," He clenched his teeth. "I believe His Grace is expecting me."

Each step thundered on the marble, the ominous clomping of his boot heels the only warning he intended to give his father. The old man had pushed him too far this time. The bastard would be lucky if he didn't kill him.

He gripped the handle of the study door and threw it open, then kicked it shut with his foot. He was alone with his father.

The room reminded him of a tomb: dark, cold, musty-smelling.

He focused on his father and anger surged though him. The familiar inborn fury he experienced every time the two of them were together reared its ugly head. Years of animosity created a barrier neither of them could breach.

It was impossible to believe he'd been sired by this man. They were so different from each other, different both in looks and temperament. Or perhaps they were so alike it was like looking into a mirror and not liking the person who stared back at you. Perhaps that was why Philip had always been closer to their father. Joshua always the one kept at arm's length.

He stared at his father, then walked to the windows and jerked open the draperies.

Bright, invasive sunlight flooded the room. He let the warmth wash over him while he tried to get his emotions under control. If he faced his father now, he might commit murder, he was that angry.

His father took another swallow of his liquor without acknowledging Joshua's presence.

Joshua turned. "Ignoring me won't do any good."

"No. It never has."

The duke's words came out slow and slurred, the

garbled sounds indicating a man who'd been drinking for several hours—or days.

"No, Your Grace. It never has."

"I wondered how long it would take for you to discover what I'd done."

His father's words were directed toward him, but he didn't lift his head, nor did he look at him. Instead, he sat slouched in one of the two matching burgundy leather chairs angled before the lifeless fireplace. With his elbows propped on the arms of the chair, he cradled a full glass of brandy in his hand. An empty bottle lay on the floor.

Joshua marched to the chair and stopped in front of him. "What the hell possessed you?"

A slow smile crossed his father's face before he lifted the glass and drank a long swallow. When he finished, his hand dropped to his side, oblivious of the liquor that sloshed onto the floor.

Joshua's temper snapped. "Answer me, damn you!"

Ashbury's reaction was slow, but not at all unexpected. He lifted his head and smiled, the lopsided grin of disdain giving him a malevolent look. Hatred glimmered in his eyes. "Did the news tear you away from your mistress, Montfort?" His voice dripped with sarcasm. "Or were you having an afternoon tryst with the lovely, and ever-popular, Lady Paxton?"

Joshua glared at him, all the bitter hostility he'd felt from his youth surging to the forefront. "You're drunk."

"So I am. It's how I choose to handle the death of a great dynasty." Ashbury picked up the bottle from the floor and tipped it over his glass. When he realized it was empty, he carelessly tossed it against the stone fireplace. Pieces of glass flew back into the room but the duke didn't notice the ones that hit him.

Joshua didn't care.

"Did you come to talk finances?" Ashbury said, pointing to an empty chair halfway across the room.

Joshua fisted his hands. He refused to talk to him from anywhere but right here. "What have you done with my inheritance?"

"I spent it. Or rather, I lost it. It's gone."

A fresh wave of fury erupted inside Joshua. "You fool!" He grabbed the front of his father's expensively tailored, hunter's green jacket and lifted him out of his chair. The old man's expression didn't change except for the sneer of disdain that crossed his face.

"I see you are finally concerned with where your mistress's next bauble will come from," Ashbury slurred.

Joshua dropped his father back into the chair. "I didn't think I had cause to concern myself with such mundane matters."

"What? You thought there would always be an endless supply of money for you to squander?"

"I was never given reason to believe there wouldn't be. I was never allowed a hand in the running of the estates. Only Philip was given that privilege."

"Only Philip *deserved* that privilege." The duke swung his arm through the air as if emphasizing his words.

Joshua struggled to root himself to the floor even though the impact of his father's venomous words nearly knocked him flat.

"If Philip were here," the duke slurred, "everything would have been different. I wouldn't have had to do what

I did."

"But Philip's not here!"

The duke bolted to his feet and staggered precariously. "And whose fault is that?!"

Joshua reeled as if he'd taken a blow to the gut. He braced his hand against the nearest piece of furniture and fought the nausea that threatened to make him ill.

Herein lay the root of the hatred that had worsened every day since Philip's death. Their father had looked upon the tragedy as *his* tragedy, the loss as *his* loss. And blame must be assigned. The favored son was dead and the son who survived would never be worthy to take his place.

He stared at the cold look of hatred on his father's face, a look that said with Philip dead, the duke didn't intend for there to be anything left to bequeath to his remaining heir.

"What happened to the money?" he asked, trying to hold his temper at bay until he could figure out what to do.

"Does it matter?"

"Yes, it matters!" Joshua swiped his fingers through his hair and took a deep breath. "I just came from Nathanly's office and he informed me that as of today, there's not enough money to pay even one more monthly allowance. That you gambled it all away on doomed ventures. Unless we come up with a solution to our problem, *Your Grace*, we will have to sell off every piece of Ashbury property that is not entailed. And even that will not get us out of debt."

The duke did not react, but staggered to a side cupboard. He took out another bottle of his fine liquor.

"Are you listening to me, *Father*? If we do not come up with enough money to pay at least part of the bills you have amassed, we will even have to sell the liquor you're pouring down your throat."

"Then sell it. Sell everything!"

"No!"

The duke settled back in his chair and looked up. The corners of his mouth lifted, his loathsome smile oozed with contempt. "Are you worried about your precious Graystone Manor, *son*?"

"You know damn well I am. It's all that's ever concerned me. Certainly nothing of *yours* matters to me."

Father and son faced each other like mortal enemies, determined to fight to the death.

Joshua was in jeopardy of losing Graystone Manor. A wave of panic raced through him that nearly took him to his knees.

He stared at the man sitting in the chair. His father had downed another glass of liquor and was now mumbling incoherently.

"Why did you do it? Why didn't you tell me sooner, when there was still something we could have done?"

His father smiled as he took another swallow of the mind-numbing liquor he'd already had too much of. "I was afraid I wouldn't have the courage to go through with it."

"Through with what?"

His father ignored him. "But I did. And it's worked out perfectly." He laughed. "Now it's too late. I've won. Lost it all. Even…Graystone."

A heavy hollow space deep in his gut churned with a sickening emptiness. Ice flowed through his veins. "You intentionally lost everything to keep me from inheriting?"

The duke's laughter had a demented ring to it. "Of course. I could never let you have any of it."

Joshua staggered backwards, his legs trembling beneath him.

"I was afraid I wouldn't manage to lose everything before you discovered what I was doing. I was afraid you'd marry some chit with a hefty dowry and save it. But it's gone now and you'll never save it."

Joshua couldn't believe his father could hate him so much. He couldn't fathom that he intentionally lost every Ashbury holding so Joshua wouldn't get it.

He braced his shoulders. "You should be very pleased then, Father. I won't be able to touch it now. You've seen to that."

His father lifted his glass to his mouth and drank. "Not yours. It was never yours. Always and only, Philip's."

His words were nearly incoherent now, so jumbled Joshua could barely make them out. What was plain, though, was something Joshua had always known. His father hated him more than any father should hate his son. He blamed him for Philip's death.

What his father couldn't know was that no one blamed him more than he blamed himself.

❧

Joshua sat at a small, round table in the corner of his club, trying to get drunk. For three days he'd spent every waking hour hounding their solicitor, searching for a way to save at least some of the Ashbury holdings. But there was nothing he could do. There wasn't enough income to pay off the debts that threatened to take Graystone Manor away from him.

He was amazed at how quickly and foolishly his father had wasted a fortune. In exasperation, the solicitor had finally dropped his pen from his fingers and declared all their attempts futile.

Joshua refilled his glass and drained the contents in one long swallow. Futile. Useless. Hopeless. Graystone Manor was lost to him.

He reached for the bottle to refill his glass and halted when a figure cast a shadow over his table.

"Go away," he said, not caring who he offended. "I want to be left alone."

The man did not move, but pulled out a chair from the table and sat.

Joshua snapped up his head. "I said—"

"I know. I heard you."

Joshua glared at the Earl of Hartley.

Instead of leaving, the man motioned for a waiter to bring an empty glass.

With a disgruntled sigh, Joshua leaned back in his chair and attempted to ignore him.

When the glass arrived, Hartley filled it two fingers high with brandy. "There are rumors circulating that your father is about to lose everything. That means you, too, are in the same predicament."

"I don't think I want to discuss my family finances with you, Hartley. So if you'd kindly leave me the hell alone, I'd be most—"

Hartley held up his hand in a halting gesture, then reached for the glass in front of him. Without hesitation, he drained what was left and slid back his chair. He tugged on the sleeves of his black wool jacket before he hooked the silver handle of his cane over one arm and leaned forward. Joshua had no choice but to look into his face.

"If you want to save your inheritance, I have an offer that might benefit you."

There was no malice in his eyes, not a hint of haughty disdain in his features. Only a closed, dark expression that left more questions than gave answers.

"And that would be?"

Hartley glanced around the room. "This is neither the time nor the place to discuss anything of this magnitude. And you will need a clear head when we talk." He slid the bottle out of Joshua's reach. "Tomorrow morning? Say ten o'clock?"

Joshua glared at him without answering.

"Until then." Hartley nodded, then walked across the room, greeting several acquaintances as he left the club.

When he was gone, Joshua reached for the bottle to fill his glass. He stopped. He had a feeling that whatever Hartley wanted to discuss with him would require every bit of his senses. And probably a whole lot more.

❧

Time had run out.

For the past week, each new day was more tension-filled than the last. She could hardly sit in the same room with David without a little of the friction they both felt coming through. But it would not last much longer.

David had given her an ultimatum. She had until today to agree to marry. She had until noon to give him the name of the husband of her choice. Or he would choose a husband for her.

Allison thought she'd be ill.

She'd gone over both her options again and again and knew she had little choice in her future. David had made that more than clear when he'd told her of the stipulation in her grandmother's trust: that she either marry prior to her twenty-fifth birthday to a husband who met with David's approval. Or, he would be required to choose a husband for her.

The very idea made her furious. What kind of archaic stipulation was that? To assume David would know with whom she should live her life better than she?

She clutched her hands into tight fists, her nails biting into her flesh. She remembered the argument she and David had had two nights ago when she announced she'd decided not to marry. She could still see the priceless vase crash to the floor when he slammed his fist against the corner of the table. Could still hear his angry words. He repeated his vow that he refused to let her give up her trust, refused to allow her to rely on her siblings for a roof over her head and food to eat.

She fought a shiver. Deep down, she knew every reason she had for refusing to marry no longer mattered. In the end, she wouldn't be left with a choice. She'd have to marry. Even if was to someone she didn't love.

She uttered a curse as the door opened.

"Good afternoon, Allison," Lynette said from the doorway of the morning room.

Allison straightened from the corner of the sofa and slid her feet to the floor.

Her sister-in-law walked toward her and sat on the other end of the sofa. "David sent me to tell you he'd like to see you in his study."

"I went to see him earlier and he couldn't be disturbed."

"He had business to attend to." She turned enough so they faced each other. "It must be concluded now."

Allison closed her book and laid it on the table.

"May I speak with you first?" Lynette asked when she started to rise.

"Of course. But I think I already know what you're going to say." Allison sat back down. "You don't have to concern yourself with me any longer, Lynette. I know what I have to do."

"You never did have a choice. None of us do. Unless you thought to rely on David's generosity for the rest of your life."

"No, I never thought to do that."

"He loves you, you know. Sometimes I think even more than me."

"Oh, Lynette. That's not—"

"It's all right," Lynette interrupted. "There's a special bond between you and David. Which is the reason I found the courage to speak to you. If you love David, you'll marry and free him from feeling responsible for you."

Allison's world shifted beneath her.

"I don't mean to be selfish, Allison. But I want my husband to myself and he'll never totally be mine if I have to share him with you."

There'd always been a special connection between she and her brother, but she never considered that bond might interfere with David's marriage. Or that Lynette might resent their closeness.

Allison's world slowed to a standstill. "I see. I didn't realize."

"It's not your fault. Or David's. It's just the way things are."

Allison pasted a smile on her face and turned to Lynette. "You are right, of course. It's past time I married. Past time I had a home of my own."

Allison waited until her legs were steady beneath her, then walked to the door. "I'll see David now." She knew what she had to do.

Refusing to marry was no longer an option. But she'd marry who she wanted. David could demand all he liked. She was done with his dictating.

She walked down the stairs and across the marble foyer. She didn't knock when she reached his study but grabbed the handle and opened the door. David's head snapped in her direction, the surprise evident on his face.

"You don't have to concern yourself with me any longer, David. I have decided I will marry." She closed the door hard behind her. "But I will not allow you to choose my husband for me. *I* will decide with whom I must spend the rest of my life."

"Allison—"

"No. Hear me out."

She marched to the small side table where David was pouring two glasses of brandy and anchored her fists on her hips. "I won't make the same mistake each of my sisters made. I won't marry a man who only wants to marry me to get control of my dowry. And I won't take a husband who will humiliate me by sharing a bed with every woman who will have him."

"Allison—"

"Hear me out, David. It's the least you can do. You above anyone know how desperate I am to avoid marriage. And you know the reasons why."

David shifted his focus to look over her left shoulder. She didn't doubt he had trouble holding her gaze. He *should* feel guilty. He was the one who had issued the ultimatum.

She faced him and gave him the most intent look she could muster. "You can put your mind to rest. I've decided who I will marry."

"Who?"

"Someone I can trust not to humiliate me with his string of mistresses. Someone with whom I am sure I can be content spending my life." A long silence stretched between them while she searched for the courage to say his name. "I will marry the Earl of Archbite."

"No, you will not."

Allison stared at him with her mouth open. She couldn't believe what she'd just heard. "Surely you don't mean to object to Lord Archbite?"

"I'm afraid if your brother doesn't, Lady Allison, I will."

She spun around in search of the low, velvety voice that came from the corner behind her. Her gaze locked with the Marquess of Montfort's and she reached out to steady herself.

"What are you doing here?"

"Your brother and I were about to toast my betrothal and upcoming marriage. Would you care to join us?"

Montfort crossed the room with slow, deliberate steps

and came to a halt next to her. His nearness forced her to look up.

His towering height engulfed her, his broad shoulders and dark presence acted as a barrier. Beneath his cool exterior, she sensed some turmoil that surrounded him, a chaotic upheaval that never seemed at rest. He was the most compelling force she'd ever encountered.

She couldn't hide her surprise. Nor could she stop the niggling of unease that erupted inside her. "I didn't know you were in the market for a bride, Lord Montfort. The last time we spoke, you indicated quite the opposite was true."

"So it was. Then."

"And now?"

"Now, I have decided to marry."

"And who is this unfortunate female?"

"Allison."

David's warning came from behind her. She ignored him.

The marquess smiled.

A knot tightened in Allison's belly. "Do I know her?"

"Yes. Quite well as a matter of fact."

Her legs weakened beneath her, her mouth suddenly dry as lint. "Why the sudden change of heart, Lord Montfort?"

"Would you believe I have fallen quite madly in love?"

"Not for a moment. I doubt you know the meaning of the word."

"Allison," David warned again. "What has come over you?"

The marquess gave her another heart-stopping grin, this time accompanied by a suggestive tilt of his head.

"Would you believe, then, that I have finally met the woman of my dreams, the woman I want to be the mother of my children?"

"*That* thought is even more preposterous. Your dreams are much too crowded with the scores of admirers and mistresses for any one woman to be noticed."

The corners of his lips curled up sardonically. "Then would you believe that I am as desperate for your dowry as you are for a husband?"

Allison felt her knees give out beneath her and reached for the back of the nearest chair to support her. Of all the men in England, no one could be further from what she wanted in a husband than the Marquess of Montfort.

## Chapter 5

"ALLISON. WHY DON'T YOU SIT DOWN?"

David pointed to one of the two leather chairs angled in front of his desk. "Montfort." He pointed to the other.

The Marquess of Montfort didn't move. Neither did she. She stayed rooted to the spot, unable to force her body to obey David's command to sit. Her blood thundered in her ears, her heart pounded inside her breast.

This couldn't be happening to her. Surely David wouldn't be so uncaring that he'd deliver her into the hands of the kind of man she'd sworn to avoid? Surely David couldn't be that eager to be rid of her that he would take the first offer for her hand, knowing that man possessed every reprehensible quality she could not abide?

Surely she'd misunderstood, and Montfort's announcement of his intentions was a mistake, a hideous joke. She flashed her gaze to David's drawn expression.

"David, you can't mean to do this. Tell me you don't seriously intend for me to marry Lord Montfort."

Montfort stepped closer. "Perhaps it would be best if I

talked to Lady Allison in private."

Allison ignored him. "David. Tell me you don't."

"It's for the best, Allie. An arrangement between you and the marquess would be of benefit to you both."

"But the Earl of Archbite—"

"I've already explained that I won't accept a match between you and Archbite."

"Hartley," Montfort's voice interrupted again. This time his tone held an edge of authority. The single word a demand. "Leave the two of us alone for a while. I need to speak with the lady. In private."

David gave her an uncompromising look then left the room.

The door closed with a deafening thud and neither of them moved. She stood behind a chair that acted as a barrier, and he stood to her left. Only the steady ticking of the mantle clock intruded on the silence that stretched like a fragile string above a flame, waiting to snap. Finally, he moved.

He walked to the small side table beside David's desk and poured a rich amber liquid into two glasses. He handed one to her.

"Here. Drink this."

She reached for the glass, but her hand halted before it touched his. His long, sturdy fingers held the delicate crystal as easily and as expertly as she could imagine him holding a deck of cards or caressing a woman's flesh. A picture of him touching her and holding her flashed through her mind, sending a molten shiver that oozed through her.

She reached out her trembling fingers and took the

glass from his hand. Without thought, she took one long swallow that made her cough and gasp for air.

"Easy. Don't drink it so fast. It will only make matters worse."

"I doubt that is possible." She lifted the glass to her mouth again, then stopped. He was right. She was the only one who would suffer by downing the liquor like she was a hardened drinker.

"I don't want to marry you."

"I know."

She expected to see anger but didn't. His lips curved into a smile that caused her heart to skip a beat, then he sat on the corner of the desk in front of her. His nearness disturbed her, but not in a way she could explain.

"You don't want to marry me either," she said, then watched to see some sign of affirmation.

His brows shot up. "Don't I?"

"No. I doubt you want to marry anyone. Men like you don't consider settling down unless it is forced on them."

A corner of his mouth curved upward as he casually crossed his arms over his chest. "Would you care to explain what you mean by 'men like me'?"

"You know very well what I mean. Men so handsome they cause women's heads to turn; men who have never felt the desire to search for that one perfect match because there have always been so many women offering themselves there has been no need; men who do not know the difference between love and lust, nor do they want to discover it. Men like you are never satisfied with just one woman. And pity the woman who gives you her heart for safekeeping."

Montfort took a swallow of his drink and stared at her, a serious look of contemplation clouding his dark features. "I see you have a very low impression of me, my lady."

"Not a low impression, my lord. Only low expectations."

"And would you find marriage to me that repulsive?"

Allison didn't answer; couldn't answer.

"Do you find *me* that repulsive, my lady?"

Allison lifted her gaze to meet his. "No. You know I don't."

"Then what is it? Why do you find marriage to me so distasteful?"

Allison didn't like this. She didn't want to be made to feel that the fault was hers because she didn't want to marry him. She didn't want to answer for shortcomings that were plainly his. She didn't like being accused of being unreasonable when her requirements for a husband had never been a secret.

"I do not want to marry a man so handsome every woman in Society sees him as a challenge."

"A challenge?"

Allison couldn't sit beneath his gaze any longer. She couldn't have him look down on her while she was at her most vulnerable, with her fears so exposed. She got to her feet and faced him squarely.

He remained on the corner of the desk and their eyes were level. "I do not want a husband who cannot be content to stay in his own bed. I have three sisters whose husbands married them for their dowries. Husbands very much like you, more handsome than most young women dream will ever ask for them. And all three of my sisters have held their heads high for years while everyone knows their husbands spend more time in someone else's bed than they do in their own. I am not nearly so good at pretending I either don't know what my husband is doing, or I don't care."

"You think I would be the same?"

"I think I am not brave enough to marry you to find out. I have already survived one scandal with the man I chose to wed. I do not want to risk another."

"But you think Lord Archbite is different? Or is it that you fancy yourself in love with him?"

Allison didn't answer him.

"Are you in love with him?" He rose to his feet, towering over her like an avenging accuser.

"He is someone I can at least trust."

She noticed a hitch in his breathing before he whispered. "I see."

The marquess kept his gaze fixed on her for what seemed forever, then walked across the room. Bright sunlight poured through the window, framing the powerful build of his broad shoulders and streaking the coffee-rich color of his hair with coppery strands. She fought the strange yearning that rumbled inside her like a waking beast. He braced his feet wide and clasped his hands behind his back. The stoic pose gave him a majestic air of invincibility.

"I do not want to marry you, Lord Montfort. I cannot risk it. And you do not want to marry me. You do not want to marry anyone."

"But I, like you, do not have a choice. I need your dowry. Without it I will lose the one thing I refuse to give up."

"And what is that?"

"The estate my mother left me. Graystone Manor."

"It is that important to you?"

He raised his eyebrows and gave her a pointed look.

"It must be," she said more to herself than to him. "Or you would never be willing to give up your freedom to save it."

She thought for a moment, then locked her gaze with his. "Surely there is another option for you."

"No. Just as there isn't another option for you."

Allison felt the room sway beneath her feet. He was right, and he knew it. She could tell by the smug look on his face, hear it in the confident tone of his voice. He knew David had backed her into a corner without a means of escape. She could refuse to marry and lose her dowry and be at the mercy of her family for the rest of her life. Or she could marry. Those were her only choices. Therefore, she had no choice.

She would marry.

But it would be a cold day in hell before she would marry the Marquess of Montfort. And by the time she finished with her demands, it would be an even colder day before he would want to marry her either.

Allison looked into his face, studying his features: the aquiline nose, his bronzed flesh stretched tight across high cheekbones, the square cut of his jaw. A muscle twitched at the side of his face. She could tell he was losing patience with her. With the situation he could not control.

"Very well, Lord Montfort. I will agree to marry you, but with one condition."

His dark brows arched over midnight blue eyes. "And

what condition would that be?"

Allison lifted her shoulders and boldly readied her demand to which she knew beyond a doubt he would never agree. A condition which a person with his reputation did not stand a chance of fulfilling. A condition to which she was confident he would rant and rage at her audacity, then storm out of here in frustration.

"My demand is that before we marry, you agree in writing to be faithful. That in return for my dowry, you agree you will never take a lover for as long as we are married."

His eyes widened in disbelief, his demeanor turned dark and foreboding. "You can't be serious."

"Oh, but I am. On the day I take your name, you will give me your promise to always be faithful."

Allison looked into his face and saw none of the rakish humor and seductive teasing she was used to.

"And what is the penalty if I break my promise?"

"Are you asking what price you will pay if you are unfaithful?"

"Yes."

She smiled, knowing concern over his penalty was a moot point. He would never agree to her terms. The risk of failure was too great.

"You will lose it all, Lord Montfort. You will give me back my freedom and repay every pound that came with me. You will also give me every Ashbury property and asset my dowry made debt free."

"Is there anything else?"

"Yes. You will give me Graystone Manor."

A long, tension-filled silence stretched between them.

He would not accept her terms. Could not. She could see it in the hard look in his eyes, in the harsh line of his pursed lips. He would not marry her and risk losing it all.

"And what sacrifice are you willing to make? Or am I the only one required to meet certain demands?"

Allison chose to ignore the icy bitterness in his words. "I will agree to become your wife, my lord. And with my hand in marriage you will get my dowry. Is there more that you require?"

He didn't answer, but held her gaze captive in his. "And if I refuse to meet your terms?"

"Then we will not marry. I am sure there are other candidates with dowries large enough to save your inheritance."

A smile so slight she was not sure it was real lifted the corners of his mouth and he slowly turned to gaze out the window at the garden. She could not see his expression, but knew the turmoil that raged through his mind. He was searching for any way he could meet her demand to remain faithful and realized he could not. She knew his struggle was great. Knew he was wise enough and responsible enough to know he had to refuse her offer.

She watched as he swallowed hard, then tilted his head back. Thick, dark lashes fluttered downward before he released a heavy sigh, then turned to face her.

"Very well, my lady. I agree to your terms. On the day you take my name, I will give you my promise. From that day on, you will be the only woman to share my bed. In return for your dowry, I will take you as my wife. And my lover."

The floor dropped out from under her. She couldn't

have heard him right. She thought he'd promised to agree to her terms. To agree to be faithful to her. A promise she knew she couldn't trust him to keep.

She knew the kind of man he was, knew his reputation. She'd be lucky if he remained faithful the first year of their marriage—the first month! Then what would she do? It would be too late by then. How could she take back her vows once she spoke them? How could she repair the damage he caused? How could she heal her heart once he broke it?

"Why are you doing this?" She felt a rope tighten around her neck and fought to breathe from the pressure weighing on her chest.

"Because I don't have a choice. And neither do you. If I don't marry you, I will lose everything. If you don't marry me, you will lose your inheritance."

"I could marry—"

"No, you couldn't. Your brother wouldn't allow it. And neither would I."

"Then I will lose the inheritance. I don't need it."

"Yes, you do. Without it you will have to beg for a roof over your head from either your brother or one of those sisters you so pity. You would always be the poor relation, the spinster aunt."

Lynette's words echoed in her mind. Her demand to have her husband to herself, to enjoy her home and her children without an intruding sister-in-law. Allison fisted her hands at her side. She didn't have a choice. Not even the choice to marry who she wanted. "I wish I would not come with a dowry at all. I don't want the money."

"But I do. And I will marry you to get it."

Fingers of dread clenched around her heart, squeezing until she could not breathe. She paced the room like a caged tiger. She could feel Montfort's trap closing around her, feel her circle of freedom shrinking by the minute.

A wide smile lifted the corners of his lips, his eyes twinkled with the rakish teasing she'd battled before. This was the marquess she'd kissed in the garden. The man who'd hounded her at every ball. The rogue who invaded her dreams each night.

"Think on the bright side, my lady. Perhaps some unfortunate accident will befall me. Perhaps I will be shot by an irate husband or jealous lover and you will be left a widow. Then you will have the best of all worlds. All your wealth and mine, free and clear, and no husband to bother you."

"Don't even tease about something like that." She sensed his devil-may-care attitude and it frightened her.

"You have to admit that would be an answer to your problems. Unfortunately for you, I do not intend to give you cause to get rid of me. We will probably be forced to spend our lives together, me content with you and you tolerating me."

Allison turned her head away from him. She did not want to think of anything beyond today.

"Is there anything else we need to discuss before I summon your brother to break the joyful news?"

"You could ask him once more if he will reconsider the Earl of Archbite."

The marquess's expression turned hard. "Even I would not let you marry the earl." He set the glass he had in his hand onto the table and walked up to her. He stopped when they stood toe to toe and placed his hands on her shoulders. "You may not believe this," he said, moving one hand to cup the side of her cheek. "But as lacking as you find me, Archbite would be the worse choice in the end."

With effortless ease, he placed his finger beneath her chin and tipped her face upward. Before he finished the last word, his mouth covered hers.

She thought to fight him, but didn't. Couldn't. Some part of her wanted him to kiss her. Another part of her knew that once she yielded, she would be lost to him.

She was.

His lips were firm and warm, pressing against hers with a gentle possessiveness that stole her breath. She stiffened in his arms and he kissed her lightly again, as if coaxing her to give in to him. Slowly and ever so gently he repeated his kisses until she could fight him no longer. On a heavy sigh, he deepened the kiss...

...and she yielded.

His mouth moved over hers, drinking deeply. His tongue outlined her lips, making demands she wasn't quite sure she understood.

"Open for me," he whispered, and she did.

He deepened his kiss until she wasn't sure where her breaths ended and his began. They were one. Then he invaded her mouth with all the mastery of an experienced lover.

Allison knew they should stop now, that she should pull away from him, but she couldn't.

He held her closer and let his tongue brush against hers.

White-hot, fiery shards spiraled all through her body.

Through her chest and down to her fingertips. To her stomach then lower, churning with a turmoil that was almost an ache. She was on fire, burning with a heat that was all-consuming.

Allison slid her hands between them and pushed back the front of his jacket. She wanted to touch him, feel him against her. With her palms pressed against the silky material at his chest, she let her fingers mold to the hardened ridges beneath her touch. His flesh was warm, alive, his heart thundered so violently she could feel it. Every second in his arms was a new experience, a daring step she'd never taken before. On a loud moan, she wrapped her arms around his neck and gave in to him.

She didn't think it was possible, but he kissed her with more passion than before. His tongue renewed its frantic search and with each thrust she met him, battled him, yielded to him. Their tongues mated with a ferocity that stole her breath, his very nearness a force so powerful it was almost a threat. She didn't know a kiss could be like this. Didn't know it was possible to lose herself so completely. It was suddenly too much.

He must have felt it too. On a moan filled with torturous agony, he lifted his mouth from hers.

She gasped when they separated. His release was painful and she clung to him as if he were a lifeline that could save her instead of a danger that could destroy her. The void, the emptiness when he was gone was indescribable.

She couldn't think, could barely stand on her own.

As if he realized what had happened to her, he pulled her against him, pressed her close, held her tight.

She wrapped her arms around his waist and leaned her

cheek against his chest. His heart thundered beneath her ear, beating in a rhythm as desperate as her own. His arms gripped like iron clasps. Both their breaths came in ragged gasps and she closed her eyes to wait until the turmoil inside her calmed.

Time went by as if spinning in circles around them. Her cheeks burned and her lips throbbed. She knew if she looked into a mirror, her eyes would hold a wild look, a frantic look. That he could do this to her frightened her, and yet…

If he took her in his arms again, she would do it all over again. Gladly.

Allison finally found the strength to step out of his embrace. It took another second to find the courage to look him in the eyes. Her gaze met with the most heart stopping grin she'd ever seen. A smile that took her breath.

"I doubt the earl could kiss you like that," he said, his voice a seductive whisper. He touched his finger to the tip of her nose. "You will do well, my lady. Both as a wife. And as a lover. I can't imagine being tempted to find my pleasures anywhere else."

Her cheeks turned hot and her heart fell to the pit of her stomach. The man she was about to marry was a rake through and through.

Her choice of a husband was no better than the choice any of her sisters had made.

# Chapter 6

FOR TWO DAYS, she lived her worst nightmare. For two days, she'd been the object of gossip that seemed to grow instead of diminish.

News of her betrothal to the Marquess of Montfort spread through Society with the speed the plague traveled through London. And was received with the same welcoming.

Most who heard the news doubted the accuracy of something so unbelievable. Some even openly repudiated its validity. All were clearly shocked when the rumor refused to die.

From every corner of the city a great wailing and lamentation could be heard because one of the most sought-after bachelors was no longer available.

A great sucking of air always followed the announcement when Allison's name was mentioned as the proposed bride.

Then, last night, the shock became a reality.

Conversation came to a deafening halt when she and Montfort stood arm in arm at the top of the stairs at the

Countess of Courtland's ball.

The looks of stunned disbelief would have been humorous if they'd been directed at someone else. Mouths dropped and whispered comments behind cupped hands followed her the entire evening.

If Montfort felt the same unease, he showed no sign of it. He was his usual jovial self, showering her with attention; playing the part of the devoted fiancé to perfection; already living up to the terms of an agreement he hadn't signed as of yet. Not once did he show the slightest indication that he wanted to escape the *ton's* attention. She, however, couldn't wait for the evening to end.

Today was no different. He insisted they go for a ride through Hyde Park. He assumed the more they were on exhibition, the sooner Society would become accustomed to seeing them together and find some other unsuspecting couple on which to concentrate. He also had the mistaken idea that their upcoming marriage would not be nearly so shocking if at least outwardly they seemed enamored of each other.

What was obvious to her was that it would take an insurmountable amount of convincing for Society to believe that she had brought the renowned Marquess of Montfort to his knees to propose marriage. It would take even longer to convince them that theirs was truly a love match. She breathed a shaky sigh as another wave of regret washed over her.

"You might look as if you were enjoying my company, my dear. That will go a long way in convincing observers that you find the prospect of marrying me enjoyable."

She couldn't keep the surprise from her face. Nor could

she hide her doubts. The marquess only laughed and moved closer.

Every time he touched her, her flesh sang with awareness. The hand he held in his grasp tingled with excitement.

"Smile, my dear. The Countess of Overton is approaching with her two daughters. She is without a doubt the last person we want to start the rumor that our upcoming marriage is not a mutually happy event."

She looked ahead to the countess's shiny black carriage, then turned back to find herself mere inches from the marquess's incredibly deep blue eyes. A touch away from the rugged planes and contours of his face. A whispered breath away from his lips. Her heart gave a leap. Then he touched her. Cupped a hand to her cheek and held it there.

Allison pulled back from him as if she'd been burned and he and laughed. "Smile," he whispered, and rubbed her lips with his thumb. She did.

He waited until the carriage stopped, then greeted the occupants. "Good day, Lady Overton. Ladies."

The countess leaned forward to extend her greetings. Her two daughters were too busy fluttering their lashes in the marquess's direction to notice Allison.

"Good day, Lord Montfort. Lady Allison," the countess said. "I must say. The rumors of your betrothal must be true." She patted a plump hand over her well-endowed bosom. "At first I didn't believe it, but here you are. Living proof."

The marquess reached over and placed his hand over hers.

Warm, vibrant shivers raced up and down her spine. She did not want his touch to affect her. But it did. More than she wanted to admit. She fought not to pull her hand from his grasp. Instead, she smiled sweetly at the countess's intense glare then lifted her smile to Montfort's.

"As you can see," he said, lifting Allison's hand to his lips and kissing her gloved knuckles, "the rumors are true. I am the most fortunate of men. Never did I think I would be so lucky."

The marquess leaned his face closer to hers and gave her a seductive glance that stole her breath. Her cheeks turned uncomfortably hot.

The countess studied Allison with a penetrating look that was filled with doubt. "You can imagine everyone's surprise when your betrothal was announced. No one realized you and Lord Montfort were so familiar with one another."

Allison kept a smile on her face. "We've been acquainted for quite some time."

"How surprising. No one in Society suspected the two of you were enamored."

"Then we are to be congratulated," Montfort said, smiling first at the countess, then leveling a purely wicked grin in her direction. "Lady Allison and I have been drawn to each other ever so long now. I am surprised we were able to keep it a secret from such knowing eyes as yours, my lady. It is not every day anything escapes your notice."

The smile on the countess's face faded. It was obvious she didn't know how to take the marquess's comment.

Always on the alert for any bit of gossip to spread, Lady Overton's gaze turned sharper. Allison felt as if she were on exhibition, as if the countess were waiting for any hint of a strained relationship that indicated not all was as it seemed between the two.

"All of us thought you had sworn off marriage," she said to Allison. "It is rumored you have had a number of offers in the past and refused them all."

Allison placed her free hand on the marquess's arm and leaned closer to his powerful body. "Obviously I was waiting for the right offer." She looked up into his smiling face — and froze. The look in his eyes was not what she expected. It held a sincerity she hadn't expected to see. With a slight nod, he lifted her hand and pressed it to his lips.

"Did I not tell you I was indeed fortunate?" he said. "I only regret it took me so long to notice such a rare find. Now if you will excuse us." He tapped the seat behind his driver. "I am loathe to share my betrothed for more than a few moments."

The marquess nodded politely to the countess and her daughters, then tucked Allison's hand close to him as the carriage moved forward again. Neither of them breathed until they were far enough away to not be overheard.

"We'll never fool them." She remembered the look on the countess's face. "She'll never in a million years believe you did not marry me for any other reason than my dowry."

The marquess laughed as if her fears were inconsequential. "Then we will make a greater effort to prove everyone wrong."

Allison rolled her eyes. She knew how impossible it was to change Society's mind once it was made up.

He laughed again and patted her hand. "Fenton," he said to the driver. "Stop the carriage. The lady and I would like to walk."

She shot him a glance of surprise but he only winked at her. Sometimes she didn't think he allowed himself a serious concern in the world. Other times, she was convinced of it.

Fenton brought the carriage to a halt and the marquess stepped out onto the grassy lawn of Hyde Park. He lifted his hand to help her down and looked at her with a heart-stopping smile.

Every nerve in her body reacted to him. She reached for him, letting him swallow her small hand in his large grasp. Fiery explosions shot from the tips of her fingertips to deep inside her. It was this way every time. Just his touch was enough to make her tremble.

The minute her feet reached the ground, he tucked her hand in the crook of his arm and smiled. Without speaking, they walked at a leisurely pace down a long, shady path. Anyone who saw them would think they were indeed lovers sharing a quiet stroll through the Park.

"I have obtained a special license," he said finally, his tone as nonchalant as if talking about the weather. "We can be married as soon as you are ready."

"I didn't think it was possible to acquire one so quickly." She felt her muscles tighten.

He answered her reaction by sliding his arm around her waist and pulling her even closer to him. "You forget. You are marrying the future Duke of Ashbury. My father's title affords me a few privileges."

Allison lifted her gaze to his face and for a fleeting second saw a coldness she didn't quite understand. Was it the title that caused such a reaction, or their upcoming marriage?

"I met with your brother earlier this morning and he informed me you will turn twenty-five the middle of next week. To avoid any concern over your inheritance, we should marry no later than Saturday. If that is agreeable with you."

Allison tried to speak but she couldn't find her voice. That was only a few days away. She wanted to hug her arms around her middle like she used to do when she was little and afraid, or run away and hide in a dark closet. But those were no longer choices. Instead, she took a deep breath and nodded.

"We'll spend our wedding night at my townhouse in London, then leave the following morning for Graystone Manor. You should at least see what your dowry has saved."

"You mean what is so important that you sacrificed your freedom to save." She knew her barbed words struck a tender spot. The slight hitch in his breath told her so.

To be on the offensive was better than thinking of her wedding night. The very thought of sharing a bed with him sent a wave of trepidation racing through her. She averted her gaze, unable to look at him. The sound of horse's hooves thundered behind them and she turned.

She barely got a glimpse of a horse and rider racing toward them before Montfort pulled her off the path and stepped in front of her as if she needed protection.

He pulled her close to him as the Earl of Archbite brought his horse to a stop and jumped to the ground. His eyes held a wild look that matched the violent expression of rage. Allison had never seen Percy look so furious.

Montfort's arm snaked around her, his action both protective and possessive. The touch of ownership was not lost on Archbite. He crossed the distance between them in long, angry strides.

"Tell me it isn't so!" he bellowed loudly enough for everyone to hear him. "Tell me you are not going to marry this philanderer."

Montfort tightened his grip and Allison felt the muscles that held her coil like bands of steel.

"That's enough, Archbite." Montfort lifted his shoulders in battle readiness.

Percy paid no mind.

A wave of fear raced through her and she made what she knew would be a futile attempt to calm the situation. "Lord Archbite. I should have explained—"

"Just tell me it isn't so!"

A small crowd gathered in the distance, but neither of the men seemed to notice. Or care. Montfort held her around her waist and tried to move her. "Lady Allison. Step back."

Allison shook her head and held firm. She was desperate to find some way to stop tempers from flying. But the open look of hatred in Percy's eyes told her any effort would be wasted. "Please—".

"I thought we had an understanding. I thought you knew how I felt and that you felt the same."

Percy took a threatening step closer.

"I'm sorry—" She stopped, unable to find the words to finish.

"That's enough." Montfort held out his arm as a barrier to stop Percy from coming closer. "The lady has nothing for which to apologize."

Percy ignored Montfort's warning and took another

step toward them.

She swallowed a gasp. Without warning, the situation escalated to a dangerous point. Every muscle in Montfort's body bristled with unbridled fury. He transformed before her eyes into an ominous warrior Percy would be wise to avoid.

He didn't.

"What did he do to you?" Percy said, waving his hand in the air. "What hold does he have on you? Tell me and I'll do everything in my power to save you from him."

She shook her head, trying to escape Percy's accusations. "He has no hold."

"Surely it isn't because you want to be a duchess?"

"No! You know better than that."

"Then why! You know his reputation. He is a rake of the worst kind. You would never agree to marry him if you were not forced. I know you would not." He paused as if struck by an eye-opening thought. "It is your dowry, isn't it? You are being forced to marry him because of your dowry!"

"Enough!" Montfort bellowed again.

The earl laughed, the sound a vile, cynical cackle. "He does not want you, my lady. He only wants the money that will come with you. Can't you see that?"

Her eyes stung with mortifying dampness and her cheeks blazed with heat. If the marquess had not had his arm around her waist, her legs would have given out from beneath her. "You are mistaken, my lord."

"No, it is you who are mistaken. He has you under his spell, just as he does every female. He will only use you then discard you in the end."

Montfort tensed like a stretched bow, ready to fire. She placed her hand atop his to keep him from striking.

"If you are wise, Archbite," he said through clenched teeth, "you will leave before I do something you will most assuredly regret." His voice was soft, but not gentle by any means. It shattered around them like the deadly hiss of a striking cobra.

"No! We had an understanding!"

"Leave. Now."

Montfort clasped his fingers beneath her elbow to escort her away but she held firm. She couldn't let it end like this. She had to set things right. She was the one to blame. She *had* led Percy to believe that she would consider his offer of marriage, if only he was patient. If only he gave her time. But David had given her no choice.

She should have talked to Percy before. Made him understand. But she'd been so consumed by her own fears, she hadn't even considered Lord Archbite's feelings.

"It's too late, my lord," she said, taking a step toward Percy. Montfort stepped with her. "The decision is already made."

"Surely you don't mean to marry him?"

"I do."

"No!"

Without warning, Percy lunged toward Montfort.

Montfort turned her away to push her behind him, but the time he used to protect her gave Percy the advantage he needed. Before Montfort could right himself, Percy's fist connected with his jaw, hitting his chin with a bone cracking jolt that jerked his head to the side.

"No!"

She stepped between them and grasped her fingers around Montfort's upper arms to hold him back. He was the one she knew could do the most damage. He was the biggest threat. "Please," she whispered, not caring that she had tears streaming down her cheeks. "Please," she whispered again. She lifted her gaze to his. "The fault is mine."

His nostrils flared with fury, his lips pressed so tightly they were white. His breaths came in harsh, ragged jerks. She knew that only the thinnest thread held his rage from exploding. "Please, leave it be," she pleaded. "Everyone is watching."

He stared at her for long, tension-filled moments, the fury that raged inside him evident to her. His muscles bunched beneath her hands and she knew how desperately he wanted to hurt the Earl of Archbite. Knew how deeply Percy's words had cut.

"Please…"

She sensed the moment he capitulated, the moment he gave in to her. He breathed in deeply, then released the air in an agonizing whoosh. His gaze lifted from her face to Archbite's, where hatred and bitterness hung between them like a heavy fog. Without a word, the marquess grasped her arm and turned her toward the waiting carriage.

Just when she thought the scene was over, Percy stepped in front of them, barring their exit. "We will settle this tomorrow morning. In the meadow behind Miller's pond."

The marquess nodded. "As you wish. The Marquess of Chardwell will act as my second. Your man can reach him at his townhouse."

Allison let Montfort lead her to their carriage and hand her in. In one swift move, he climbed the step and sat down beside her. The carriage lurched forward but he did not look back. He kept his gaze focused straight ahead while they moved toward the park's nearest exit.

"What did Lord Archbite mean when he said you'd settle this in the morning?"

"Nothing."

Allison sat back in the seat, trying to calm her roiling stomach. And then she knew. Her hands flew to her mouth to stifle the scream that threatened to escape. "No! You're going to duel tomorrow. You can't!"

"Why not, my lady? You don't think you're worth fighting over?" His voice was calm and steady, but he avoided her gaze.

"No! I'm not worth the death of either one of you."

"I was not the one who issued the challenge."

"Then be the one to ignore it."

"I already ignored Archbite's first challenge because you asked me to. You have no idea what that cost me."

She stared at him a long moment, remembering how she'd pleaded with him not to fight Percy. "Don't go. Just stay away."

His brows arched high. "And be known as a coward as well as a philanderer?"

"It is better to be a living coward than a dead fool."

"Are you sure, my lady? Are you sure you could be content with a coward for a husband? Perhaps it isn't me you're concerned with. But Lord Archbite? Perhaps you are more afraid some danger might befall him?"

For the third time since she'd met him, she wanted to

slap him. Her hand lifted of its own volition, but as quickly as she moved, his arm reached out to stop her. His fingers wrapped around her wrist in a deadly grip.

"I've been attacked enough today. I don't need you added to the long list of enemies who want to do me harm."

"Please—"

"Quiet." His voice was not loud as much as the tone was deadly. "Spend your time preparing for your wedding, my lady. I know you will not wish to do overly much to celebrate the event, but I imagine you will at least want to drape the windows in black. You will hear soon enough if Archbite's bullet hits its mark and you have real cause to celebrate."

She felt as if he'd buried a knife deep inside her. "I don't wish to see you harmed."

He looked at her and smiled, but it was not a smile of happiness. Far from it.

❦

How the hell had he gotten to this point?

Joshua stepped into the carriage after escorting Allison home and sank against the cushion. In less than two weeks' time he'd gone from being a carefree bachelor who had an allowance that covered his earthly needs and a mistress who saw to the more important essentials to...this!

Bloody hell!

The battle to fight his father's hatred was ending in defeat!

He'd narrowly escaped losing his beloved Graystone!

Nights spent with his long-time mistress were a thing

of the past!

The woman he'd asked to marry him didn't want him as her husband!

There was a good chance he wouldn't survive the duel he was fighting in the morning!

And he only had a few days more of freedom left and he'd be leg-shackled forever!

*If* he lived that long. If dear Percy, Lord Archbite, didn't put a bullet through his heart and kill him!

He couldn't believe this was happening to him, couldn't believe he was taking a wife. Couldn't believe he'd actually signed an agreement that he'd never seek his pleasures in any bed other than his wife's. Couldn't believe he was fighting a duel. But what choice did he have?

He'd do anything to save Graystone, agree to anything to keep from losing it.

He closed his eyes and fisted his hands at his side while he considered the most important question he was unable to answer. Why did his father hate him so much he'd gamble away everything rather than allow him to inherit it?

No matter how hard he tried, he couldn't find an answer that made sense. Now, Joshua was forced to do everything in his power to save the Ashbury holding, especially Graystone—unless, of course, Archbite killed him in the morning. Then it wouldn't matter if he lost it all.

He wanted to blame Allison for everything that had happened. She had, after all, demanded that he give up his former way of life. But he couldn't blame her for that. She was as much a victim as he. She didn't want to marry any more than he did.

Yet, what choice did either of them have?

Joshua dismounted when he reached his townhouse and climbed the stairs. He had to get a good night's sleep so he'd be alert enough in the morning to dodge Archbite's bullet.

Or prepared enough to meet his Maker.

# Chapter 7

SHE HAD TO STOP THEM before it was too late.

Allison stared out the carriage window as it made its way to the small body of water known as Miller's Pond. It wasn't dawn yet, but it wouldn't be long and the sun would begin its ascent over the horizon.

In her mind, she heard shots, saw blood, and felt the pain as if it were her own. Montfort could die, and it would be her fault. She knew if that happened, her world would never be the same.

Her head throbbed from worry and lack of sleep, and her throat felt thick with panic. She clutched her arms around her middle and rocked back and forth in the plush leather seat of David's carriage, praying the driver would make the horses go faster. What if she didn't get there in time?

"Hurry, Benson," she yelled at the groomsman she'd roused from bed before first light. Although at first he'd been reluctant to drive her halfway across town unescorted, she'd given him no choice. Now, she was afraid all her efforts had been for naught. What if she was too late?

Foolish, stupid men. She couldn't let this happen. Couldn't let them fight over her.

Her skin turned cold and clammy, her teeth chattered uncontrollably. The weight of her guilt nearly suffocated her. She knew she would never be able to live with herself if she didn't reach them in time to stop the duel from happening.

"Hurry! Are you sure you know where it is?"

"Yes, my lady. We're almost there."

She scooted to the edge of her seat and looked out the window again. The sun was now clearly visible in the sky, bright rays streaming through the carriage window. Benson followed a sharp curve to the right, then slowed.

"We're here, my lady."

Before the carriage came to a complete stop, she had the door open. She jumped to the ground.

A large crowd had already gathered, no doubt to watch the excitement. She clutched her hand to her aching stomach and fought the urge to be ill.

"Do you see Lord Montfort?" She frantically scanned the area.

"Over by that copse of trees, my lady." Benson pointed to his right. "But you shouldn't be here. Lord Hartley will be furious if he finds out. And you all alone. We should have at least brought Emma with us."

Allison ignored his protests and looked to where he'd pointed.

They stood like little toy soldiers, the marquess's towering frame unmistakable even from this distance. He faced Lord Archbite, perhaps forty paces separating them.

Before she could feel a sense of relief, her gaze focused on a third man standing between them. The man raised his arm and at the same time, Lord Archbite and Lord Montfort raised theirs. A white flag hung almost perfectly still from the man's fingertips, then slowly, as if in slow motion, it fluttered to the ground.

"No!" she screamed as she ran across the grass and into their line of fire.

❧

Joshua stood in the early morning haze and waited for the sun to rise high enough in the sky so they could get this over. What a turn his life had taken since he'd met her.

He looked to where Archbite stood with Baron Fitzwater, his second, and wondered how this would all end. If the lady they were dueling over cared. Or if she secretly hoped for a certain outcome. Joshua released an angry breath.

They were both of them excellent shots, Archbite known for his daring and his accuracy. Today could go either way.

"Watch your back," Chardwell warned. He picked up the pistol Joshua was to use to examine it. "Archbite doesn't have a reputation for letting the flag hit the ground before he fires his first shot."

"So I've heard." Joshua unbuttoned his jacket and shrugged it off his shoulders.

"I still can't believe he's gone to this extreme," Chardwell said. "Who would believe the Earl of Archbite would be willing to risk his life for someone wearing a skirt. Everyone knows his preference runs to young lads in breeches. Do you really think he's serious about offering for her?"

He tossed his jacket into Chardwell's waiting arms. "He's serious."

"Why?"

"Pressure from his dear mother, the countess. Archbite's older than me by a few years. I suspect he's been ordered to find a suitable wife and produce an heir. I think my betrothed showed him just the right amount of encouragement to seal her fate. And now he wants her."

Chardwell looped Joshua's jacket over his arm. "And we both know that what dear Percy wants, dear Percy gets."

"Yes," Joshua mumbled beneath his breath. "But he'll not get her. Even if I'm not around to stop him, her brother will see to that. Hartley knows what Archbite's about."

Joshua methodically rolled the sleeves of his white lawn shirt to his elbows, then breathed in a deep breath. One he knew could be his last. He didn't know why, but things didn't feel right today. There was an air of uncertainty that wouldn't go away.

"If things go for the worst today—"

"They won't, Montfort."

"If they do," he continued, taking the pistol from Chardwell's hand. "Keep a watch on her, would you?"

"You know I will. But there won't be—"

"Just don't let him have her." He cast a glance over to where the Earl of Archbite stood, stretching like a cougar about to pounce. "I don't want him to touch her."

"He won't."

Joshua scanned the gathering crowd, then focused on where Archbite stood. "It looks like they're ready. Fitzwater is coming to issue the last instructions."

Fitzwater strode across the meadow, his cocky walk filled with overconfidence. He bowed elegantly when he arrived. "Lord Archbite has most graciously agreed to forget this entire misunderstanding, Montfort, if you will agree to drop your intentions to marry Lady Allison."

Joshua let a lethal smile lift the corners of his mouth. "How magnanimous."

"He is also willing to make it worth your while. Say, fifty thousand pounds."

Joshua's eyebrows shot high and he turned his gaze to Chardwell's shocked expression.

"Lord Archbite has placed quite a value on my betrothed. I'm impressed."

Fitzwater smiled. "Lord Archbite appreciates Lady Allison's exemplary qualities. She will of course make him the perfect countess."

"Of course." Joshua crossed his arms over his chest and rocked back on his heels as if he was truly considering the offer.

Fitzwater gave him a few more minutes before he lost patience. "Is there a reply you wish me to take to Lord Archbite?"

Joshua dropped his hands and stepped closer to Fitzwater. "Yes. You can ask Lord Archbite if he prefers a bullet to the heart for a quick and easy death, or one to the gut. I think I prefer to lodge my bullet in his gut. I am told the victim's pain is excruciating."

Fitzwater breathed a repulsed "hrumph", then spun on his heel and left. Joshua doubted the messenger would relate the message verbatim. More's the pity.

"Fifty thousand pounds." Chardwell followed his words

with a low whistle. "Archbite must really want her. I wonder if your intended realizes how valuable she is."

He wanted to laugh. "Knowing her as I do, I doubt she would be impressed to know she was measured in monetary value. I think she is hoping to be valued for something less—calculating."

Chardwell started to laugh, but his laugh was cut off when Fitzwater stepped forward. "They're ready, Montfort."

Joshua looked, then nodded.

Chardwell clasped him on the shoulder. "I'll wait for you here. And remember what I said. Watch Archbite's hand. Don't concentrate on the flag. He won't wait for it to hit the ground."

Joshua gave him a broad smile, trying to shake the feeling that something was not as it should be. This was not the first duel he'd ever fought; there'd been others. But they'd been mostly for show. No one had ever died. None of his other challengers had ever wanted him dead. Not like the Earl of Archbite intended so he could claim his betrothed.

A cold shiver raced up and down his spine and he knew it was not the early morning coolness that was the cause of such a chill. He looked around the small glade before stepping into place, noticing nothing unusual.

A medium-sized crowd had gathered. Not out of the ordinary considering all the attention their argument had garnered yesterday. Or the wagers placed on the outcome at White's.

A black carriage pulled up at the outskirts of the crowd and a well-dressed female disembarked. Under different circumstances, he would have laughed. Some females had a taste for blood as great as a man's.

"Ready," Fitzwater announced from a safe distance to the side of them. "You may fire when the flag hits the ground. Not before."

Joshua let his gaze concentrate on his opponent. Archbite's eyes were nothing more than narrow slits, his mouth pursed in a thin, angry line. His nostrils flared like those of a fire-breathing dragon. The hatred emanating from him was alive and palpable, the loathing and jealousy as deadly as a cancer-eating sickness. Archbite had no intention of losing, had no intention of letting Joshua make Allison his wife. And he would play by whatever rules were necessary to win.

Every nerve and muscle in his body stretched taut. If ever there was a reason to come out the victor, the reason stood before him. How could he give Allison over to that cur?

Fitzwater raised his arm, the white flag clutched between his fingers. Archbite followed suit, holding his pistol out, steady and straight.

Joshua did the same, never losing sight of the pistol aimed at the center of his chest. Never taking his eyes off Archbite's finger resting on the trigger.

From the corner of his eye, he saw Fitzwater release the flag, saw the white cloth flutter downward.

He tightened his grip and squeezed ever so gently. And stopped.

A feminine voice echoed in his ears. A voice filled with terror and panic.

Blood thundered in his head.

She screamed again.

Joshua's heart gave a lurch inside his chest. That voice. Her voice.

Bloody hell!

"No!"

He heard her scream again, and this time she seemed nearly on top of them.

He turned his head to the side as she broke through the crowd. She looked like an avenging angel, wisps of her fiery hair flying around her face, her eyes filled with terror, her arms reaching out as if she could prevent what was going to happen.

His heart lodged in his throat. "Stop!"

He prayed Allison would heed his warning, but knew she wouldn't.

She ran forward until she was directly in the line of fire.

He reached out and pulled her to him just as Archbite's finger moved on the trigger. He turned with her in his arms, to shield her from danger. A loud explosion rent the air and an instant later a burning, stinging sensation gripped his arm.

Shouts and jeers erupted. "Foul! Foul, Archbite!" The crowd was clearly appalled at Archbite's disregard for fairness, as well as for the risk he took in firing when a lady could have been hit.

Joshua looked down at Allison huddled in his arms and seethed with anger.

*She could have been shot.*

*She could have died.*

He didn't know with whom he was more furious, Allison for doing something so foolish. Or Archbite, for firing even though he knew she was running toward them. He took a deep breath and swung back with Allison still next to him, and aimed his pistol.

Archbite's eyes grew wide. His face paled with a dread Joshua relished seeing. He knew the coward wanted to run, but he didn't. He faced Joshua squarely, knowing Joshua had every right to kill him.

"Don't, please," her soft voice whispered against his chest. "Oh, please. I couldn't bear it."

She wrapped her arms tighter around his waist and buried her face against him. Her body trembled in his arms.

He uttered a vile oath then lowered his pistol.

He hesitated. He contemplated the ramifications of allowing Archbite's actions go unanswered, then he lifted his arm and aimed his pistol. Not at the ground. Not at Archbite's chest where he wanted to bury his bullet with deadly accuracy. But at the soft, fleshy part of Archbite's leg. And he fired.

Her grip tightened and her muffled scream echoed against his body. Her warm, wet tears soaked into his shirt.

Archbite clutched his leg then crumple to the ground.

The crowd of observers rushed forward, Fitzwater and one or two more going to where Archbite lay. The rest crowding around him.

"Are you hurt?" Chardwell was the first to reach him.

"I'm fine." He looked down at the deep red moisture soaking through the material of his shirt, turning it nearly black.

"No doubt about it," one voice hollered from behind him. "Archbite fouled."

"We all saw it," another voice added. "It was a blatant

act of cowardice. Archbite will never be able to show his face in Society again."

"If any questions arise, we'll vouch for you."

"Right," another added. "I say, Montfort. You're bleeding. Do you need a surgeon?"

The man's words affected her. Her eyes locked with his. They were filled with concern. She scanned his body, searching for the wound. Her face paled when she saw the blood.

"It's all right," he whispered in her ear, but he knew it wasn't. Blood ran down his arm and dripped from his fingers.

A heavy film of perspiration covered his forehead, the burning wetness stinging his eyes. He should at least take time to stop the bleeding but all he wanted was to get as far away from here as possible.

His head swam and he fought to keep his feet from buckling beneath him. He would not go down with everyone watching.

"Someone!" a voice bellowed. "Send for the surgeon."

"Have him look after Archbite," Joshua said. It was a struggle to stay on his feet. "He may need him. I don't."

He took one step and sagged into her. She clasped her arm around him and helped him away from the crowd already embellishing the tale of what had just happened. Archbite was already being painted in a very dark light.

"Are you all right?" Chardwell gave him his arm. "Do you need help?"

"I need to get away from here."

Sheer willpower kept him on his feet. Raw fury kept the blackness from swallowing him.

What possessed her to rush toward them like that? Which one of them did she intend to protect?

A fresh wave of anguishing pain engulfed him. The intense throbbing in his arm kept him from coming to any conclusion. The answer was one he didn't want to know.

When they reached the carriage, Benson already had the door open. Allison stepped up first and with Chardwell's assistance, he stepped inside next. He fell back against the seat as the carriage lurched forward.

She leaned over him to try to make him more comfortable. Their gazes met and held. She was the first to look away.

"You could have been killed," he said through clenched teeth.

"And you as well." She loosened his cravat from around his neck.

Chardwell removed his cravat and handed it to her, too.

"Would you have minded?"

She shot him a lethal glare. "Of course I would have minded! If you had gotten yourself killed, I would have been forced to make a show of mourning you for at least a year. By then it would have been too late to meet the stipulations of my trust. My dowry would have been lost to me."

"As well as the man you intended to marry."

"That may have been the only blessing." She struggled with the material of his shirt.

"You aren't…impressed I wanted to fight for…your honor."

"Honor! All I asked was that you didn't embarrass me in front of the *ton*. We aren't even married and already you've made me the subject of a scandal. Isn't it enough that we've shocked everyone with our betrothal and hastened marriage?"

"I wasn't the one…who issued the challenge,…my lady." His breaths came in shorter gasps. "Perhaps you could…remember that."

She opened her mouth to speak but stopped. "I can't get this loose," she screamed at Chardwell.

"If you will allow me." Chardwell leaned forward and ripped the sleeve from Joshua's shirt.

She gasped when his wound was exposed. The look of terror on her face punched him in the gut.

"It's just a scratch," he heard himself say, but his voice sounded weak and far away. Not like his at all. "The bullet… barely passed...through flesh."

Her face turned even paler. "You've lost a lot of blood."

"Take this cloth and press firmly against him," Chardwell said. "We need to stop the bleeding."

With trembling fingers, she grabbed the cloth and pressed it against his wound.

He wanted to ease her fears, to assure her everything would be all right, but just then another stab of pain knifed through him and all he could do was focus on the angel of mercy trying to care for him.

Her face was pasty white, her gaze filled with concern. And her eyes brimmed with tears that threatened to run down her cheeks. The dark circles surrounding her eyes spoke volumes. They told him of her sleepless night and hours of worry. A wave of guilt consumed him.

"Are those tears for me, my lady?"

"If they are, my lord, it proves what a fool I am. They are

the last I shall ever shed over you."

Joshua tried to smile but couldn't. Another wave of pain spiked through him. "Do not fear," he said when the pain subsided. "The wound is not…nearly so severe as to prove fatal. I would not…dream of being so inconsiderate as to…die before our wedding."

Her lips pursed but her hands kept at their ministrations. "Perhaps you would consider keeping quiet and saving your breath."

"Perhaps," he whispered. He leaned his head against the cushions as the carriage raced down the cobbled streets.

"I am such a fool," he thought he heard her say, but wasn't sure if he'd heard right. His hold on consciousness was fragile at best.

"It's still bleeding," she said, the worry evident in her voice. "I can't press hard enough."

Chardwell shifted so he was in front of Joshua. Then pressed down enough to cause him to jerk in agony. "Sorry, Montfort."

Joshua ground his teeth and moaned. When he opened his eyes her cheeks had paled even more. "It's all right, Allison. It'll be fine now."

"It's too bad the wound was not at your neck. Then I wouldn't have trouble tying the cloth tightly enough."

Even though she'd said the words beneath her breath, he had no trouble hearing her.

That was the last he knew until he woke hours later.

He was alone in his bed, his arm cleaned, bandaged, and throbbing like bloody hell.

He remembered the last words she'd spoken to him and smiled.

# *Chapter 8*

HE COULDN'T BELIEVE he was actually going through with this, that he was getting married. That he'd signed the damned agreement, vowing to give up everything, even Graystone Manor, if he proved unfaithful. But what choice did he have.

He climbed into Chardwell's carriage and sank back against the seat. Nearly a week had passed since he'd fought his duel with Archbite. A week that he'd spent recuperating from the wound that was more a nuisance than anything else. A week since he'd seen his betrothed. And it wasn't for want of trying. She was the one who refused to see him.

"I find it difficult to believe you're actually giving up your freedom," Chardwell said, a wide, open grin on his face.

Joshua ignored how his cravat suddenly seemed like a noose around his neck. "Your smug attitude isn't at all appreciated. Besides, it matters very little what I'm giving up or not. I wasn't left with much choice, one way or the other."

"Have you seen your intended since the duel?"

"No. She refuses to see me."

Chardwell rolled his eyes heavenward and laughed. "What a turn of events for you. Usually the ladies fall at your feet. Yet the one female in London you wish to have there, refuses to even let you through her front door."

"She's too damn proud for her own good." He rubbed his shoulder. His arm was mostly healed, but it still ached. Especially when moved a great deal.

"Perhaps she did have feelings for Archbite," Chardwell teased.

Joshua shook his head. "No. She was never serious about him. She was forced to marry and she wanted someone she thought would never give Society cause to gossip."

"But why Archbite?"

"She thinks he is above reproach. Because of the first scandal, it's important to her that the man she marries isn't a womanizer, and has a reputation for being faithful."

"No wonder she doesn't want to marry you!"

Joshua scowled at his friend. "Those are only a few of the reasons. I'm sure if asked she could come up with a dozen more."

Chardwell laughed, then his eyebrows arched upward. "Does this mean the fair Angelina is now in need of a protector?"

"You are welcome to her with my blessing. We parted when I became betrothed to Allison. That was one of the terms in the betrothal agreement."

"That you give up Angelina?" Chardwell asked.

"Angelina and anyone to replace her."

Chardwell slumped back against the seat. "I don't believe it!"

"You don't believe what? That I made such a bargain? Or that I intend to keep it?"

"Either. Both!"

"I had good incentive," Joshua said, thinking of the bargain he'd made. "I'd do anything to protect Graystone, including giving up my freedom. I need Allison's dowry to save the Ashbury holdings. It wouldn't have taken the creditors long to figure out my country estate was the only asset worth anything. By the time they finished, I would have lost Graystone Manor."

"Are things that desperate, then?"

"Yes. My father set out to lose everything and he did a perfect job of it. His poor investments and wild spending and gambling were intentional. He wanted to be sure there was nothing left for me to inherit."

"Why? What possessed him to do something so malicious?"

"Hatred, mostly. He blames me for Philip's death."

"That's ridiculous."

"Not in his mind. Philip's dead and I'm alive. The wrong son fell and broke his neck."

The two friends sat in companionable silence while the carriage rolled through the busy London streets.

"I met up with Fitzwater last night at my club," Chardwell said.

Joshua lifted his brows.

"Fitzwater said it will take a while for Archbite to heal, but when he does, he'll be ready to challenge you again." Chardwell laughed. "Idle boasting, I'd say."

Joshua remembered how close Allison had come to getting shot and fought a new surge of anger. "I welcome another chance to fight him," he said, "and this time my betrothed will not find out about it."

"You'd better hope she doesn't. By then she'd be your marchioness and I doubt she'd take kindly to Archbite making her a widow so soon after she has married."

"Or perhaps she would. Perhaps she'd welcome a way to rid herself of me."

Chardwell shook his head. "I don't think so. If she wanted to be rid of you, friend, she wouldn't have thrown herself in front of you to save you from getting hurt. Do you know what I think? I think she is already half in love with you."

Joshua dropped his head back and laughed. "Love? Really, Chardwell. You and I both know there's no such thing. There's friendship and there's mutual attraction, both physical and emotional. There's lust, there's companionship, and there's sex. But nowhere in the vast array of human emotions is there any such thing as love. At least none that lasts any longer than it takes for the sheets to cool after you climb out of them.

"What my betrothed was trying to do was prevent a scandal from reaching the ear of the *ton*."

"It's that important to her?"

"She has three older sisters. One is married to the Earl of Fortiner. One to Viscount Hanbury. And one to the Marquess of Banbain."

Chardwell's laughter echoed in the closed carriage. "Bloody hell, Montfort. No wonder salvaging her reputation is so important to her. You could parade a string of mistresses through Westminster Abby and not cause half the stir each of your illustrious future brothers-in-law cause nearly every day. Just last week Banbain was bold enough to bring his mistress to the opera."

"That is hardly the most shocking thing anyone has ever done," Joshua argued.

"Perhaps. But Banbain's wife was at the opera that night too, with her sister, the Countess of Fortiner. Their box was next to where Banbain sat with his mistress. My sister was there. She said not one in attendance watched the performance. They had their eyes focused on the two boxes, waiting for them to notice each other."

"What a fool," Joshua said. "Did Lady Banbain discover her husband and his mistress?"

"Salon gossip relates that they passed each other in the hallway afterward and Lady Banbain walked past her husband and his paramour as if she didn't see them."

"Bloody hell," Joshua whispered.

"It's no wonder your intended doesn't want to be the target of any more rumors. For years it's been a mystery how each of her sisters has been able to walk through Society pretending nothing is amiss in their marriages."

Joshua felt a hand clench around his heart.

Chardwell reached for his hat and gloves. "Does your father know you are marrying?"

"No. I saw no need to tell him."

"You don't think he'd want to know you've found a way to save Ashland Park and the other country estates?"

"He'll find out soon enough." Joshua looked out the window. They were almost there. "Besides, he's left London and even his mistress doesn't know where he's gone. I think he couldn't face the end. Or perhaps he just couldn't face me." He shrugged his shoulders as if his words didn't cut him to the quick.

When the carriage stopped in front of Hartley's townhouse, he gathered his hat and gloves then dismounted. The front door opened before he could reach for the knocker.

"If you will follow me," a dignified butler issued, leading the way to a bright sunny room on the other side of the house. "You are expected."

He breathed a sigh of relief. At least he wasn't turned away at the door.

Two double doors stood open at the far end of a hall and he walked into the room. He accustomed his gaze to his surroundings.

Hartley stood with his elbow propped casually against the mantle of the fireplace. His three brothers-in-law surrounded him.

Joshua took the relaxed look on their faces as a good sign. Huge bouquets of flowers had been placed at various spots throughout the room, giving it an air of elegance and serenity. The perfect decor for a wedding. Joshua first breathed a sigh of relief, then he smiled.

At least she hadn't draped the windows in black.

# Chapter 9

*HE WAS HERE.*

Her sister Phoebe saw him from the upstairs bedroom window and let out a squeal of delight. Mary and Tess ran across the room to catch a glimpse of him as he and his friend, Lord Chardwell, made their way to the house. Allison's stomach did a nervous flip.

"Oh, Allie. He's even more handsome than I remember," her sister Tess exclaimed. "I do believe you have captured the best looking husband of us all."

She said the words as if choosing a husband was a game. The one who married the most handsome husband scored the most points.

Her three sisters had arrived a little over an hour ago in a whirlwind of excitement and jubilation. They couldn't believe their baby sister had finally decided to take the wonderful step from lonely spinsterhood to wedded bliss. And to the renowned Marquess of Montfort! Each one espoused the sanctity of matrimony as if their own experiences brought nothing but happiness and fulfillment. As if each one was happy and content in her marriage.

Allison knew better.

They bustled about, chattering like happy magpies while they helped her get ready for her special day.

One made a last minute adjustment to her hair while another checked that each tuck and pleat and ruffle on her dress lay perfectly. The third picked out just the right flowers for her gown and her hair. Together they decided on the necklace and ear bobs that would go with what she wore.

She only wanted to be left alone. She didn't want to be reminded of the monumental step she was about to take or the enormous mistake she was undoubtedly making. But none of them would hear of leaving until everything was perfect.

Finally she was ready. They gave her a last perusal and declared her the most beautiful bride of them all. Then, they looked at each other nervously and ordered her to sit down.

She thought she would die when they informed her that since their mama was not here, they considered it their duty to enlighten her as to what to expect on her wedding night.

"Don't be squeamish," Mary volunteered, her cheeks flushed with a deep blush. "It's terribly discomfiting, but it's something we all have to tolerate."

"Just concentrate on something else, a new gown you want or a new bonnet you've had your eye on. I always reward myself the next day," Phoebe announced, as if being the oldest and having been married the longest gave her special insight.

"And whatever you do, lie still and keep your eyes closed until he's finished," Mary added as if she'd suddenly forgotten the most important part. "Your husband will think you're no different from a common trollop if he suspects you enjoy it."

"If you're lucky," Tess added, crossing her fingers as if making a wish, "he'll plant his seed in you right away and you won't have to suffer the embarrassment too many times."

"And never allow your husband to see you unclothed," Phoebe added as an afterthought.

She stared at her three sisters in shock. Was this truly what it was like between a husband and a wife? Was letting a man hold you, kiss you, be intimate with you truly so horrible? It hadn't been when Montfort had held her. When he'd kissed her.

The deafening silence in the room brought her attention back to her sisters. Phoebe looked to Mary, then to Tess, as if needing to be reminded of what else they needed to tell their younger sister. "And don't be afraid," she said in a very matter-of-fact manner. "It's only painful the first time. After that, it's just uncomfortable."

"And be sure the room is totally dark," Tess added, chewing her lower lip. "It's ever so much worse when you can see him … his …" She took a deep breath and finished her sentence on a shaky sigh. "Well, … when you can see."

She fought to keep from being sick. Surely it couldn't be so horrible? Surely it couldn't be such a dreaded part of marriage? She couldn't bear it if it were. She wrapped her arms around her middle and hugged tight.

"Oh, look," Phoebe said, rushing to put her arms around Allison. "We've scared her to death. She's as pale as a ghost."

"Don't be afraid," Mary said, trying to comfort her. "You will learn that *that* part of marriage isn't very important at all. It's just necessary to produce an heir or two. And if you're lucky, Montfort will keep his mistress for the other times he feels the need."

*No!*

Her blood pounded in her head. Surely Mary wasn't serious.

"What would half of the women in Society do without them?" Tess said on a laugh.

It was Mary's turn to add her opinion. "I don't even want to venture a guess. Pity the poor women whose husbands can't afford to keep someone on the side."

Phoebe laughed. "At least I know my dowry went for a good cause."

*No!*

Allison's heart thundered in her chest.

She jumped from the stool where Mary had been putting the last flower in her hair. "Stop it! All of you! Doesn't it bother you that your husbands aren't faithful? Don't you care that all of Society knows the man you married would rather sleep in someone else's bed than his wife's?"

Her sisters' cheeks turned bright red as their jaws dropped.

"You can't let that bother you," Phoebe answered timidly for all of them. "To let your husband come to your bed so often is not proper. No well-bred married woman allows it. Besides, how can you stop your husbands from taking their pleasures elsewhere?"

Allison swiped her hand through the air. "I don't know, but I'd make an effort to find out."

Three pair of eyes stared at her as if she'd grown a second head.

"You don't know what you're talking about," Mary said.

"Just wait until you've been married awhile," Tess said.

"You haven't even gone through your wedding night," Phoebe said.

"All I know," Allison answered as calmly as she could, considering how badly she shook from head to foot, "is that I will do everything in my power to satisfy my husband both in my bed and out. How can you go through life holding your heads high while all of London knows where your husbands are sleeping? How can you pretend you don't hear the whispered comments and ridicule because your husbands all prefer someone else's bed to yours? How can you pretend you are the happiest wives in England when everyone knows you are not? You can't be!"

Silence settled around them like a thick London fog.

For ever so long, no one spoke. Phoebe was the first to recover, the first to make an effort to defend herself. "You don't know yet, Allie. You don't know what it's like to watch your husband leave your bed and not know what to do to get him back. To know it's not really you he wants in his arms. To know he can't wait until he's done his duty by you so he can spend the rest of the nights with another woman." She swiped at a tear that spilled from her eye. "Your marriage will be no different. None of our husbands came with half the reputation as a rake and womanizer as the man you are marrying."

Allison felt the air leave her body and reached out a hand to steady herself.

"If you are lucky, though," Tess added, with tears running down her cheeks, "you'll be smarter than we were."

Allison was ready to hear Tess warn her not to marry Montfort, but she didn't. She gave her a warning even more impossible than that.

"You won't let yourself fall in love with the man you marry," she finished. "You won't let yourself care that he prefers someone else to you. Or you won't go to bed each night praying that this will be the rare night he comes to you, even though you've done your best all day to convince him you don't want his attentions. That you don't need them."

Tess brushed a tear from her cheek before she added, "Or that maybe, just this once, he'll fall asleep when he's finished, still holding you in his arms. And you'll get to lie next to him for at least a few hours."

"If you are truly lucky," Mary said, her voice thick with emotion, "you'll be able to hide how much it hurts to know your love will never be returned. We've all gotten quite adept at it, don't you think?"

Allison looked from one to the other. "How can you live like that?"

"What choice do we have?" Phoebe asked.

"Surely there's something you can do. Some way to fight for the men you married."

Mary shook her head. "If there is, none of us know what it is. It's not at all proper to encourage a husband's attentions. If we did, we would be no different than the women they visit when we refuse them."

Tess brushed a finger across her damp cheek. "It would be different if we'd started our marriages loving our husbands and they loving us. But we didn't." She hesitated. "And neither are you."

She couldn't breathe. This wasn't how she wanted to start her marriage. Wasn't the way she wanted to spend the rest of her life.

"My marriage will be different," she said, trying to sound more confident than she felt. Failing miserably. "Lord Montfort has promised—"

Phoebe stopped her sentence with a laugh. "Don't you know, they'll promise you anything. Until they get your money."

She didn't want to believe her. Couldn't believe her.

On legs that barely held her, she turned away from her sisters and took a shaky step toward the door.

"Oh, Allie," Phoebe said, rushing to her and pulling her into her arms. "We're sorry. Truly it isn't so bad. We didn't mean nearly any of the things we said. We're just three old married ladies complaining about nothing. It's really wonderful. Being married is so romantic. Really it is."

"Yes, Allie." Mary grabbed her hand and held it. "Being married is just grand. We should have only told you the best parts instead of all the rest."

"Never mind us," Tess said, with sadness in her eyes. "This is your wedding day. You're supposed to be happy. We never should have been so open with you. We should have told you just what mama told us."

"And what was that?" she asked, looking at each of her

sisters, not sure she really knew them. "What did Mama tell you on your wedding day?"

The three sisters looked at each other and shrugged their shoulders. Finally Phoebe spoke for them. "Nothing. Just that we'd find out soon enough. I guess that's what we should have told you, too. But we didn't want you to walk into it blind like we did."

She nodded, then stepped away from them. She had to get out of here. "I need to be alone for a while. Tell David I'll be down shortly."

Tess took a step toward her. "Are you all right?"

She wanted to laugh, but was afraid if she started, her laughter would turn into tears. Instead, she nodded and took another step toward the door.

Mary reached out and touched her arm. "We're sorry if we said something we shouldn't have."

Her head felt light, her hands cold and clammy. How could she go through with this? How could she walk into the same trap each of her sisters had, knowing once she said the words, there'd be no turning back?

She turned away from them and fled the room. She raced down the hallway until she could go no further, then turned the knob to the last door on her right. She slipped inside the dark, unused chamber and leaned against the closed door.

With her eyes squeezed tight and her blood pounding in her head, she struggled to keep the weight that pressed against her chest from suffocating her.

No matter what, she wouldn't let her life end up like her sisters'. She wouldn't let her husband keep his mistress. She wouldn't be the object of ridicule and gossip.

She walked to a chair pushed against the wall by the window and lifted the dust cover from it. With a heavy sigh, she sat down. She knew sitting on her silk moiré gown would wrinkle it, but that didn't matter. Her legs weren't steady enough to support her any longer. She and Lord Montfort had made a bargain. He'd put her terms in writing and they'd both signed it with witnesses present.

She vowed by everything she held sacred, she'd never give him cause to leave her bed. She had done everything possible to protect her dowry and her future.

The only thing it was too late to protect was her heart.

∽

Joshua stood in the small circle that included Allison's brother, three brothers-in-law, Chardwell, and the minister who would perform the ceremony. He stood relaxed, while focusing his gaze on the open doorway. He would not rest easy until he saw her.

Allison's sister-in-law, Lady Hartley, played the perfect hostess, making sure all the men had a glass of excellent brandy. She would no doubt offer the ladies a glass of wine as soon as they arrived. Her husband, the Earl of Hartley was an expert host. Conversation flowed smoothly, the small gathering never at a loss for some topic to discuss.

Joshua had liked Hartley the first time he'd met him. He admired his intelligence as well as his straight forward manner. And he was impressed by the way he truly cared for his sister. What surprised him though was that he also liked his future brothers-in-law. He hadn't expected to.

He'd never had business dealings with any of them, so had never formed an opinion, other than the negative one Allison had given him. But he found each of them pleasant to converse with, and unique in their own way. He wondered what kind of women they'd married. How like Allison the three sisters were.

Just then, they entered the room.

Allison wasn't with them.

He moved his gaze from the empty doorway to the three sisters. Their excitement was obvious, yet beneath their enthusiasm, he noticed tiny frown lines etched on their faces, as well as the frequent glances they shared. A wave of unease sharpened his senses, alerting him to some unknown problem he knew involved Allison.

The ladies came toward them and Hartley made the introductions. The circle opened to include them, and, instead of staying with her sisters, the oldest of the three, Lady Fortiner, went to stand by her husband. His reaction was one of surprise, as if his wife's nearness was not something he was accustomed to.

"Is everything all right?" Fortiner asked as he took a glass of wine from a passing servant and handed it to his wife.

"Yes."

But Joshua thought he noticed a slight hesitation in her answer.

Of the three sisters, she looked the most like Allison: her hair the color of burnished brass; her eyes the same vivid blue; her coloring the same creamy perfection. Lady Fortiner didn't seem as tall as Allison, nor as perfectly filled out, but she was a beauty nonetheless.

She took a sip of wine, then, with her free hand, entwined her fingers with her husband's and held them in the folds of her skirt. The puzzled look on Fortiner's face showed his confusion, but he did not pull his hand away. If anything, he stepped even closer to nestle his wife's shoulder against him.

"Is Lady Allison nearly ready?" Tiny pinpricks of unease stabbed at Joshua and refused to leave. The troubled glance Lady Fortiner cast at each of her sisters stung him anew.

"Yes. Nearly."

"She just needs a little time before she joins us," Lady Hanbury added. The hesitancy in her voice was obvious. She moved close to her husband, Viscount Hanbury, who seemed equally as perplexed by his wife's attention as Fortiner.

Joshua experienced an emotion that bordered on alarm. What if she'd changed her mind? What if she refused to marry him? Graystone Manor would be lost to him forever. Bloody hell. What more did she want from him? He'd already agreed to everything she'd demanded. "I would like a word with her before the ceremony," he said.

The three sisters looked nervously from one to the other. Finally, Lady Fortiner nodded. "I'm sure her maid, Emma, can take you to her."

Lady Hartley called for the maid and Joshua followed her up the stairs to a room at the end of the hall. He nodded his dismissal and slowly turned the knob on the door.

No candles lit the room. For a few seconds, he thought the maid must have been mistaken. He didn't think Allison was here. Then he saw her—seated in a chair by the window, her back ramrod straight, her hands clasped in her lap. A look of regret on her face.

"This is hardly the place for a bride, my lady. You should be standing in the bright sunshine so the light can reflect off your beauty."

Slowly, ever so slowly, she turned to face him. Her gaze contained a frightened look, as if she were about to go to the gallows instead of her wedding.

"Do you wish to change your mind?" she said. "It is not too late."

Her question startled him. There was no softness in her voice, no trepidation. Not even the hint of meekness. She'd asked the question as matter-of-factly as she'd ask the milliner if there'd been a mistake in her bill. It was not a plea, but an ultimatum. A last-minute demand for him to tell her if he had changed his mind. An opportunity for him to back out now if he intended to, if he couldn't meet the terms of their agreement.

"I would not be here if I had, Allison. There has never been a pistol pointed at my head."

"Hasn't there?"

He smiled. "Perhaps, but you weren't the one holding the gun."

She turned her head and stared ahead. He wondered what she saw. There was nothing there except an empty wall without even a picture to break its bareness.

After what seemed an eternity, her shoulders lifted.

He took the steps necessary to reach her and stood before her, his feet planted wide. She had no choice but to lift her head and look at him.

"Are you waiting for me to give you the same option?"

"Would you give it?"

Her voice lacked any sign of hopeful expectancy. He was glad.

"No. We are both here because we have no choice."

More silence stretched between them. Finally, he heard her sigh of resolve.

He did not move, but stayed so close it was impossible for her to rise from her chair. "I have already given my word that yours will be the only bed I share. In a few minutes I will swear before God and man to plight you my troth. I can't do more than that, Allison."

"Is that all there will be to our marriage?"

"Only time can answer that."

Their gazes locked and held. With far more confidence than he felt, he held out his hand and waited for her to take it. She did.

Her touch was warm. Her small hand a perfect fit in his larger one. As if it belonged there.

As if she belonged there.

❧

"Joshua Camden, wilt thou have this woman to thy wedded wife, to live together after God's ordinance in the holy estate of Matrimony? Wilt thou love her, comfort her, honor, and keep her in sickness and in health; and, forsaking all others, keep thee only unto her, so long as ye both shall live?"

"I will."

Allison listened to the minister's words as if they echoed in a tunnel. Her soon-to-be husband answered with confidence, his voice strong and forceful, his demeanor filled with assurance. He wanted this marriage—because he wanted her dowry.

*"Don't you know, they'll promise you anything. Until they get your money."*

"Allison Townsend, wilt thou have this man to thy wedded husband, to live together after God's ordinance in the holy estate of Matrimony? Wilt thou obey him, and serve him, love, honor, and keep him in sickness and in health; and, forsaking all others, keep thee only unto him, so long as ye both shall live?"

She hesitated. She wasn't sure she could do it. Not step into the same shoes as her sisters. Not live a life of shame and embarrassment like they did and not know how to stop it.

*"None of our husbands had half the reputation as a rake and womanizer as the man you are marrying."*

Yet, what choice did she have? She only had a few days until her twenty-fifth birthday.

Lynette's words came back to haunt her, her plea for Allison to take a husband. If she didn't marry, she'd lose it all. She'd be forever dependent on her sisters and brother for everything. She'd even be without a home of her own.

"My lady?"

She lifted her head. She knew he saw her hesitancy, her doubts and fears and uncertainty.

Without a word, he reached for her hand and held it in his own. He gave her fingers a gentle squeeze, as if trying to reassure her the only way he knew how.

The minister subtly cleared his throat and Allison turned to face him. What choice was left to her?

"I will."

Her heart gave a lurch, her breath caught in her throat.

The choice had been hers to make and she would live with the consequences of her decision.

"Join your right hands and repeat after me," the minister instructed, and Montfort took her hand.

Allison heard the minister's soft, gentle voice say the words and heard Montfort's deep, confident voice repeat them. "I, Joshua Camden, ninth Marquess of Montfort, … take thee, Allison Townsend, to my wedded wife, … to have and to hold from this day forward … for better for worse … for richer for poorer, … in sickness and in health … to love and to cherish till death us do part, according to God's holy ordinance—"

There was a pause, a pause long enough to make her lift her gaze. The look on his face was as serious as she'd ever seen.

"My lady," he said, lifting her hand and clutching it to his chest, atop where his heart beat. "And thereto I plight thee my troth."

Her eyes filled with tears, her heart hurt with an ache that threatened to bring her to her knees. Tess's words came back to haunt her. *If you're smart, you won't let yourself fall in love. You won't let yourself care.*

Allison repeated the minister's words, promising to have and hold from this day forward a man who might destroy her in the end. Promising to love, cherish, and to obey, till death us do part.

Knowing it was already too late to heed her sister's words. She perhaps did not love him, not yet.

But she more than cared for him.

Much more.

## Chapter 10

IT WAS OVER.

She sat on the window seat in the bedroom she would share with her husband, and stared out the window. She rested her chin on her bent knees and hugged her arms around her legs while she waited for him to come to her.

For nearly ten whole hours now she had been the Marchioness of Montfort, married to the Marquess of Montfort, one of the most renowned rakes in all of London. She should be terrified, filled with fear and regret and misapprehension. She thought she would be. But she was not. Instead, she felt a strange sense of… completeness.

A flurry of excitement swirled inside her, the elation and anticipation soaring with the same wild abandon as the tiny bubbles in the glasses of champagne David served following the ceremony.

She couldn't explain the sense of fulfillment she'd experienced the minute the minister had pronounced them man and wife. Just as she couldn't explain the happiness that erupted in a fiery explosion when he kissed her. For just a second it was as if a door opened and she knew her choice to marry had been right. She prayed she would remember that contentment forever.

She closed her eyes and relived every second of the day, from the time he'd entered the room where she'd gone to be by herself to the minute he'd brought her here, to his townhouse, as his wife. The day she'd dreaded her whole life had been—wonderful. Filled with special memories she would always cherish.

She wondered if it had been the same for him. She couldn't tell. He remained as unreadable as a Greek scroll.

It wasn't that he'd been hostile or antagonistic, or even distant and aloof. He hadn't been. He'd been stunningly perfect. He'd smiled when David had toasted their happy union, and talked when he'd been spoken to. He'd laughed easily and often. But she couldn't help but feel that at least part of it had been an act. That his every smile or laugh or gesture was a brilliant performance. That he conducted himself as was expected of him.

The ring he'd placed on her finger had been perfect. It was not large and ornate like she was afraid it would be. But small and delicate, a beautiful opal with tiny diamonds surrounding it.

When the ceremony finished and the guests toasted the happy couple, he'd pinned to her gown a delicate filigreed butterfly brooch made of the finest spun gold imaginable. The moment was heartwarming. Even now her eyes blurred with unshed tears.

He'd smiled at her, then cupped her cheek in his hand and explained that the ring was an heirloom passed down from his mother and from her mother before her. But the butterfly was a gift from a husband to his bride. He wanted her to have something made just for her, something special she would know he had picked out to give her on their wedding day.

*Was that only an act?*

Tears choked her throat again and she got up from the window seat and walked to where Emma had placed the brooch on the mirrored table. Even though the room was shadowed in darkness, she'd become accustomed enough to the dark that she could trace her fingers across the delicate strands.

Giving her something so special had been a beautiful thing to do. Almost too perfect. As if he'd followed a treatise outlining the perfect way to win her over, the perfect gift to endear her to him, the perfect words to say, the perfect smile, touch, gesture.

*How much of what he'd done had been sincere?*

Before they'd left, Lynette had served a wedding breakfast in celebration of their marriage. Montfort had joked and conversed and bantered with her family as if he'd known them his whole life. He'd especially included her in the conversation and often during the meal he'd reached over to give her fingers a gentle squeeze. As if he wanted to reassure her that she'd made the right choice in marrying him. As if he wanted to reassure her that he had, too.

*How much of it had been an act?*

When they finished eating, it was as if he knew she could not survive sitting through an hour of idle conversation. As if he knew she needed to escape the flushed cheeks and embarrassed looks each of her sisters wore because they knew what awaited her yet this evening. Or that she didn't enjoy the sly looks she caught her brothers-in-law giving her husband because they knew, too. Whatever those looks were about, it would happen in this room. It would happen in that bed.

Allison turned and slowly scanned the room. The decor was his, all bold and masculine. There was no feminine softness to the furniture, no delicate touch in the knickknacks sitting around, and not a domestic scene in any of the pictures on the wall. Yet she felt perfectly at home here. Perfectly at ease and comfortable surrounded by everything that was his.

*It couldn't have been an act. It couldn't have.*

She made her way to the other side of the room and clasped her hand around one of the end posters on his bed. She stared at the maroon counterpane, then at the covers Emma had thrown back after she'd helped her ready for bed.

A mighty whirlpool swirled deep in her stomach, a warm heat that turned hotter by the second. She tried not to think what would happen in that bed tonight. Tried to remember the instructions her sisters had given her.

Her cheeks burned hot as the raging heat raced from her face to low in her stomach. Had she ever heard of anyone who had not survived their wedding night? No, she didn't think so. But it didn't matter. Even if it was something 'terribly embarrassing' like Mary had said, she would not let him know she found it repulsive. She would suffer in silence. She would never do anything to drive him from her bed. That had been part of their agreement. She cupped her hands to her cheeks and leaned her forehead against the poster.

"Have I given you enough time, my lady?" he said from the doorway.

She couldn't stop the tiny cry of surprise as she spun around to face him. "Perhaps too much," she whispered, more to herself than to him. But he'd heard her.

A smile crossed his face before he stepped into the room.

His broad shoulders filled the doorway, the light from the hallway outlining his tall frame. He'd removed the black jacket, silver brocade waistcoat, and satin cravat that he'd worn for his wedding, and now wore only a burgundy night robe that tied at the waist.

His dark hair was slightly mussed and she fought the urge to brush an errant strand from his forehead. He was the most roguishly handsome man she had ever seen. He looked at her as if he could read her thoughts, and smiled. There were at least a thousand butterflies nestled in her stomach and they all took flight at once.

He took another step into the room and closed the door. They were in near darkness.

"Would you prefer to have a candle lit?" he asked, coming closer.

"No. It's supposed to be dark."

"It is?"

She nodded.

"Who told you that?"

"My sister. Tess."

"Lady Hanbury?"

She nodded again.

He stepped closer until he was so near she could smell his masculine scent, feel the heat from his body. It seemed strange to stand so close to him wearing nothing but her thin silk nightgown. She felt naked because she knew he was aware she wore nothing beneath it. "What else did your sisters tell you?" He touched his hand to her face and cupped her cheek.

"Mary said that I shouldn't open my eyes until it was over, although I'm not quite sure what 'it' is."

He smiled. "She did?"

"Yes. She said it wouldn't seem so…that it would be better if I didn't look."

He rubbed the pad of his thumb against her lips, then lowered his head and gently pressed his mouth to hers. The first kiss was light, like a gentle breeze. Her head buzzed, her blood roared against her ears.

"What else?" He brushed his lips against hers again, but this kiss was just as light and chaste as the kiss before, leaving her wanting more.

"That I shouldn't be afraid."

"Ah. A beacon of hope," he said, pressing a kiss to the center of her forehead. "Which of your sisters told you that?"

"Phoebe. She said it was only painful the first time and after that, it was just uncomfortable."

His eyebrows arched. "I see."

"She said it would help to think of something else until it was over."

"No wonder their marriages are such disasters." He touched her lips lightly then left them again. "Were there any other pearls of wisdom your sisters felt it necessary to impart?"

"No," she whispered on a ragged breath. "Except that *this* part of being married..." she glanced down at the bed, "...isn't very important and that after awhile you will tire of it."

He threw his head back and laughed.

"Was that funny?" She didn't understand what struck him as so amusing.

"You have no idea," he answered, then pulled her into his arms and kissed her with more fervor. Every inch of her body tingled. "No wonder their husbands have mistresses."

"What does that have to do with it?" She was confused about more than just his words.

He kissed her again. "Every man needs not only a wife, but a mistress. It's a rare wife who can become both."

The breath caught in her throat as she considered his words.

He deepened his kiss and held her close. "I'm sure you will make a fine wife, my lady. Now, I will teach you to be an excellent mistress."

He kissed her again, then again. Until she was desperate for something more.

She knew he intended to take his time, to teach her what to do without frightening her but he'd teased her enough. She wanted him to kiss her like he'd done before.

When she couldn't control her desire any longer, she moved against him, urging him without words to kiss her with that certain possessiveness she'd come to anticipate.

He angled his head and deepened his kiss, then moved from her lips to her cheek, then to a spot just below her ear.

She sucked in a breath. Oh, she couldn't think when he kissed her there. "What are you doing?"

"I'm making love to you, and attempting to prove that every piece of advice your sisters gave you was a lie."

He kissed her there again, just beneath her ear, then moved his attention lower, down her neck and to the front.

She gasped for air. With a finger beneath her chin, he tipped her head back and to the side and kissed the hollow spot at the base of her throat.

She sucked in a breath and reached out to clasp her hands on the silky material at his shoulders. Soft little whimpers echoed in the darkness. They were hers and she couldn't stop them. Then he lifted his head and covered her mouth with his lips.

His kisses were long, and deep, and demanding. He pressed his lips against hers then opened them, touching her lips with his tongue. His message was clear. He wanted her to follow his lead, wanted her to meet his demands and answer them with demands of her own. She did.

"Don't be afraid," he whispered in her ear.

"I'm not." She tried to say the words with confidence, but couldn't. "I don't want to be," she finished.

"I'll take care of you." His voice was a raspy whisper, his breathing uneven and labored. "Always, Allie. I promise."

She looked into his eyes, struck by the concern in his gaze, the gentleness in his voice, the tenderness in his touch. She answered the only way she knew. "Love me. Please. Show me what to do."

He breathed a heavy sigh and pulled her back into his embrace.

With slow intensity, he kissed her until she feared she

might drown. He ran one hand over her body, while the fingers of his other hand worked at the buttons on her gown. When the placket was open nearly to her waist, he lifted his mouth from hers and pushed the material from her shoulders. Cool air hit her flesh but she welcomed it. Her flesh was on fire.

With his gaze locked with hers, he placed his hands on her shoulders and slowly let his palms move downward.

This was not what she'd thought it would be like. Not the torture her sisters had led her to believe.

"Look at me, Allie. Don't close your eyes. Watch me as I love you."

She opened her eyes and looked at him.

"What we share as husband and wife is beautiful. There will be no shame or embarrassment between us."

With her gaze locked with his, she gave in to his lovemaking.

# *Chapter 11*

JOSHUA THOUGHT HE WAS GOING TO DIE when she wrapped her arms around his neck and gave herself to him. He'd never wanted a woman like he wanted her, a thought totally alien to him. Was it just because she was his? His wife?

With his lips still pressed to hers, he picked her up and carried her to the bed.

She was lighter than he expected, smaller, more delicate. That realization shocked him. He hadn't thought of her as fragile. She'd seemed stronger somehow, more forceful. Perhaps it was because of the way she carried herself. Her self confidence. Her inner strength.

"You're beautiful," he whispered, lifting his mouth from hers.

"Not nearly as beautiful as you."

He laughed as he lay down beside her. "Men are not beautiful, wife. They are handsome."

She lifted her hand and cupped his cheek, letting her fingers roam over his cheekbone and down the side of his face. With tentative movements, she traced the cut of his jaw then outlined the shape of his lips.

"You are beautiful," she said, then wrapped her arm around his neck and pulled his mouth down to hers.

He kissed her thoroughly, then lifted his head. "Do you know what will happen between us?"

"No."

"Then I will teach you."

"If I do something wrong—"

"You won't do anything wrong. You will make love to me as I make love to you, giving as much of yourself as I intend to give to you."

"I don't want to be a disappointment to you."

"You won't be."

"How can you be so sure?"

"Because it will be my fault if you are. It will mean I was not an adequate lover. And I assure you, I am."

Before she had time to realize what he'd meant by his boast, he covered her mouth again and kissed her with wild abandon. While his mouth paid homage to her lips, his hands moved over her body, touching her, caressing her, stroking her until she writhed beneath him.

"Please," she moaned. She clamped her fingers down on the muscles of his shoulders and held him.

"Please, what, Allison?"

"I don't…know. Just…please." Her breathing was as ragged as his, her eyes glazed with passion.

Joshua dropped the robe from his body and lowered himself onto her. He braced his elbows on either side of her and made love to her.

෴

Allison had no idea it would be like this. She thought she might die if he continued. Was certain she would die if he stopped.

He kissed her again, and even though she tried to lie still like Mary had warned her to, she couldn't.

"Now we will make love," he whispered against her neck and began the movement she'd craved without knowing she craved it.

The expression on his face was strained, his eyes as black as midnight, the creases at his forehead deep, giving him such a concentrated look.

She lifted her hands and let her fingers run up and down his arms. He was beautiful. As perfect as anyone God had ever made. And he was all male. The muscles across his shoulders rippled beneath her touch, the hair on his chest coarse, yet soft, the skin at his waist and lower firm and taut.

This was not at all like she'd imagined. She could not think, could not concentrate on anything except what he was doing to her. How could Phoebe think of a new dress or bonnet? How could she think of anything except the riot of wild emotions raging through her? How could she do anything but cling to the man carrying her to the stars and beyond and race along with him? How…? Why…? Oh…

"Oh…!"

"Yes!"

"Joshua!" she cried as her body trembled then shattered like a fireball that rocketed through the starlit sky. She soared through the heavens like an exploding comet, surging from darkness into blinding sunlight. With arms open wide, she plummeted toward earth, leaving behind the trailing glow of a falling star.

He followed behind her.

He collapsed against her, his wonderfully heavy weight pressing her deep into the mattress. His harsh, ragged breathing brushed hot against her flesh, the thundering of his heart pounding against her breast, his muscled body a cocoon surrounding her, protecting her, holding her safe. She had never felt so perfect, so complete.

For several long minutes he lay there, not moving. She let her fingers trail along his arms, across his shoulders, and down his back. His flesh was covered with a light sheen of perspiration.

How could her sisters have said the things they had? Given her the warnings they had? What she'd shared with her husband had been wonderful. Beautiful. Amazing.

A shiver raced up and down her spine. Perhaps she'd done something wrong. What if this was not the way a proper lady acted? What if her behavior had shocked him? What if she'd let him do things to her a respectable lady would never have allowed? A cold chill caused her to tremble.

She'd done none of the things her sisters had told her to do. She hadn't kept her eyes closed. She hadn't thought of a new gown or bonnet. She hadn't lain still until it was over, but had touched him, and kissed him, and … What if she'd behaved no better than a common trollop? Suddenly she had to know.

"Are you all right?" he asked, still nestled against her. His breathing was calmer than before, but not much.

"Yes. Are you?"

He laughed, his breath warm against the side of her neck. "I'm not sure yet."

"May I ask you something?"

"Yes." He tried to lift his head.

Allison held up her hand to stop him. "Please, I don't want you to look at me."

"Very well." He kept his head nestled in the crook of her shoulder, but shifted his weight off her.

"Is it always like this, my lord?"

She felt him stiffen. "I'm afraid you'll have to explain." There was a wariness in his voice. "Like what?"

She felt her cheeks turn hot. "Please, don't be angry with me."

He lifted his head but she was not fast enough nor strong enough to stop him.

"I'm not angry," he said, but the frown on his forehead indicated otherwise.

"Very well. I would like to know if this is the way it always is."

"Didn't you like it?"

She turned her gaze away from him. "That is not the point."

"Then what is?"

"I need to know if it is this way with the other women with whom you've slept."

"You would like to compare notes?"

"No. Not that. I just want to know if you found me…"

She heard a chuckle and felt him smile. "What are my choices, Allison? Unbelievable? Fantastic? Incomparable? Remarka—"

"No! Wanton. Did you think me wanton?"

He lifted himself up and looked down on her. "What?"

His eyes seemed darker than usual and his gaze locked with hers as if he found her inquiry an inappropriate question to ask.

"I'm sorry," she said, feeling the need to apologize, "but I need to know."

He placed his finger beneath her chin and kept her from looking away from him. Her eyes filled with tears the moment she looked at him. Blast! This was not the way she wanted to react at all. She did not want to cry, not when what they'd shared had been so wonderful, yet tears threatened to spill from her eyes.

"Why would you think your behavior wanton?"

She clenched her hands in the covers and squeezed. "I didn't do any of the things they told me to do. I didn't keep my eyes closed, and didn't lie still. I didn't—"

"Hush." He placed his index finger over her lips. "How dare they," he whispered, then turned with her in his arms. He wrapped her in his arms and held her. "I do not think you wanton. I think you are nearly the most perfect lover imaginable. If any of your sisters would be half so perfect, their husbands wouldn't have to take their pleasures in another woman's arms."

"You do not think I was too…forward?"

"Quite the opposite. In time you will learn not to be nearly so shy and reserved."

She looked at him in surprise, then sighed in relief when he laughed. "Perhaps then we could practice again so I improve?"

"Perhaps," he whispered as his mouth came down on hers.

❧

She opened her eyes to the bright sunshine streaming through slits in the draperies at the windows. She knew it was later than she usually woke, yet couldn't remember why she'd slept so long. Why she should still feel so tired. With a delicate yawn, she rolled onto her back and stretched languorously, then opened her eyes as a strange soreness pulsed through her.

"Good morning, sleepy head," he said from the chair beside the mirrored table. He was already dressed in a fresh white linen shirt and buff-colored breeches, and was putting on his boots. His hair was combed, his face clean-shaven, and when he stood, her heart gave a lurch. He was without a doubt the most handsome man she'd ever seen. And he was her husband.

"Good morning," she said shyly, pulling the covers up under her chin. He smiled.

With a pleased look on his face, he walked to the bed and kissed her lightly on the lips. "Are you all right?"

She lowered her gaze and nodded, but couldn't keep her cheeks from burning. "I'm fine."

"Good." He sat on the edge of the bed. "Are you ready to rise?"

"Yes. I usually don't lie abed this long. I must have been..." She couldn't finish.

"Yes," he said with an open grin. "I'm sure you were very tired."

He brushed a strand of hair from her cheek and wrapped his fingers around the back of her neck. "You are beautiful in the morning, with sleep still on your face and the look of love in your eyes. I will enjoy getting used to seeing you like this."

She felt herself blush again but she lifted her face to accept his kiss. His lips were warm and firm, and when he kissed her, a fire ignited deep in her belly.

"I have to go." He walked to the door. "I've ordered hot water sent up for your bath, and Emma is waiting outside with some hot chocolate. When you're ready, come down. Cook has prepared a breakfast fit for a regiment of starving men. Do you think you'll be able to ride in a carriage? I'd like to leave for Graystone Manor before lunch. If you're able."

"I'm able," she said, feeling her cheeks warm again.

"Good." He turned to open the door.

"Joshua?"

"Yes?" He turned back to her.

"Thank you."

He lifted his brows in question.

"For everything."

He bowed graciously and opened the door. He stepped back to let Emma enter and stopped her before she got into the room. "Take care of your mistress, and don't disturb anything." He cast a look to the bed.

"Very well, my lord."

He closed the door behind him and left.

"What did Lord Montfort mean by that, Emma?" she asked when Emma set down her tray of hot chocolate.

"Never you mind, mistress. The master knows what he's about. Now, let's get you bathed and dressed proper so you can break your fast."

Allison scooted to the edge of the bed and stood, then

winced at her soreness. She turned around to let Emma help her into a robe and froze. Blood stained the center of the sheets where she'd lain, her blood. Proof of her innocence. She slipped her arms into the sleeves of her robe, then reached out to throw the covers over the stain.

"Leave it, my lady." Emma turned her away. "There's a nice warm bath waiting for you in the next room."

She bathed and dressed, then went down the stairs almost at a run. Joshua waited for her in the small dining room. Along with David and a man she'd never seen. She came to a halt when she saw them.

"Good morning, Allison," David said, as the three men rose from the table. Joshua walked to her and escorted her to a chair.

"Good morning, David," she said, barely able to meet his gaze. She prayed that what she'd done last night didn't show on her face, but knew it must. She felt her cheeks burn with embarrassment. "Is something wrong that you're here so early?"

"No. Everything's fine."

She looked over to the man she did not know.

"Allow me to introduce Mr. Franklin Bower, Allison. Mr. Bower, my sister, the Marchioness of Montfort."

"My lady." Mr. Bower bowed formally.

"Mr. Bower is our family solicitor, Allison. He has come to verify that …" David stopped, stumbling over his words. "He's come to certify that …" He stopped again and cleared his throat.

"Allison," Joshua said, turning her in his arms so she faced him. "Mr. Bower has come to legally verify that our marriage was consummated last night."

Her eyes widened and she shook her head.

"It's all right," Joshua said, stepping closer to her. "It's as much for my protection as it is for yours. The size of your dowry makes it mandatory. Carlton," he said, calling the butler. "Please take Mr. Bower upstairs. Emma is waiting for him."

"Yes, my lord." The butler ushered the solicitor from the room.

"How could you?" she said, turning on David. "How could you embarrass us like that?"

"Don't, Allison." Joshua tightened his hand around her waist. "It's no one's fault. Our marriage is, after all, a business arrangement. It must be handled as such."

Allison had never heard any colder words in her life. Or any truer. Her marriage was a business arrangement and she would do well to remember that. Her heart would do well to remember it. But that's not what last night had been. What she had given Joshua and he had given her had nothing to do with a business arrangement.

She stood straight and tall until Mr. Bower returned. With a curt nod of his head that indicated both he and the law were satisfied that her marriage had been consummated, he turned and left the room. David turned to follow.

"I'm sorry, Allie," he said from the doorway, then left.

She stood without moving for a long minute, then Joshua placed his hands on her shoulders and whispered in her ear. "Come, my lady, let's eat so we can be on our way. I'm very anxious for you to see your new home."

She looked at his face and felt the pressure in her chest weigh heavier. "Is our marriage nothing more than a business arrangement to you?"

He remained ominously quiet. The pain surrounding her heart intensified.

"Did what we shared last night mean nothing more than the fulfillment of an obligation, a legal requirement to be met?" She prayed it had not meant so little to him. "Did it?"

His dark, thick brows arched just enough to be menacing while his unreadable glare focused on her. "I was not the one who insisted the consummation of our marriage be verified. That was a stipulation set down by your brother. Just as I was not the one who insisted that our marriage be confined by an agreement demanding my fidelity instead of building a marriage based on trust. You were. I agreed to live by the strictures you have demanded, and I intend to keep my word. What develops between us will have to overcome the obstacles *you* placed in our way."

They stared at each other for a long moment, then she watched as his hard, angry look softened. "Come." He held out his hand. "Our food is getting cold."

She hesitated, then put her trembling hand in his and followed him. As she always intended to do. She could do little else. But now she understood a harsh fact she wished would have forever remained a mystery to her.

She would never know for sure if he remained faithful to her because he cared for her, or because of the agreement she'd forced him to sign.

# Chapter 12

IT WAS MIDDAY when they reached Graystone Manor. For the past hour, Joshua had grown more agitated. He frequently glanced out the window as if searching for landmarks to tell him how much farther they had to go, then leaned back against the seat and waited. It was as if they wouldn't arrive soon enough.

Finally the carriage slowed, then turned into the long, tree-lined lane. He moved from where he sat across from her, to right beside her. She felt his excitement. Saw it in the expression on his face. He reached over and twined his fingers with hers as if he needed to be connected to her when she saw Graystone for the first time. An amazing warmth raced through her.

"These trees were planted by my great grandparents." He leaned in front of her to point out the window. "The story has it that they planted the first tree on their wedding day, then on every anniversary of their wedding. There are fifty four trees that line the drive."

Allison followed his gaze and looked at the dense-leafed trees. "What are they?"

"They're Linden trees. They're known for their shade. Every fall the colors are unbelievable, and in the spring their thick, green leaves return to shade the lane."

"They're beautiful. It's as if they're welcoming us."

He smiled. "When I was young, I used to think their long, sturdy branches were open arms spread wide to greet me each time I came here."

"Was that often?"

"Whenever Mother needed to get away from Father. More often as I got older. Father hated it because Graystone Manor was Mother's and he couldn't touch any part of it." He paused. "We were safe from him here."

She lifted her gaze to him. "What a strange thing to say."

He turned away from her, but not before she caught the expression in his eyes. His gaze indicated he'd told her some intimate detail he hadn't intended to reveal.

"Has your father always been so difficult?"

"Yes. He was always hard and cruel and filled with anger and hatred. But he's become worse since Philip's death. Intolerant toward anyone who doesn't meet his standards."

"And did you meet his standards?"

"Only Philip met his standards. He doted on him. Gave him every advantage. He was to be the next Duke of Ashbury."

She looked at the firm set to his features, the closed look on his face. She felt sorry for the lonely, frightened little boy he must have been. "Were there any happy times in your childhood?"

He turned toward her and the corners of his mouth

lifted. "The times I spent here were happy." He glanced away from her then pointed. "Look out the window."

She leaned forward and followed to where he pointed. The breath caught in her throat. Ahead of her was the most magnificent home she had ever seen.

Graystone Manor resembled a castle as much as it did a country home, the structure so large she could barely see from one end to the other. The house was divided into three sections. The center third jutted out to make an impressive entrance.

Most remarkable, though, were the massive windows. The entire front of the house seemed more windows than wall, windows that reached from ceiling to floor on all three levels. She didn't need to step foot inside to know the house would be a bright and happy home.

The carriage rolled up the graveled drive beneath the beautiful Linden trees and stopped at the entrance. Even though a small army of maroon-liveried servants rushed forward, Joshua didn't wait for a footman to help them. He reached across to open the door himself. He was like an exuberant child escaping his schoolroom.

He jumped to the ground and pulled down the steps for her. "Welcome home, my lady." He held out his hand to help her.

She stepped out and let her gaze take in her surroundings. The house was magnificent, spacious and imposing. Yet, for all its grandeur, there was something warm and inviting about the design.

The home was built of large gray stones, no doubt the reason for its name, and stood proudly on a grassy knoll. Everything about it added to its appeal.

Seven curved steps led to the open doorway, and in the front, tall mullioned windows stretched from floor to ceiling. Seven gabled ballustrades curved from the rooms on the third floor at either side of the house giving the manor a special flavor. Undoubtedly, these were the bedrooms. She could imagine herself standing on one of the balconies surveying the elegant gardens with Joshua at her side.

"Allow me, my lady." Her husband took her hand and led her up the stone steps then through the open doorway. She stopped.

The interior was breathtaking. With her hands clasped at her breast, she stepped to the center of the room and turned a full circle. Never had she seen anything so beautiful in her life. No wonder Joshua loved it here.

The room was mammoth in scope, as large as their whole townhouse in London or larger. A gigantic marble fireplace took up a small portion of the wall to the right and on the left a huge winding staircase led to the landing on the second floor. A balustrade of ornately carved oak decorated the balcony that surrounded the entire room.

She tipped her head back on her shoulders and looked up. A domed ceiling stretched three floors above them, its circle of beveled glass allowing brilliant rays of sunshine to rain down on the room below.

From the center of the dome on a large gold chain, hung a crystal chandelier. During the day, the sun reflected from the glass and created shimmering prisms of light that dotted the burgundy walls on the upper floors.

"Oh, Joshua," she whispered, coming full circle until her gaze met his. "It's beautiful."

She smiled at the look of satisfaction on his face then concentrated again on every detail of the room. There were at least a dozen double-wide doors around the perimeter. They were closed now, but at a nod from Joshua, two footmen hurried to open each one.

She watched in rapt attention as the footmen unveiled each room, then she walked with her hand on his arm as he led her past each one.

"You can investigate the rooms at your leisure." He stopped at each doorway only long enough to give her a peek inside. "There's far too much to take in at once."

"Oh," she said again and again as they stepped from room to room. It was the only word she could utter to describe how she felt.

He laughed, then put his arm around her shoulder and brought her close. "I knew you'd like it." He pressed his lips to the top of her head. "Now." He turned her around. "Your staff is waiting to meet its new mistress."

One by one he introduced her to the long line of servants waiting to greet her: Converse, the butler, Ferdie, the downstairs maid, Quilla the upstairs maid, and so on, and so on, and so on, until she'd greeted each one personally.

"Mrs. Dewey?" he asked before they all filed back to their posts. "You wouldn't have some blueberry muffins and those cakes I'm so fond of, would you?"

A plump little woman with rosy cheeks beamed brightly. "Of course, my lord. I told them in the kitchen we'd best have a fresh batch of each on hand when I heard you was comin'. I'll send some right out with a pot o' tea."

The cook toddled off in a hurry with the others on

her heels. Joshua turned to the butler. "Converse, see to the baggage. Have it put in the east wing. In my old suite. And Quilla," he said to the upstairs maid. "This is your mistress's maid, Emma."

Emma stepped forward and bobbed a polite curtsy.

"See that she's settled."

"Right away, my lord."

Emma followed the upstairs maid up the stairs, her mouth still gaping as her gaze tried to take in everything.

He held out his arm and when she placed her hand in his, Joshua escorted Allison across the wide foyer to an open door to the right of the fireplace. "This is the morning room." He stepped back to let her enter first.

Her breath caught when she looked around the room. "It's beautiful."

She walked over to the windows and looked out. The view of the garden from here was picturesque. To the right of the windows were two double doors which led out onto a small patio. She opened them and stepped out.

"Oh, Joshua," she whispered. She stopped beneath a trellised roof crowded with climbing roses in full bloom and looked up. "This is lovely."

He came to stand beside her. "Mother always loved this room best in the morning because of the bright sunshine. But I prefer it better at this time of the day. When the sun is low and the shadows are long. Would you like to have tea out here on the veranda?"

She nodded, then walked to a round table near the railing. He pulled her chair for her and she sat.

When Ferdie brought the tea, she poured, and together they ate the muffins and cakes Joshua was so fond of. She thought she'd never been happier, thought she'd stepped into a dream. Prayed she would never wake.

She knew now that she'd have to guard her heart more closely than ever. She could see already how easy it would be to lose herself to him. How easy it would be to allow him to become the most important person in her life. How easy it would be for her life to revolve around him. That was something she was not ready to do. Something all three of her sisters had done and paid for every time their husbands left their bed for another woman's.

She tried not to think that the same could happen to her. For now she had him all to herself. It was not until they returned to London that she would have to worry. Then…

He placed his hand atop hers and pulled her away from her fears.

"Tomorrow or the day after you will choose one room on the main floor and make it your own. It doesn't matter which one, but you will completely redo it."

She looked at him in surprise. "You can't be serious."

"But I am. You have just stepped into a house that my mother's family occupied for eight generations. Each of them left their mark on it. They lived and loved here, raised their families here. It was a home to each of them. It will be a home to us too. But it will be a home of our making. And you will have one room that will say to all who enter that this is *our* home."

"You truly love it here, don't you?"

"Yes. My father took great delight in telling me I would never have any part of Ashland Park or any of the other Ashbury holdings. But I knew he could never take

Graystone Manor away from me."

"Why would he say such a thing?" She was unable to believe any father could be so cruel.

"Perhaps because I was the second son. Perhaps because I was not subservient like Philip, or because Father and I clashed like oil and water. Perhaps because I was not born with his blond hair and blue eyes. Who knows? Whatever the reason, my father barely tolerated me. Graystone Manor became my refuge. The only place I could truly call my own."

"No wonder it is so important to you."

"You have no idea how much. I would have done anything to save it."

"Even marry someone you did not want?"

His gaze shot over to lock with hers. "Even that. But I was lucky enough to find you and didn't have to make such a choice."

He rubbed the pad of his thumb against the top of her hand then lifted her fingers to his lips. "Walk with me in the garden while there is still light." He helped her to her feet. "It has been a long time since I've been here and I want to walk down the stone paths and see the ducks and swans swim in the ponds and the flowers in full bloom. I want to watch the red glow of the setting sun when it shines against your hair. And hold you in my arms as the sun slides beneath the horizon. And kiss you until the moon is bright enough to reflect in your eyes."

She laughed, trying to hide her blush. "I hardly think that is possible."

"You think not?" Suddenly his words sounded very much like a dare. And what sounded improbable, seemed more than possible.

They followed first one path then another, stopping on the edge of a shimmering pond to watch the ducks and swans swim in lazy circles. Then they sat on a painted wooden bench at the edge of the water to watch the sun set behind a cloud, their fingers entwined.

When the sun was nothing but a fading fireball sinking below the horizon, he put his arm around her shoulders and tucked her close. She leaned against him. For a long time they didn't speak, didn't need to.

She lay against him in perfect contentment, with one arm draped around his waist, and her cheek nestled against his chest.

Then, as the last rays of sunlight faded from the sky, he lifted her chin with his finger and covered her mouth with his lips. He kissed her thoroughly, completely, desperately. His mouth moved over hers, his tongue touched her lips, entreating her to open to him. She did.

He deepened his kiss, causing her blood to rush through her veins then thunder in her head. Her heart pounded like the beating of a herd of wild horses. And every secret place in her body churned with a molten heat that set her on fire. She wrapped her arms around his neck and kissed him until neither of them could breathe.

"Look at me," he whispered. And she did. He smiled. "I see the moon reflected in your eyes." He lowered his head until their foreheads touched. "Do you know what else I see?"

She couldn't speak. She could barely breathe. She only managed to shake her head.

"Desire. You desire me as much as I desire you."

Her cheeks warmed.

"Come. Mrs. Dewey will have our supper laid out. We will eat before we make love."

She lowered her gaze. She wasn't used to such plain speaking.

"I venture this will be one of the longest meals either of us has ever suffered through," he said. Then, with the full moon bright in the sky and her arm looped through his, he led her inside.

He was right. The meal lasted interminably long.

Neither of them did justice to the fabulous feast Mrs. Dewey prepared for their first meal at Graystone Manor. When they finished, he escorted her to their room.

She blushed when he dismissed Emma, telling her she could retire for the night, that he would help her mistress undress. But those first blushes paled in comparison to the burning heat that radiated from her cheeks when they made love.

❧

The glistening rays of the full moon shone through the open window, casting silvery streaks against his dark hair. She tenderly threaded her fingers through his hair as he lay heavily against her. He was a wonderful burden she didn't want to give up.

She stroked the glistening bronze of his back, the rippling cords across his shoulders, the thick muscles of his arms, and a solitary tear spilled from her eyes.

She suddenly realized how open and vulnerable she was. What a target for betrayal. How could she survive if he ever held another woman like he held her? Kissed another woman like he kissed her? Made love to another woman like he made love to her? It was not only her body she gave him when he made love to her. She wished it were. But it was her heart as well.

A heart she knew was as fragile and in danger of breaking as a delicate porcelain vase.

∽

Joshua rubbed his fingers against the muscles at the back of his neck and sat back from the desk where he'd been studying the estate books for the past three hours. Everything was in remarkably good shape, considering how little he'd concerned himself with the running of Graystone for the past three years. Since Philip had died.

He chided himself for being neglectful. But things would be different now. He had a wife, and in time there would be children. He wanted to make sure there was something he could leave each of them, not just the one who would be next in line for the Ashbury holdings.

Provided there was anything other than an empty title left by the time his father was through trying to lose it all.

But that didn't matter to him. Graystone Manor was safe. Allison's dowry had seen to that.

He closed the ledger on his desk and smiled. All that could jeopardize the agreement he'd made with her would be if he were unfaithful. And there was no chance of that happening.

He thought he would resent both her and that damned agreement she'd forced him to sign. But with each passing day, the terms intending to shackle him to her meant less. Why would he turn to someone else when he'd been given the best gift any man could hope for in a wife? It had been nearly a week since they'd spoken their vows, and every minute since then had been ideal. She was the perfect companion by day and the perfect lover at night.

He didn't know how he could have been so fortunate to have her.

There was a knock on the door and he looked up to see the woman who'd given him such pleasure standing in front of him.

"Am I interrupting you, Joshua?"

"No." He walked around the desk to where she stood. He closed the door then took her in his arms and kissed her. She kissed him back with the same eagerness that she received all his attentions.

He forced himself to lift his mouth from hers. "What can I do for you, my lady?"

It took her a moment to catch her breath. "I was about to go over the menu with Mrs. Dewey for next week and I thought I should find out your plans."

He picked up her hand and held it in his. "Are you in a hurry to return to London?"

"No. I would be content to never go back to London."

He smiled. "I wish that were possible, but it's not. Tell Mrs. Dewey we will be leaving next Friday. Perhaps she will pack us a lunch for the trip. Some of her muffins."

She laughed and patted him on the stomach. "I think, my lord, it's good you're leaving Mrs. Dewey's muffins behind. I hesitate to think what you'd look like were you to have a steady diet of them."

"Don't you realize that I need them to keep up my strength? I would hate to be too tired and fatigued to be a proper husband to you." He kissed the tip of her nose and she turned a deep crimson.

"I love it when you blush like that." He pulled her closer and kissed her again.

She sighed and leaned into him, kissing him back.

A knock at the door stopped him from deepening his kiss. It also made her burrow deeper against him to hide from Converse's knowing eyes. Joshua could hardly keep from laughing.

"Excuse me, my lord," Converse said from the doorway. "There is a Mr. Graham here from London to see you. He says you are expecting him."

"Yes. Give me a minute then send him in."

The butler left, closing the door behind him.

"You can lift your head now, Allie. Converse is gone."

"Oh, Joshua." She clasped her hands against her crimson cheeks. "This is the third time in as many days Converse has come upon us when you were kissing me. I can't imagine what he must think."

"I can."

Her jaw dropped and there was a chastising look on her face. "You, my lord, are terrible."

"And you, my lady, love it." He put his arm around her shoulder and held her, then leaned down and kissed her on the forehead. "But, to save you from further embarrassment, I'd best let you go so I can conduct my business with Mr. Graham."

"Who is he, Joshua?"

"No one of consequence. Just someone I need to see."

When they reached the door, he turned her in his arms and held her. "Perhaps we could have an early supper tonight."

"Of course. I'll tell Mrs. Dewey. Is there a reason for us to eat early?"

He kissed her again. "Uh-huh. So we can retire early."

It didn't take her long to understand his meaning. Her cheeks turned a rosy hue and she stepped out of his arms. "You are incorrigible, my lord."

"And you are lovely when you try to chastise me." He kissed her once more on the lips, then opened the door. She cast him another censuring glance and left the room, averting her eyes when she passed Converse.

He smiled as she walked away. He wasn't sure how it had happened, but he was already more than a little in love with her.

"Mr. Graham to see you," Converse announced a few seconds later.

Thadius Graham entered and Converse shut the door behind him.

Joshua took note of his visitor: at the commanding way he carried himself, with his back erect and his head high. He looked little different from the last time Joshua had seen him. There wasn't a wrinkle in his exquisitely tailored suit coat and breeches, even though he'd just ridden several hours to get here from London.

He looked at Joshua with a confident lift to his chin and Joshua felt more confident of the choice he'd made to do what had to be done.

Thadius Graham was reputed to be one of the best solicitors in England. After meeting with him the first time, Joshua had no doubt his reputation was well founded.

He was the perfect person to make sure there were no

mistakes. He had a shrewd intelligence and understood what had to be done to protect Joshua's holdings.

Describing him as brilliant was an understatement. His vow that no detail would go unnoticed wasn't an idle boast.

Joshua knew what Thadius Graham's presence meant. He knew that it was too late to go back now.

A heavy silence stretch between them, then Joshua asked the question he dreaded having answered. "Did you have any trouble?"

"No, Lord Montfort. All your instructions were followed to the letter."

It was over. Graystone was safe.

Joshua looked down at the thick leather folder in the solicitor's hands. The information inside was all that concerned Joshua.

"I believe you'll find everything to your satisfaction, Lord Montfort, although as I stated before, it is impossible to imagine every repercussion your actions will generate. We will have to stay alert to anything your father attempts."

Thadius Graham's words sent a chill of forewarning down Joshua's spine. "That doesn't come as a surprise."

"I'm sure it doesn't, my lord."

Joshua nodded, then walked to a small table and poured two glasses of brandy. "Please, sit down, Mr. Graham." He indicated a chair beside the desk.

Mr. Graham sat and Joshua handed him one of the glasses, then sat behind the desk with his glass at his right hand.

He knew he should take a drink, that Graham would not lift his until Joshua had taken his first swallow, but he couldn't. Not yet. He knew if he did, the man facing him would notice how his hands shook. For surely they would.

Now that it was over, he could finally admit to himself that he could not believe he had taken such a risk.

But he'd had no choice.

Joshua took a calming breath then lifted the glass to his mouth. Graham sampled his own drink, then placed his glass on a small table to his right and opened his folder.

"These," he said, handing Joshua a stack of papers, "are all the outstanding notes your father has accrued. They have been paid in full. Every Ashbury property is now debt free."

Joshua thumbed through them, trying to hold his temper in check. Each page indicated nothing but flagrant mismanagement. It was obvious his father had intentionally tried to destroy the dynasty his ancestors had built rather than let Joshua inherit it. "You're sure these are all of them?"

"Yes. And as per your instructions, when each debt was paid, the creditor was notified that you personally paid the debt, and you will not, under any circumstance, honor any further debts accrued by your father. We also made sure each creditor understood that your father's income is tentative at best, and totally dependent upon you."

Joshua pushed his chair away from the desk and walked to the window. He didn't look at the solicitor, but stood with his hands clasped behind his back. Mr. Graham listed off completion of Joshua's other instructions.

"In addition, his club as well as any other establishment where your father does business have been notified that His Grace does not have the resources to cover any large expenses. Nor will any further debts be covered by you."

"Have you talked to Mr. Nathanly, my father's solicitor?"

"Yes. We conversed a second time this morning before I left London. He is well aware of the allowance you set up for His Grace, as well as the stipulations concerning the notes you now hold. He was quite shocked by the steps you took to save your inheritance. He doesn't relish the idea of informing your father of the changes in his status."

Mr. Graham paused as if searching for the right words. "I can't say I blame him. Your father's precarious mental condition since your brother's death is common knowledge. Even though you have done what is obviously best, I doubt your father will see your actions in that light. He will no doubt consider what you've done as…"

"Traitorous?" Joshua finished for him. "Blackmail?"

Mr. Graham's silence was answer enough.

"Is His Grace back in London?" Joshua asked, turning back from the window.

"No. Mr. Nathanly did not know when he intended to return. I think he is glad for any reprieve."

"Putting off the inevitable will not make it go away." Joshua took his glass from the table and drank. "And nothing where His Grace is concerned is ever easy."

"That brings us to the other matter you insisted upon. Are you sure you do not wish to change your mind, Lord Montfort?"

"No."

"But it is highly irregular to—"

Joshua held up his hand to silence the solicitor. "My instructions will be carried out to the letter."

"Very well," Mr. Graham said, shaking his head as he

took out another set of papers. "This is the agreement as per your instructions. Ashland Park is entailed, of course, as are the estates in Kent and East Sussex. These cannot be given away or sold, but will pass with the title, if not to you, then to the next Duke of Ashbury. There are, however, several properties adjacent to Ashland Park, as well as a number of shipping and mining investments that are not entailed, and, of course, there is Graystone Manor. All of this, should anything, God forbid, happen to you, will go to your wife, the Marchioness of Montfort."

Joshua walked to the table and lifted the decanter of brandy. He filled his glass part way and downed it in one swallow while listening to the solicitor outline the details.

"I attached this document to your marriage contract which was drawn up by the marchioness's brother, the Earl of Hartley. It basically states the same details. Everything that is in your name, including Graystone Manor, will go to the marchioness either upon your death, or in the event that you are found … unfaithful."

"Yes. If ever I am unfaithful."

"May I say that is a most unique stipulation to be placed in a marriage contract?"

"That is because my wife is a most unique person."

"But aren't you concerned that—"

"No, Mr. Graham. I am not. You have not met my wife. If you had, you would realize that death is the more likely possibility."

The expression on the solicitor's face was a mixture of disbelief and admiration.

Joshua set his glass on the table and clasped his hands behind his back. The solicitor took the hint that their meeting was at an end. "Will you return to London soon, my lord?"

"Yes. At the latter part of next week. I do not anticipate it will take long for His Grace to realize what I have done. It will be more…convenient to face the repercussions in London than here."

Joshua hoped it would also be safer. His father would be furious at best, murderous at worst. He prayed it would not come to that.

Thadius Graham collected his papers and walked to the door. With his hand on the knob, he turned to Joshua.

"Lord Montfort. One word of warning before I go. Please, do not underestimate His Grace. In listening to the opinions of those who have had recent dealings with him, it is apparent he harbors great resentment toward you. The situation in which you have put yourself could be quite volatile. I fear His Grace is capable of almost anything."

"I appreciate your warning," Joshua said.

"For what it's worth, I think your actions admirable. Quite unorthodox and perhaps desperate, but necessary." Mr. Graham bowed graciously. "Good day, my lord. I wish you every success, and…"

He smiled. "I look forward to meeting your wife."

# Chapter 13

ALLISON WATCHED THE COUNTRYSIDE slide by and wanted to scream for the driver to stop and turn around. The last two weeks had been the most perfect of her life. She couldn't shake the feeling that once they returned to London everything would change.

The farther they traveled from the peaceful serenity of Graystone Manor, the more nervous she became. She needed Joshua to hold her and tell her everything would be all right but his mood was one of the reasons for her discomfort. Even the click of the horse's hooves over London's cobbled streets seemed to echo a warning.

"Is something wrong?" she finally asked. She focused her gaze on the deep furrows that etched his forehead. He'd been quiet and withdrawn ever since they'd left. Now, as they made their way through the city to their London townhouse, he seemed more distant than ever.

"I'm sorry, Allie." He lifted the corners of his mouth to form a smile that wasn't quite real. "I haven't been very good company, have I?"

"I don't need to be entertained, Joshua. But I can tell something's bothering you. I wouldn't mind if you shared your concerns with me. Perhaps I could even help."

His glance shifted from hers, to stare absently out the window. "There really isn't anything to be concerned over."

"Yes, there is. And it started the minute Mr. Graham came to see you last week."

His gaze shifted slowly back to hers. "How observant you are."

"The change was hard to miss. Are you sure I can't help?"

He reached over and clasped her hand in his. "It's nothing. Really."

But it was. And she knew it. She'd known it from the minute Mr. Graham left. Joshua packed every hour full from dawn to dusk, as if each day were his last chance to take care of his estate. He rode over the land, met with the manager and each tenant, gave instructions for improvements and changes he wanted made, and pored over the ledgers.

There was a fervor in the way he drove himself, a tenseness about the way he held himself, and a desperation in the way he made love to her.

He worked himself to exhaustion during the day and made passionate love to her each night, holding her close when they were finished as if she were a lifeline, a safe harbor he desperately needed.

Something was wrong. But she couldn't force him to share it with her.

The carriage turned another London street corner, then slowed. They were home. She reached out and placed her hand atop his. "Do not forget I am here if you need me."

He raised her hand to his lips and kissed her fingers. "I will not forget, my lady." He kissed her fingers a second time, then exited the carriage and turned back to help her.

Carlton met them at the door, greeting them with the same regal look he'd worn when Joshua brought her here on their wedding night.

"Are there any messages?"

"The messages are on your desk in your study, my lord. I divided them by importance: those that are urgent and need an immediate reply, invitations to events you may or may not wish to attend, replies that can wait until you have time."

"Thank you, Carlton. Has the Marquess of Chardwell sent a message?"

"Yes, my lord. As soon as I received word you were returning, I informed him, as per your instructions. He sent a message back with your footman. I expect him momentarily."

"Very good." Joshua held out his arm for her to take. "I'm going to see Lady Montfort to our rooms. Show the marquess to my study when he arrives and tell him I'll be down shortly."

"Yes, my lord."

He led her up the stairs. When they reached their bedroom, he cupped his hand to her cheek. For a long minute he held her in his arms and looked into her eyes as if searching for something.

Then, on a sigh that shuddered, he slowly lowered his head and kissed her. His kiss was warm and seeking, tender and passionate. An open display of his gentle nature.

For many long minutes he kissed her as if each touch held a special meaning. When he finally lifted his mouth, she had to lean her forehead against his chest to hold steady.

"I've wanted to do that all the way to London," he said, trying to catch his breath.

"Then why didn't you?"

He laughed. The first real laugh she'd heard for nearly a week.

"Because I knew I wouldn't be able to stop. With our driver seated barely two feet away, I didn't think you would relish an audience while we made passionate love."

She felt her face turn hot.

"I love it when your cheeks turn red like that." He kissed her again. "Now, I'll send Emma up with some tea, then I want you to rest for awhile. The journey here has probably tired you."

"I'm fine, Joshua. Please, don't leave me."

Her stomach churned and an uncomfortable weight pressed against her chest. Something was wrong. She could see it on his face, feel it in his touch, hear it in his voice. She had to try once more to help him. "Why did you send for Chardwell?"

"Because I have some business to discuss with him."

"Like you had business to discuss with Mr. Graham?"

Joshua took her in his arms and held her close. Her cheek nestled against his chest, her arms wrapped around his waist and he rested his chin on the top of her head. "Do you know what your problem is, wife?"

"I am too persistent?"

"Yes. And … ?"

"I meddle into affairs you would rather I stayed out of?"

"Yes. That too. And … ?"

"There's more?" She dropped her head back to look at him.

"Yes," he said, kissing the tip of her nose. "You are too wise for an average male to keep secrets from. Too inquisitive for your own good. And too, too caring to stay away from a situation that it might be best if you avoid like the plague."

"And that would be?"

"Perhaps nothing. I will know more after I talk to Chardwell."

"And if he brings you bad news, will you share it with me?"

"If I think it is something you need to know."

"Please. Don't shut me out."

"I couldn't even if I wanted to. You wouldn't let me."

He kissed her lightly again then left.

She watched his back as he walked away from her and wanted to call him back. She was not an immature youngster fresh out of the schoolroom, but had spent many years on her own. What could be so bad he couldn't share it with her?

She sat on the edge of the bed and tried to calm her nerves. If she was to be his wife, she wanted to be a wife to him in all things.

❧

Joshua closed the bedroom door behind him and leaned against the wall. Why couldn't he have married a woman whose only concerns were adding new gowns and fripperies to her already extensive wardrobe, and deciding which balls to attend? Why couldn't he have chosen a woman who was dull-minded and only concerned herself with the latest parlor gossip?

Joshua pushed himself away from the wall and made his way down the stairs. He knew very well that he couldn't tolerate a wife who was shallow and dull-witted. But Allie was so intuitive it was difficult to keep anything from her. Yet in this, he had to. He had to protect her from his father's vile temper and vindictive wrath.

He threw open his study door and entered.

The Marquess of Chardwell sat in one of the two matching wing chairs angled before the desk with a glass half filled with brandy in his hand. "Well, Montfort," he said, the open grin on his face a welcome sight. "I must say it looks like married life agrees with you."

"It does. I find I have married a remarkable woman. When this is all over between my father and me, I have decided to devote as much time as it requires searching for the perfect match for you, too."

Chardwell sputtered on the brandy in his mouth. "Spare me, Montfort. I have no desire to sacrifice my freedom for the sake of keeping you company in the marriage doldrums. Just because you have gone the way of all foolish men does not mean I intend to follow the same path. I enjoy my life far too much to see it change." He lifted his glass in a symbol of a toast. "By the way. Angelina sends her greetings."

Joshua managed a laugh. "I am glad the two of you are getting along."

Chardwell smiled. "We are."

Joshua shook his head, then took a drink of his brandy. When he finished, he set his glass down on the desk. "What do you hear of my father?"

Chardwell hesitated before he spoke. "It's not good. He arrived two days ago and has made a number of uninvited appearances at several balls in search of you. He is never sober and, if rumors are to be believed, has made an embarrassing spectacle of himself."

Joshua raked his fingers through his hair. "He's bound to be furious."

"Furious is not the word Society uses to describe him. The opinion spreading through the *ton* questions his sanity. If I were you, I'd stay clear of him."

"Perhaps if I talk to him he will—"

Chardwell bolted to his feet and slashed his hand through the air. "He wants you dead, man. As dead as Philip is. He blames you for your brother's death and won't be satisfied until they bury you, too. Now he's ranting that you have stolen everything from him."

Joshua pushed his chair back and turned to look out the window behind him. A gentle breeze blew the leaves on the trees, the calm serenity outside so opposite the turmoil raging inside. "I have." He braced one hand against the window frame. "I bought up all his debts with my wife's dowry, and now I own everything, except of course the properties that are entailed. Those cannot be touched, nor can he borrow any more against them."

"Bloody hell, Montfort."

There was a long silence before Joshua could speak. "I realized what he was doing before I married. He was intentionally losing everything so there would be nothing left for me to inherit."

"Why?"

"I don't know. Nothing my father's ever done where I was concerned has made sense."

"He's not rational, my friend."

"I'm sure he isn't. His credit has been cut off all over town and he's left with few options. I've set him up a substantial allowance, but I doubt if his pride will allow him to accept it."

Chardwell took a drink of the liquid in his glass, then leveled his gaze. "He's dangerous, Montfort. He's always been volatile, but even those who claim to know him say his mind has snapped."

"I'm not worried. There's little he can do."

"Just be on your guard. And don't let your wife take any chances either."

"What does Allison have to do with this?"

"Rumor has it he blames her for his troubles. Her dowry, after all, gave you control over him."

So help him, he would never let anything happen to her. She'd done nothing, nothing except give herself to him.

He clenched his fists at his sides and breathed a deep sigh. He knew what he had to do. He had to go see his father, had to convince him Allison had nothing to do with his troubles. He couldn't let Allison get caught in this web of bitterness and hatred. He couldn't let his father think she was responsible for any of this.

"Do you know where he is?"

"Stay away from him," Chardwell offered, his voice

almost a command.

He shook his head. "I can't. This war between my father and me has gone on since I was born. Waiting another day or two will not make it go away."

"Then I'll go with you."

"No. But if you do not have another engagement, I would not mind if you stayed here until I return. I don't want Allison left alone."

Chardwell nodded.

Joshua threw the remaining liquid down the back of his throat and walked to the door. Without a glance back, he left the room.

Allison would be safe until he returned.

# Chapter 14

ALLISON POKED HER NEEDLE through the front side of her embroidery and brought it to the back, knotting the medium brown thread at the bottom of the tree trunk she was creating. It was the same piece she'd worked on every day for the past two weeks since they'd arrived from Graystone Manor. She was fortunate the wall hanging didn't take a great deal of concentration. She doubted she could keep her mind focused long enough to handle anything more intricate. By now her scene would probably have purple trees and a green sun.

She lifted her gaze to where Joshua sat opposite her, pretending interest in a book. She noted he hadn't turned the page once in the last thirty minutes.

"How is the book?" She threaded her needle with yellow thread.

"Very interesting. It is—" He had to look down to read the title. "…um…*The Count of Monte Cristo* by Dumas. Have you read it?"

"Yes. David gave me a copy at Christmas."

"Did you enjoy it?"

"Yes." She pretended concentration on her embroidery again. "I found it fascinating."

She started a yellow daisy in a ring of flowers beneath her tree. "A footman delivered an invitation this morning to a ball hosted by the Countess of Evernon." She kept her voice even, as if her request was unimportant. "I thought perhaps—"

"Not yet, Allison."

"But invitations have arrived by the score. By refusing them all, you've made us a novelty."

"We were a novelty long before now. With our unexpected betrothal, Archbite's challenge and duel, our rushed wedding, then fleeing from anyone's watchful gaze immediately after our vows, we've made ourselves objects of speculation and intrigue. Everything that's happened to us since we met has added to our 'novelty.'"

Allison lowered her gaze. "Phoebe wrote that we have become the most sought after married couple in London. Everyone is vying for our attendance at their gatherings. The fact that we haven't surfaced since our arrival in London has only fueled speculation." She stabbed the needle through her cloth. "Everyone is placing bets on whose gala will be enticing enough to force us out of the house to spend at least one evening in public. I don't even want to imagine what they think we're doing when we stay cloistered here."

Her husband smiled. "Personally, I find that rather flattering."

She couldn't help but look embarrassed. And it was not far off the mark. Their time together had been remarkable,

hours filled with talking and laughing and loving and...
simply enjoying each other's company.

She'd loved every minute of it and was loathe to give
up being with him. But she also knew the reason he
kept her cloistered was not because he wanted to give
Society something over which to speculate. It was almost
as if he kept her hidden to protect her. Her theory was
corroborated by the fact that every time Joshua left the
house, the Marquess of Chardwell magically appeared. As
if Joshua's absence had been pre-arranged so she would
never be alone.

It wasn't that she did not enjoy the marquess's company.
She enjoyed him immensely. He was charming and witty,
and filled with the latest gossip from every drawing room.
But he joined her as part of a pre-conceived plan between
him and Joshua.

"Would you like to go for a walk in the gardens?" Joshua
asked, pulling her from her musings.

"Is that my only choice?"

There was a twinkle in his eyes. "We could always go
upstairs to rest. I feel quite fatigued right now." He closed
his book and moved to rise.

"I doubt you are in the least fatigued." She rolled her
eyes to the ceiling. "I'm not naïve enough to fall for that
excuse, husband. I know good and well neither of us
would get a wink of sleep if we went upstairs."

He sighed as if he were disappointed. "Then we might
as well go for that walk."

He held out his hand to her. She came to her feet and
made a move to step into his arms, then stopped when a
loud noise erupted from the foyer. His hands grasped her

upper arms and turned her.

"Stay out of sight," he ordered, then pushed her to the far corner of the room. "Go!" He lunged toward the desk and pulled open a drawer.

She couldn't move but clasped her hands over her mouth to stifle a scream. He reached inside the drawer and brought out a pistol.

"Joshua?"

"Go!"

He stuck the pistol in the pocket of his breeches and moved toward her.

Loud shouts and violent curses echoed in the hallway, followed by the shattering crash of a piece of furniture. She tried to get to the far side of the room but the study door burst open and the Duke of Ashbury staggered in, dragging Converse and another footman with him. Joshua rushed to her side and pushed her behind him.

"Damn you to hell!" Ashbury flailed his fist in the air. He shook the two men from him as if they weighed nothing and took another step into the room.

Allison stepped out enough to look at the man who was her father-in-law.

His hair was tangled and uncombed, his disheveled clothing wrinkled and far from clean. His dark blue coat was torn at the sleeve and the buttons of his waistcoat were mismatched, giving him an off balance appearance.

His shirt had been white at one time, but was no longer, and his cravat hung untied around his neck. He looked like a man in need of a hot bath and fresh clothing, but she knew that would only change his outside appearance. No amount of soap and water would change the demented look in his eyes.

She'd never seen such malevolence, such undisguised contempt as she saw when father looked at son. Her heart ached with a pain that nearly took her to her knees.

No son should ever have to see such blatant hatred in his father's eyes.

❧

Joshua stared at his father, at his wild appearance, at the haunted look in his eyes, at the demented bitterness etched in the contorted scowl on his face, and at the snarl on his lips.

Chardwell had told him his father had stepped beyond the edge of sanity, but he'd refused to believe it. He didn't want to think that the hatred the duke had always felt for him had eaten away at his mind.

Chardwell had also warned him that his father had threatened to do Joshua harm. He didn't want to believe that either. But he could see it was true.

"I've been searching for you, Father."

The duke stumbled further into the room, his nearness a greater threat. Joshua stepped in front of Allison and put out his hand, wanting her to stay behind him.

"For what reason, *son*?" he slurred, spitting out the word 'son' as if it were bile in his mouth. "Have you thought of another way to humiliate me? Another method to destroy me?"

"My intent was not to destroy you, but to save you from losing everything. Your very dukedom is at stake."

Ashbury laughed, the sound a demented bark. "You mean *your* dukedom is at stake. You took such steps because of greed. You want what you have no right to own!"

His father's words were a blow, but nothing he hadn't heard before. He stood in silence, meeting his father's glaring hatred, pretending his words did not matter.

His father stepped closer, staggering noticeably. "You figured out what I was doing," he slurred. The corners of his mouth lifted in a malevolent snarl. He raked his fingers through his twisted, wind-blown hair, then swung his hand through the air. A vase he hit on a nearby table teetered precariously, then fell to the floor and shattered.

"Damn! I nearly succeeded. I nearly managed to lose it all so there wouldn't be anything left. But then *she* came along."

Joshua inched to the side to keep himself positioned between Allison and his father.

"If it weren't for her," his father said, jabbing an accusing finger in Allison's direction, "it would all be gone by now. Only a little while longer, and everything would have been lost to you!"

Joshua's breathing came in harsh jagged gasps. Certainly his father loved Philip and barely tolerated him, but he never thought he'd go to these lengths. Not to the point of losing Ashland Park and the other Ashbury estates in order to keep him from inheriting them.

"Why?" he said through clenched teeth. "Why would you want to lose everything?"

"Why!" He staggered backwards and threw out his arm, his hand in a fist railing at heaven. "So you could not have it. It was Philip's. Not yours! Everything was to go to him. Not you!"

"Philip is dead!"

His father staggered as if he'd received a great blow. "Yes. And you killed him."

"Philip died because he forced his horse to attempt a jump he couldn't possibly make."

"No!"

"Yes!

His father lunged forward but caught himself against the corner of the desk, then glared more intently. "You think you've won, don't you? You think you'll get it all. That your wife's dowry has saved you from losing everything." He shook his head. "You haven't. Do you know why?"

Silence.

"Because I know the conditions of your marriage contract."

Ashbury staggered to the small table where Joshua kept the liquor and pulled the stopper from a cut glass decanter. He lifted the bottle to his lips and drank, then swiped his mouth with the back of his hand. When he turned to face them, the look on his face changed. His lips curled in a sardonic grin that caused Joshua to take pause.

"I cannot believe you were so foolish to agree to a condition you have no chance of meeting." He threw his head back and laughed. He straightened, then aimed his glare at Allison.

Joshua put his arm out and held her to him. She was trembling.

"Do you really think you are woman enough to keep this rakehell from straying? There isn't a woman alive who can satisfy him. He's just like his mother. His blood runs as hot as hers did. He won't be any more faithful than she was."

The air left Joshua's body. "How dare you!" He wanted to strangle his father, wanted to strike out and do him harm, but Allison's small, firm hand in his stopped him.

"Why are you here?" he asked. He wanted his father out of his house. Wanted to never set eyes on him again.

"Just wanted to meet my new daughter-in-law."

"Get out!"

"But I've just come. And you have yet to introduce me."

He had no intention of introducing Allison to anyone so vile as his father, but without warning, Allison stepped out.

"Your Grace." She bowed a polite curtsy and faced his father with as much courage as he'd ever seen.

"So you're the woman who so foolishly sacrificed her wealth for a husband who will never be faithful to her." He took another step toward them.

"That's enough!"

"Surely you know that?" Ashbury took another step.

To her credit, Allison didn't flinch, but held her ground. "I know no such thing, Your Grace."

"Of course you do, Lady Montfort. I think that's why you included a fidelity stipulation in your marriage contract. To protect yourself from the day when your husband is unfaithful."

Blind fury erupted like a bright explosion deep inside him. He wanted his father out of his house, away from him. Away from Allison. "Your Grace," he said through clenched teeth, "I don't think we have anything further to discuss."

He stepped in front of Allison to shield her from any more of his father's vicious attacks. "As I'm sure you are aware, I now own every Ashbury property with the exception of Ashland Park and two other estates that are entailed. They are yours until your death. What you do with them is entirely up to you. I have saved what I could."

"Your precious Graystone Manor?"

"Yes. Graystone Manor is safe from you. The rest I don't care about. I never did."

"Damn you!"

Joshua gave no quarter. He wanted the break clean. "I have set up a sizable allowance for you to use as you see fit. Or you can refuse it and live in the squalor you have created for yourself. It matters not to me. You are the one who put yourself in this position. You will have to deal with it however you like."

The duke bellowed a vile oath. "I wouldn't touch a pound of your blood money if I were starving.

Joshua shrugged his shoulders. "That is up to you."

His father's expression turned even more vile. "You won't keep Graystone Manor or anything else you've paid for. There is no way you will meet the stipulations of your marriage contract. You are a whoremonger, a philanderer. There is no way you will stay out of another woman's bed. It will happen as surely as I'm standing here. Then, if your wife is not a fool, she will take it all away from you."

"Enough!" Joshua bellowed, and swiped his hand through the air. For the first time, he saw fear in his father's eyes. The duke stumbled backward, but righted himself against the settee.

Joshua took another step closer. "Get out! This is my home and you are no longer welcome here."

"You are so cock sure of yourself," he spat, then turned

to Allison. "Just wait, my lady. It won't be long before your husband leaves your bed for someone else's."

Joshua reached for Allison's hand, but when he turned toward her, her face was pale. A heavy weight fell to the pit of his stomach. "My wife knows that will never be a concern. I have given her my word."

"Your mother gave her word, too. Her solemn oath on our wedding day. Your promise will be no more trustworthy than hers." He paused, sliding his gaze back to Allison. "Unless, of course, you're fool enough to think you're woman enough to keep him in your bed." The duke's accusing gaze scrutinized his wife's body, lingering on her breasts, then dropping below her waist. He laughed. "You're not."

Joshua saw red. "Out! Get out of my house right now." He took his father by the arm and ushered him to the door. Converse magically appeared and rushed to open the front door.

Ashbury jerked his arm out of Joshua's grasp and slashed his hand through the air as if Joshua's very touch disgusted him. "You'll lose it all. I'll see to it. You'll never get what should have been Philip's. Never!"

Ashbury staggered across the threshold. The minute he stepped outside, Converse closed the door and slid the heavy metal bolt into the lock.

Joshua faced the door, his chest heaving to force air into his lungs, the blood thundering through his head. His mind was a riot of incoherent thoughts. He couldn't believe what had just happened. Couldn't believe his father had said the things he had—that his mother hadn't been faithful, had taken lovers.

A thought raced through his mind that was so debilitating his whole body went numb. Was his father implying that he wasn't his son?

"Joshua?"

Her gentle voice seeped through the filth and chaotic muddle in his mind like a breath of clean, fresh air. He fought his way back to her, back to the goodness that was such a part of her. He turned.

She stood in the doorway, her silhouette a masterpiece of near perfection. Oh, how he needed her, how he wanted to hold her. To have her wrap her arms around him so he could forget his father's accusations.

"Joshua?"

Her voice wafted over him like a gentle whisper. She didn't move at first, then took a tentative step forward and halted, unsure. With slow deliberation, he stretched out his arms to her, showing her the only way he knew how much he needed her.

She came forward, slowly at first, then with a small cry, she ran into his arms.

He wrapped his trembling arms around her and held her close, crushing her to him as if he never wanted to let her go. "Are you all right?" he asked, pressing his lips to the top of her head.

"Yes, but you…"

He sensed her fear, felt the effect his father's words had on her. "Shh. I'm fine. I am, after all, used to this."

"You can't be. No one could." She tilted her head back to look at him. "Your father is ill, Joshua. His grief over your brother's death has twisted his mind."

He shook his head. "His hatred for me did that a long

time ago. Philip's death only snapped the fragile thread that connected him to sanity."

There was a desperation in the way she clung to him. "What are we going to do?" She rested her cheek against his chest and held him tighter.

"I've done everything I know of to save my inheritance. My father...is lost to me."

She breathed a harsh breath that shuddered when she released it. "We should leave here." She burrowed against him even closer.

A certain wariness crept over him. There was a frightened anxiety in her voice.

"I'll tell Emma to pack." She lifted her gaze to meet his. "We'll leave first thing in the morning. We can go back to Graystone Manor. We'll be safe there."

The air caught in his lungs. "Safe from what, Allison?"

She averted her eyes and worried her bottom lip. "Everything."

But he knew she feared only one thing. That his father's words would come true.

As long as she could isolate him in the country, she didn't have to fear he would find another woman to share his bed.

He grasped her by the shoulders and held her out to look in her eyes. He lifted a loose strand of hair from her cheek, then brushed one finger over the tiny worry lines on her forehead. "Whose invitation did you say we received for tonight?"

Surprise was evident on her face. She shook her head but answered him. "The Countess of Evernon. She is hosting a ball."

"We will attend."

Her eyes opened wide. "But … your father?"

"We have nothing more to fear from him. He will not search me out any longer. He has said what he wanted to say. And from what Chardwell says, his name has not been included on any invitation list for weeks."

"But … are you sure you want to go? Tonight?"

"Yes." He kissed the frown on her forehead. "It is time we made our way back into Society. Time the *ton* saw us as the happy couple we are."

*Time I earned your trust*, he thought, but did not say the words out loud.

"Let's go upstairs and pick out your prettiest ball gown. We will make a grand entrance tonight."

She smiled up at him, but he saw the hesitancy in her gaze. His father had done an exemplary job of bringing to light all her fears, and destroying whatever faith she'd come to have in him.

He ushered her up the stairs almost at a run. The minute they crossed their bedroom threshold, he kicked the door closed and slid the lock. Without giving her time to even glance at her gowns, he took her in his arms and made slow, languorous love to her. He would do whatever it took so she never doubted him.

She was far too important to him. Far more precious than he'd ever intended his wife to become.

# Chapter 15

"YOU'RE TIRED." Joshua tucked her close to him as their carriage clattered over London's cobbled streets.

"Just a little."

It wasn't a lie. She had good reason to be tired. They'd attended at least one event every night for the last two weeks. Most times two or three. From the afternoon of the scene with his father, Joshua insisted they be seen together every day. It was as if he needed to show Society they were the perfect couple. As if proving his father wrong was of the utmost importance. Tonight they were attending her sister Phoebe's ball.

"We won't stay long," he whispered, as their carriage slowed, then stopped. A footman raced to open their door.

Joshua exited first and reached for her hand to help her from their carriage. From the number of vehicles that lined the street there was already a huge crush of people inside. This was normal for any function Phoebe hosted. Unlike Allison, her three sisters were in their element when surrounded by hordes of people.

She stepped onto the damp cement and breathed a heavy sigh. She would be glad when they could spend a quiet evening at home. Happier yet when they could go back to Graystone.

She didn't know what was wrong with her, but she'd felt uneasy since Ashbury had thrown out his wild accusations. He'd voiced her deepest fears as if they were guaranteed to become a reality.

If only she could keep his words buried deep inside her where she could forget them.

She silently chastised herself. There was no reason to feel this way. Joshua had given her no cause for concern, no cause to doubt him. If anything, he'd been the model husband. She was the envy of every married woman wherever they went. And yet…

"Is everything all right?" he asked handing over their cloaks to a footman.

"Yes, fine."

He walked with her to the top of the stairs leading to the ballroom and gave her hand a gentle squeeze. "We will just make an appearance, then leave."

The minute they were announced, the crowd turned to stare at them. He flashed her a heart-stopping smile and all her doubts faded.

"Allie," Phoebe said, then reached out to give her a very warm hug. "Lord Montfort."

"Lady Fortiner. Fortiner," Joshua answered.

Allison noticed the speculative look on her sister's face. If they'd been alone, she had no doubt her sister would have been forward enough to inquire about the more intimate aspects of her marriage. Thank heaven there was a crowd behind them.

"You both look as happy as everyone says." Phoebe gave Joshua a huge smile.

"That is because marriage agrees so entirely." He placed his arm around Allison's waist. "I have married a remarkable woman."

The look he gave her was one of pure adoration. The murmur behind them crescendoed and Allison knew her husband had been raised another notch in every woman's esteem.

How could she ever have doubted him? She only had to remember his attentiveness and consideration to realize the man she'd married had given his vows seriously. She was the foolish one for letting her own fears overshadow her happiness. Any doubts she harbored were of her own making.

She gave his hand a gentle squeeze and vowed from this moment on to quiet the nagging voice that repeated the bitter warnings the Duke of Ashbury had spewed in anger.

"Are Mary and Tess here?"

"They're standing together near the second set of patio doors talking to the dowager Countess of Etonbury and Lady Questry."

Her gaze moved to the back of the long, narrow room. Double-paned French doors took up the length of one wall of the ballroom. They were open to let in a cool breeze.

Phoebe leaned closer. "You missed our small scandal." She spoke loud enough for just Allison to hear. Joshua was carrying on a conversation with the earl. "Lady Questry and Lady Bingham were on their way to one of the retiring rooms and came upon Lord Questry in a semi-compromising situation."

Allison felt the first prickle of unease. "What, pray tell, is a *semi*-compromising situation?"

"Well, it seems the Ladies Questry and Bingham saw Lord Questry and Lady Paxton sharing a most intimate embrace. It didn't take Lady Bingham long to alert the entire room as to what she'd witnessed."

Allison was shocked. "Lord Questry! But he's barely been married a year!"

"What does that have to do with anything?" Phoebe asked. "Lady Paxton's loose conduct is well known. One can hardly blame Questry for taking what is freely offered."

Allison was shocked. "Surely you don't mean that?"

"If only human nature weren't so predictable. But it is. It's a rare husband who can be trusted."

Allison let her gaze focus on Lady Questry. The young wife stood alongside Mary and Tess amidst a small group of ladies all near the same age. She wore a bright smile on her face and joined in on the conversation as if nothing untoward had happened.

How could she do it? How could she face everyone after witnessing her husband embracing another woman? Allison knew she couldn't. She *wouldn't*.

"Allison, is something wrong?"

Joshua's deep, rich voice brought her back to the present and she took a huge gulp of air, then lifted her gaze to his face. "No." She placed her hand on his arm. She needed the contact.

He smiled at her. "Would you like something to drink?"

She shook her head. "The orchestra is playing a waltz,

Lord Montfort." She wanted him to hold her. Needed to feel his arms around her.

Her husband's gaze turned seductive. "How remiss of me not to have noticed." He gave their host and hostess a graceful nod. "If you will excuse us."

She stepped into his arms the minute they reached the dance floor. He held her closer than was proper while they danced, but she didn't separate herself from him. She didn't care if they caused talk.

When the music ended, she stayed in his arms even as the other couples left the dance floor. She needed to feel his arms around her. Needed to cast every doubt and shred of mistrust from her mind.

And forget the hateful words his father had said.

∼

Joshua stepped out onto the flagstone patio and inhaled a deep breath of cool nighttime air. The crush at the Fortiner ball was suffocating. At times like this, he longed for the quiet solitude of Graystone. The magical nights when he had Allison all to his own.

He made his way to a secluded corner and leaned against the stone balustrade, taking a swallow of the brandy in his hand and looking at the stars.

"Much more peaceful here than inside," the Marquess of Chardwell said, his voice a welcome interruption.

"I didn't know you'd arrived." Joshua turned to his friend.

"How could you? It's too crowded in there to see your own hand in front of your face, let alone someone else's. Why is it, do you suppose, we attend such gatherings?"

"Because it's expected of us." Joshua propped one hip on the stone railing and crossed his arms over his chest. "I've barely seen you in the past two weeks."

"I had business to attend to at one of my estates. How are things with you?"

"Are you inquiring after my wife?" He couldn't help but smile.

"Of course."

He laughed. "Only a fool could find something to complain about where she is concerned."

"You sound hopeless, Montfort."

"I fear I am. But I do not regret it. Marriage isn't what I thought it would be. Things couldn't be better."

"With your father as well?"

He took a swallow of the drink in his hand then breathed a sigh. "I'm afraid things haven't improved where he's concerned. I talked to his solicitor this morning and he still refuses any help from me. He's alarmingly destitute but is hiding away at Ashland Park."

Chardwell held his silence for a long moment, then uttered a thought Joshua had refused to contemplate. "Perhaps your father needs help, my friend. Perhaps he needs to go someplace where—"

"No!" Joshua spun away. "I won't lock him away. He's a duke, for God's sake. He's my father. He's—"

"He's sick. And you're not safe as long as he's filled with such bitterness and hatred."

He slashed his hand through the air. "Can you imagine what the *ton* would say if I put my father away? That all the rumors surrounding my brother's death were true. That I killed him to inherit his title, just as my father has insisted all these years. That I'm so greedy for the dukedom that even murder isn't beneath me."

"No one believes that, Montfort. It's only your struggle with guilt that won't let your conscience rest easy. There are some things over which we have no control. Your brother's death was one of them. You couldn't have prevented it from happening, and no matter how much you wish it, you can't trade places with Philip. Ignoring your father's sickness will not make it go away."

"I know." He leaned his hands flat against the railing and stared into the darkness. "I keep hoping that Philip's death will be easier for him to handle if I give him more time."

"I pray you're right," Chardwell said.

But Joshua didn't hear much hope in his friend's voice.

They stood together in the darkness, the veranda lit only by a scattering of lanterns that cast them both in shadows. All that could be said already had. He knew Chardwell was right. His father was sick. And no amount of time would heal him.

But no matter how much he agreed, he couldn't force himself to take action. Not against his father.

"I think I'll make a final tour of the ballroom," Chardwell said, clasping his hand on Joshua's shoulder in a comforting gesture. "Then go to my club. I've battled all the marriage-minded mamas I can for one evening. Are you ready to return?"

He shook his head. "In a moment. You go ahead."

He heard Chardwell's footsteps fade and knew when he was alone in the darkness. He wished Allison was here with him. Things would not seem so hopeless if only she were in his arms.

"Good evening, my lord," a soft, feminine voice crooned from behind him.

He turned, wishing the voice belonged to his wife. Disappointed because it didn't. "Good evening, Lady Paxton."

She laughed, her laughter a husky, seductive sound. "My, my. How formal, *Lord Montfort*. I seem to recall it was not that long ago you whispered my name in passion."

He stiffened. "That was a long time ago. Before I married. Now, my wife's name is the only name I whisper in passion."

"How sad."

Lady Paxton closed the short distance between them and stood near enough that he could feel the heat radiate from her.

"It's not uncommon," she said, pressing her palm against his chest, "for men and women who are not married to each other to remain friends. *Close* friends."

He looked down and wondered what he'd ever seen in her. How could he have thought her enticing, appealing?

"I'm afraid such an arrangement would be impossible." He lifted her hand from beneath the lapels of his jacket.

"Are you afraid your wife would object?"

"I am certain she would, but not nearly as much as I would."

She arched her fiery brows and pursed her full, lush lips. "What a shame." With a swish of her full skirts she stepped from one side of him to the other. "I can't believe you intend to disappoint me so."

He laughed. "You'd best believe it. But don't despair.

You've never had difficulty finding a legion of suitors to shower you with attention."

"Oh, it's not attention I would lack, Montfort. It would be *your* attention I would sorely miss."

"I'm flattered, Lady Paxton, but there's nothing I intend to do about it. Now, if you will excuse me."

He tried to step around her but she moved close, stopping his escape.

"Surely you don't intend to leave me so soon."

"I do. I've left my wife far too long and miss her desperately."

"I don't believe it." She wore an incredulous look.

"Alas, it's true. Marriage has changed me."

"Perhaps you just need to be reminded of how it used to be between us?" She moved closer and placed one foot on either side of his feet, then leaned against him, her body so close he could feel her thighs hard against his and her breasts pressed against his chest.

"I've missed you terribly, Montfort," she whispered seductively, then brushed her fingertips down his cheek, to his neck and down his chest.

He clamped his hand over hers none too gently and pushed it away. "I doubt you've had time to miss me, my lady. Gentlemen trade places in your bed with such frequency it's impossible for you to miss one lover before the next one takes his place."

Anger flashed from her eyes but quickly faded. With lightning speed, she looped her arms around his neck and leaned into him. She wore a seductive smile on her face and stood on her tiptoes, lifting her lips to meet his. "Oh, yes. I have missed you."

A sickening repulsion surged through him. He immediately wanted to be far away from her. Was desperate to forget the kind of person he used to be. "Step away from me." He glared at her with more repulsion than he thought it possible to feel. "Now."

As if tempting him to forcibly remove her, she kept her arms wrapped around his neck. He was filled with a deep abhorrence. He couldn't abide the feel of her against him. Couldn't stand to have her anywhere near him.

With uncharacteristic roughness, he clasped his hands high on her arms and pushed her away.

A movement from the doorway caught his attention. He turned. Nothing. The doorway was empty.

He breathed a sigh of relief, tamping down the self-loathing he felt for letting Lady Paxton lure him like she had. He couldn't imagine what Allison would have thought had she come upon them, couldn't imagine the hurt he would have caused her.

Without a look in Serena's direction, he stepped away from her. He was barely able to stop himself from wiping his hands on his jacket to get the feel of her off him. He would never let anything like that happen ever again. Never!

❧

Allison stood in the small circle that included her three sisters, Lady Etonbury, Lady Questry, and Lady Bingham, all friends and acquaintances. They each shared the latest gossip and talk about the newest fashions, subjects that required little thought. It was all she could do to keep a smile on her face and look as if she were interested in their trivialities. Her gaze repeatedly moved to the patio door, waiting for her husband to walk through it. Trying to forget what she'd just seen.

The buzz in her head grew louder until she could hardly think. Her stomach lurched and she wrapped her arms around her middle, praying she wouldn't have to run from the room.

She'd seen him. Seen Joshua with Lady Paxton. Seen her arms wrapped around his neck and her mouth lifting to meet his.

A fresh wave of devastation turned her skin cold and clammy. Her legs trembled beneath her, her face burned as if it were on fire. How she wished she'd never sought him out. Wished she hadn't seen them together. And yet, did she really want to be so ignorant of what went on around her?

*"Yes!"* a chorus of voices deep within her screamed.

Her head swam in a muddy confusion she couldn't find her way out of.

"Isn't that right, Allison?" her sister, Mary asked, touching her arm to gain her attention.

She jumped in surprise.

"Is everything all right?" her sister asked, studying her more intently than she wanted.

"Yes. I was just wool gathering. What was it you wanted?"

"Never mind. It would take too long to explain again. Besides, here comes your husband to monopolize your attention. We've lost you again."

Allison's heart pounded in her breast, her palms suddenly damp with perspiration.

"We wondered how soon he would be here to claim you," Lady Bingham teased. "We've had you to ourselves for all of fifteen minutes." She gave the rest of the group a knowing look. "That must be a record so far. We all had bets he couldn't be separated from you even this long."

The ladies in the small circle laughed, voicing comments that expressed their envy.

"He doesn't show signs of losing interest in his new bride, does he?" Lady Enderline noted, casting Joshua a glance as he wended his way through the crush of people crowding the ballroom. "I remember my Lord Enderline acting the same way just after we married. His attentiveness lasted all of about … two weeks."

The ladies in the group giggled again.

Allison's sister Tess tapped her cheek thoughtfully. "From the rather hungry look in his eyes, I'll wager he hasn't begun to tire of his new bride. I'll give him at least another month before his attentions begin to wane."

"Oh, no," Phoebe chimed in. "With that look, I'm sure it will be another six months."

Allison felt the air leave her body. The room spun around her.

"I wager he lasts longer than that," Mary said with a decidedly wicked grin on her face. "Just look at the way his eyes haven't left Allison since he walked in from the patio. It's been years since I've seen that look on my husband's face. I'll bet all next quarter's pin money when he reaches us he says it's time to leave."

The crowd of women all twittered behind their open fans then parted when Joshua came up beside her. She thought her legs would collapse beneath her. How could she keep up this pretense when … when she knew?

Then he touched her.

He stepped beside her as if she were the only woman he wanted to be near and wrapped his arm around her waist.

Her heart pounded with greater ferocity, her skin ignited beneath his touch. Then, he gently pulled her closer and looked down at her. Her heart soared in her breast.

The bottomless depth of his midnight eyes was her undoing. The yearning she saw, the emotions he didn't try to hide, emotions that consumed her with a need, a hunger only he could satisfy. How could she give up what they'd shared? The magic she'd found with him.

At that moment, she knew her former fierce bravado, boasting of what she would do if he strayed even once, hadn't prepared her for the hurt such a decision would bring. Her heart ached because of what she feared had happened in the garden between Lady Paxton and her husband. But she knew her heart would break if she walked away from him like she'd threatened.

With that knowledge, she reached a monumental decision. She couldn't pretend she hadn't seen him. He needed to know she had. But then what? She cared for him too much to let something like that happen again. She wanted him to know she wouldn't give him up without a fight.

"Ladies." He greeted her circle of friends. "Thank you for taking such good care of my wife while I was gone."

"It was our pleasure," Phoebe answered for them all. "Although I fear she missed you. That must be the reason her mind was so occupied while you were gone."

Joshua joined in the laughter but when he looked at her, his face sobered, a hint of concern filling his eyes. She turned away, not wanting him to see anything troubling in her gaze.

"Have you attended the opera lately?" Phoebe asked him.

"No, but my wife mentioned she'd like to attend. Verdi's *Rigoletto* just opened last week. It came to us from Venice."

"Perhaps you'd like to join Fortiner and me next week Thursday. We've invited a small group to join us."

"We'd love to," he answered, but Allison had a hard time concentrating on the plans that were being made. "Then, after the performance, my wife and I insist you join us for a midnight supper."

All the ladies oohed and aahed in anticipation of being chosen to attend the first function hosted by the Marquess and Marchioness of Montfort.

"Splendid," Joshua said in answer to their nods of acceptance and exclamations of delight. "Now, if you will excuse us." He looked at her. "The orchestra is playing a waltz."

Allison took his proffered hand. She wanted to escape her sisters and the other ladies to be sure, but more importantly, she wanted to have Joshua to herself. Wanted to cling to him and make what she'd seen go away.

He led her to the dance floor and pulled her into his arms. She stepped closer and he gathered her to him as if she were the only woman he wanted in his arms.

He was an excellent dancer. Each turn was a display of intricate movements. His hand pressed against her lower back and sent a fiery brand that raced through her. His nearness and warmth created a delicate balance between raw hunger and passionate desire.

The picture of Lady Paxton pressed against him, her arms around his neck, her lips reaching for his, flashed through Allison's mind. She was desperate to erase all memory of her. Desperate to be the only woman Joshua wanted. Desperate for him to love her so completely he wouldn't turn to anyone else.

"Joshua?" Her voice was barely audible above the music. "Take me home. Please."

He looked down on her and his smile faded. He stopped while the other dancers flew around them. "Are you all right?"

"I want to go home."

He nodded and held out his arm.

"Your sister is straight ahead." He nodded to where Phoebe stood with Mary and Tess and the others. "We'll bid our hostess good night, then take our leave."

She stepped with him to the other side of the room.

She remembered little of their farewell except Joshua's reminder of the midnight supper he'd arranged following the opera, Thursday next.

"Are you sure you're all right?" he asked while they waited for their driver to bring round their carriage.

"Just tired." She was glad he draped his arm across her shoulder. She ached to feel his arms around her.

He pulled her into his embrace and she placed her cheek against his chest and breathed in his masculine scent. She would not lose him. She would not let the indiscretions start already. She couldn't survive if they did.

He held her until their driver pulled their carriage to the

curb, then helped her inside and sat beside her. "What's wrong, Allie?" He turned to face her. "Did something happen tonight? Are you ill?"

"Of course not. What could have happened?"

He placed a finger against her cheek and turned her head so she looked at him. "You're frightening me. What's wrong?"

She had to tell him. She couldn't keep it to herself. "I saw you. With Lady Paxton."

He lowered his hand and sat back. His features turned hard, the look in his eyes unyielding. For a long time he remained silent. When he spoke, his voice held a hollowness she'd never heard before.

"Nothing happened, Allison."

She closed her eyes and looked away from him. "I saw you."

"I don't care what you think you saw. Nothing happened. You have my word."

Her heart pounded in her breast, a strange wariness overpowered her. She wanted nothing more than to believe him. Wanted nothing more than to take him at his word and pretend what she'd seen hadn't happened.

"Or isn't my word enough?"

A muffled cry caught in the back of her throat.

"Is it, Allie? Is my word enough?"

It was her choice. To believe him or not. To let seeds of doubt take root in their marriage which would grow like weeds until they choked out all the good things. All the love.

She couldn't do it. She couldn't survive a marriage like that.

"Yes. It's enough. I just…"

"Lady Paxton thought I was still interested in her attentions. I explained that I was not and left her on the terrace and came back to you. I won't betray you, Allison. I gave my word. Being faithful is too important to me."

She knew it was. But what wasn't clear was whether being faithful was important because she'd asked that he not humiliate her, or because he'd lose everything if he strayed.

She was suddenly as frightened as she'd ever been in her life. "Please, kiss me. I need you to kiss me."

"Oh, Allie."

"Please."

She lifted her lips to meet his and he kissed her with a desperation that matched her own. His lips ground against hers, deepening an already suffocating kiss, and still she begged for more.

"Oh, Allie. I'm sorry you saw that. I'd give anything if you hadn't."

"I know. I know."

She wrapped her arms around his neck and kissed him again. By the time they reached their townhouse, their passion was at a frenzy. "Love me, Joshua," she whispered when their carriage stopped.

"Bloody hell, woman." Joshua kissed her once more, quick and hard. He helped her out of the carriage without waiting for a footman and together they raced across the portico and through the open door.

They stopped long enough to give Converse their cloaks and hats and gloves, then made their way up the stairs and to their room.

She welcomed him with open arms, pulling him to her, touching him, kissing him, opening herself to him. With his mouth pressed against hers, he slid his naked flesh over hers, his muscles quivering beneath her touch. He rested against her, hard and ready, and Allison wanted to have him inside her more than she ever wanted anything in her life.

"Take me, Joshua. Make love to me. Let me be enough."

Joshua thrust his hips forward, making them one together. He wanted to go slow but she wouldn't let him. She needed him too badly. Wanted him too desperately. Needed to erase every hint of Lady Paxton.

As if he sensed her urgency, Joshua found his release the same moment she found hers. With a great cry, he shuddered above her then collapsed atop her. She held him close, never wanting to let him go.

Their completion came too soon, yet there was no chance either of them could have made it last longer. Not this time. She had too much to prove. She wanted to give him so much of herself that he wouldn't think of anyone else. Would never want anyone else.

Ignoring the tears that streamed from the corners of her eyes, she held him to her. And prayed what she had to give him was enough.

# Chapter 16

LADY PAXTON let her burgundy satin pelisse drop from her shoulders and fall into her butler's waiting arms. She'd just come from one of her frequent carriage rides through Hyde Park and wanted a few minutes to herself before she went upstairs to dress for tonight's round of parties and balls. Perhaps Montfort would be there. Her heart stirred at the thought.

"Have tea sent to the library," she informed her butler as she walked across the black and white marble flooring to the room that had been her late husband's library. She stepped inside and closed the door behind her.

With her back pressed against the hard, cool wood, she let her husband's presence surround her. She'd kept this room exactly as he'd left it, as a shrine. A place she could come whenever she needed a reminder of the hell she'd endured to become a countess.

His life-size portrait hung above the mantle. His piercing gray eyes honed in on her as she moved about the room; his sardonic smile grinned at her in mocking humor.

She took a step closer and glared at him as she'd done so often when he was alive.

May he rot in hell.

She let her gaze roam from one side of the room to the other. The mahogany paneling that engulfed the room was so dark as to be nearly black, an apropos reminder of the late earl's charred soul. His very spirit lived here. His evil presence. There was nothing within these four walls that was soft or showed any sign of tenderness. Even the sun seemed to dull as it crept through the windows. Everything about this room portrayed a harshness and cruelty that had been his trademark.

A shiver raced up and down her spine. The air weighted with a dank heaviness, a suffocating reminder of the man who'd occupied it.

Lady Paxton fought a resurging eruption of intense loathing and hatred. She'd paid in spades for the freedom her title afforded her. And had rejoiced like a newly freed prisoner when her husband's heart gave out and he died. She vowed she would never give any man control over her again. Never.

She unclenched her hands and rubbed the palms where her nails dug into her flesh. Only when the door opened and a maid carried in a tray of tea and small sandwiches did she sit gracefully on the dark maroon sofa as if her past weren't filled with painful memories.

"You have a guest, my lady," her butler announced when the maid left. "The Duke of Ashbury."

Serena couldn't hide her surprise. Or her fear. Everyone knew Ashbury had lost his hold on sanity since his oldest son and heir, Philip, had died. His volatile temper made him a man to fear and avoid.

"Tell the duke I'm not receiving, Simpson," Serena said, pouring herself a cup of tea.

Ashbury's harsh voice slurred from the doorway. "The duke doesn't give a bloody damn if you're receiving or not."

Serena's gaze darted to the hulking figure swaying inside the doorway.

Ashbury couldn't be more than in his mid fifties, yet looked fifteen years more. His clothing was wrinkled and unkempt, his overly-long graying hair stuck out from his head like a madman's. He wore a maroon tailored jacket over his silver brocade waistcoat, yet neither was buttoned, and the cravat around his neck hung at an odd angle. The wild look in his eyes made him appear as if he were teetering on the brink of madness, and from the smell of stale liquor that permeated the room, he was thoroughly inebriated and had been for quite some time.

"How dare you walk into a lady's home uninvited," she said, rising to her feet. "Simpson, show His Grace to the door."

Simpson took a step forward then stopped when Ashbury turned his head and glared at him.

"It'll take more than your puny footman to kick me out, Lady Paxton, so you might as well save your employee a cracked skull and invite me in. I'm not leaving until you and I have a discussion."

Serena studied him, noticing the way his eyes darted from side to side, the way his hands clenched and unclenched at his sides, the way he staggered where he stood. Something told her if she insisted on evicting him, Simpson would come out on the losing end of the battle and she would be left unprotected until she could summon one of the gardeners.

"Very well, Your Grace." She held out her arm to bid him enter. "If you insist." She turned to her butler. "Simpson, fetch Carver from the garden and wait in the foyer."

The butler scurried to do as he was told. When she turned back to face the duke, a lopsided grin contorted his features.

"Prudent and wise, my lady," he slurred, leaning against the small table at the end of the settee. "Aren't you going to offer me something to drink?"

"Tea, Your Grace?"

"Hardly." The tone of his voice contained a frightening anger. "I prefer something a little stronger. Perhaps some of the fine brandy for which your late husband had such a penchant?"

She lifted her eyebrows to indicate she thought he'd already had enough to drink. When he ignored her, she went to the decanters of liquor and filled two glasses.

Ashbury took the glass and studied it. "Paxton was always proud of his fine stock. He had only the rarest wines, brandies and ports. Do you know what I suspect? I suspect he smuggled them in." He took a swallow of his whiskey. "Excellent." He lifted his glass in salute. "Of course, you would know more of his activities than I."

His hooded look indicated there was a hidden meaning to his words, but she refused to rise to the bait. Just as she refused to encourage him in conversation.

"I forget now, Lady Paxton. How did you and Lord

Paxton meet?"

She sat on the settee and slowly turned her glass in her fingers. She took a small sip, then eyed the duke with a cold expression meant to hide her fear. The duke may be teetering on the brink of madness, but he was still a wily, crafty man—much like her husband. Someone to be feared. She recognized the signs. Had lived with them too many years not to.

"Paxton and I met in Paris," she said carefully. "I was on holiday and he was there on business. We met at the home of mutual acquaintances, Monsieur and Madame DeVaneaux."

"I don't think I ever heard Paxton talk of them."

"They are both, unfortunately, deceased."

"I see. I've often wondered though, Lady Paxton, how—"

"I fail to see how Paxton and I met is of any significance, Your Grace." A prick of unease pinched the nerves at the back of her neck. The desire to have him gone intensified. "If you will excuse me now." She rose to her feet and placed her glass on the table. "I have several engagements tonight and am running late."

He made no move to leave but leaned back into the settee and leisurely drank his brandy. "I recently met an acquaintance of yours, Lady Paxton."

"I have many acquaintances." She took her first step to the door.

"But this is someone who claims to have known you in your childhood."

Her footsteps faltered.

He was lying. He had to be. She'd had no childhood.

She'd grown up in a … "Really?" She slowly turned. Tried to pretend indifference.

"Yes. A very unusual woman. She claims she is your—"

Her heart skipped a beat and she moved toward the door. "You are welcome to stay and finish your brandy, but you'll have to excuse me, Your Grace. I have to get ready—"

"An extremely attractive woman with hair the same color as yours. It's amazing how the two of you resemble one another."

Waves of panic surged through her. Heaven help her.

"Her name is—". He stopped. "But you know her name, don't you? She claims you are as talented as she." He bellowed a crude, disgusting laugh. "By God, but Paxton was a lucky man."

Serena slowly closed the door and stepped back into the room. This couldn't be happening. He couldn't have found out.

But he had.

"What do you want?" She turned to face the man who possessed the power to destroy her.

"In exchange for my silence, you mean?"

"Yes."

His lips curled to form a cruel, sardonic grin. "I want the Marquess of Montfort. I want him destroyed."

Her heart skipped a beat. "You can't be serious. He's your son."

"No!" He threw his empty glass against the wall. "He *killed* my son!"

Shards of crystal shattered around her and she turned her face to avoid being hit.

"I want him destroyed. And you are going to help me ruin him."

She shook her head but knew her refusal was useless. Even though she had nothing with which to bargain, she had to at least try. She couldn't let him hurt Montfort without trying to prevent it from happening.

"And if I refuse?"

"Then I tell the *ton* my startling news. I'm sure they will find it as...interesting as I did."

The blood drained from her head, leaving her weak and lightheaded. She'd come so far. She couldn't allow this crazy, demented imbecile to ruin everything for her.

"How did you find out?" Her voice spoke barely above a whisper.

"Your late husband told me."

"That's a lie. Paxton would never have told anyone."

"But he did, my lady. One night when we were both feeling extremely despondent. I had just lost my son. And you were spending an inordinate amount of time with some handsome, young French nobleman."

Serena knew the exact time he was talking about. Her indiscretion with Jordan nearly destroyed all she'd worked for.

"Anyway, Paxton vowed he didn't need you. He let slip where he'd found you and insisted we go there to...renew his acquaintances. He said your former establishment would cheer us both up. He boasted that he was on familiar terms with a number of the...inhabitants. One in particular.

"We'd both had far too much to drink, but Paxton was worse. One thing led to another and... Well, you know how he was when he drank. He was quite angry with you. His tongue became quite loose."

Serena felt a cold chill. Ashbury could ruin her. If anyone found out where she'd come from, what she'd been, the life Paxton had taken her from, she'd lose everything.

Her mind reeled. She had to make a choice. She'd endured too much to get where she was to lose it all now. This was her life, what she'd always dreamed of having: the balls, the parties, the attention. Being the Countess of Paxton and having the prestige and influence that went with it. She'd never survive if she lost it. Never.

"Why haven't you said anything before?"

"There was no need—until now."

She looked at the malevolent grin on his face and realized with appalling alarm that Ashbury would not hesitate to ruin her if she didn't help him destroy his son. She braced her shoulders and stood brave against the evil he carried. With devastating clarity, she knew she had no choice. Destroying Montfort was the only way to save herself.

"How can I be assured you will keep my secret even if I do help you?"

His lips lifted in a mocking grin. "You can't."

She stared at him a long time before she spoke, her insides roiling with a hatred so intense it almost made her ill. "Then I will give you this promise, Your Grace." She took a step closer and faced him as if she were facing her worst enemy. Because she was. "I did not grow up where I did, and survive the life I did without acquiring some valuable skills. If I hear even one whisper that questions my past, or if you ever threaten to blackmail me again, I'll kill you."

Ashbury blinked in surprise.

"Yes. You heard correctly. I will kill you." She smiled. "And take great pleasure in doing so."

He stared at her with a dumbfounded look on his face as if he were trying to digest her words. After a long, uncomfortable silence, he threw his head back and roared with demented laughter. "You have nothing to fear, Lady Paxton. I will never breathe a word concerning your past. Nor will I ever ask another favor of you. Once Montfort is destroyed, there is nothing else I will ever need."

She stepped away from him. She was not at ease being in the same room with a man so evil. She walked to the settee and sat in stoic silence while the duke explained her part in the plan he'd devised to destroy his son.

She felt ill. She'd done many things in her life she wasn't proud of, but never had she intentionally set out to be so cruel. Never had she purposefully determined to cause such pain, especially to someone for whom she truly cared.

By the time Ashbury finished detailing his plan of destruction, Serena visibly shook. A part of her wanted to stand up to him, tell him she refused to have anything to do with his vile scheme. But she couldn't. She wasn't brave enough to lose everything she had.

"Get out," she said when he finished outlining her part in his devious plan.

"But—"

"I said, get out! And don't ever come near me again."

"As you wish." He bowed politely if not a little unsteadily, then walked to the door. "I will wait to hear when the deed is accomplished."

Simpson was there, waiting to escort the duke out.

She stared at his back, anxious to have him gone. She clasped her hands around her middle and prayed she could hold on until he left before she became physically ill.

"Oh, by the bye," he said, stopping on the other side of the door. "Your mother sends her regards."

# Chapter 17

JOSHUA BRACED HIS RIGHT ARM against the window frame and stared out into the early evening sky. Allie and he would leave soon for the opera, then return here afterwards for a midnight supper. It had been a little more than a week since they'd made arrangements. A little more than a week since she'd seen him on the terrace with Lady Paxton. A little more than a week since he'd noticed the subtle changes in her.

*Let me be enough.*

She'd whispered these words the first time that night when they made love. There'd been a desperation to her plea, but he hadn't paid as much attention as he should have. He'd been too wrapped up in his passion. Too consumed in pleasuring her. In finding pleasure himself.

Remembering the way she touched him, held him, clung to him even after they'd both found their release caused his body to react even now.

*Please, let me be enough.*

He'd heard her words again last night, barely a whisper

she probably didn't know she'd spoken aloud. Only this time there had been a 'please' at the front. As if she directed her entreaty to a higher power. As if her request was a prayer she wanted God to answer.

*Please, let me be enough.*

Did she think she wasn't? Did she doubt he was content with her? A niggling worry settled in the deep recesses of his mind. Surely, she didn't. Surely she knew Lady Paxton meant nothing to him.

His blood ran cold. He knew her greatest fear. Knew the crushing blow it would be if she thought he'd been unfaithful. Knew how much she feared having a husband who would flaunt his affairs before the world and prove his disregard for her. What could he do to make her believe nothing had happened between Serena and him?

He spun around, filled with the most urgent need to rush to her and assure her she had nothing to fear. To take her in his arms and hold her and kiss her until she never doubted his faithfulness again. He took one step and stopped short.

She stood in the doorway, the most beautiful woman he'd ever seen. An unsurpassable vision of loveliness and grace.

She wore a gown of the deepest emerald green, a perfect shade to enhance her coloring. The satin material shimmered in the glow of the lanterns, the unique design perfect for her slight figure. The décolletage was low enough to show off the rise of her breasts but not so low it was offensive.

She'd pulled her magnificent auburn hair loosely atop her head, leaving wispy tendrils of burnt gold to cascade downward. Vibrant curls touched the long curve of her neck and framed her face.

Her complexion was as pure as a porcelain doll's and around her neck she wore the necklace of small emeralds and diamonds he'd bought on impulse just the other day.

Her eyes shone with a brightness that lit the room, and when she smiled, he feared his heart would burst with joy.

*Let me be enough.*

Surely she knew she was. Surely she knew how much he'd come to love her, and that he would never do anything to hurt her.

"My dear, Marchioness of Montfort." He bowed formally, then closed the distance between them and grasped her hands. "You are, without a doubt, the most beautiful woman God has ever put on the face of the earth. How I was ever fortunate enough to have you as mine will forever be a mystery."

"Oh, Joshua." She leaned forward to press a kiss to his cheek. "I am the one who is fortunate."

When she pulled away from him, he noticed a faint dampness in her eyes. He kissed each eye lightly and vowed she would never shed a tear on his account. That he would make sure her eyes were only filled with laughter and joy.

He checked the time on the mantle clock. They were still early. "Would you like a glass of wine before we leave?"

"I'd love one. It's been a harried day." She smiled. "But I think everything is ready for our guests."

"You didn't mind that I suggested returning here, did you?" He handed her a glass of deep red burgundy wine.

"Not at all. I'm glad you suggested it. Really."

He sat down on the settee beside her. She moved her voluminous skirt, then turned to face him.

"How soon can we go back to Graystone?" She reached for his hand and held it.

"You are tired of life in London?"

"A little. But mostly, just selfish. I had such a wonderful time when we were there before. I miss it."

"So do I. But we can't leave just yet."

"Because of your father?"

"Yes."

He got to his feet and stood with his back to her. This afternoon he'd had a long meeting with his solicitor, Mr. Graham, and Mr. Nathanly, his father's solicitor. Nathanly feared the duke and at first was hesitant to agree the duke's behavior was out of the ordinary. Eventually he admitted his concern.

Upon prompting from Mr. Graham, Nathanly admitted that the duke's prime purpose had been to bankrupt every piece of property that would eventually pass down to Joshua. He intended to leave Joshua so destitute he wouldn't be able to afford the upkeep on anything, so all the properties he could not sell would crumble around him. Especially Graystone.

It had taken quite a bit of talking, but eventually Nathanly agreed that the Duke of Ashbury was indeed unstable and needed to be placed someplace where he would be taken care of. If not for his own protection, then for Joshua's. And even Lady Montfort's.

The moment the solicitor mentioned Allison's name, a cold wave of panic washed over him. In his next breath, he informed both Mr. Graham and Mr. Nathanly he wanted to begin proceedings immediately to institutionalize his father. Not in Bedlam or any of the public institutions, but at some private hospital where he would receive only the best of care.

"I can't leave until I know everything is taken care of," he said to Allison. "My father is far too ill to be left on his own."

Allison rose from the settee and stood beside him, clutching his arm and holding it to her breast. "Of course you can't. I know how sick he is. It's just that I worry about you. I don't trust him, Joshua. Promise you won't let anything happen."

"Nothing will happen, Allison. I won't let it."

How could he tell her that his greatest fear was that in one of his father's drunken tirades he would try to rid himself of the son he believed had killed the son he loved. Or worse. Try to kill the only thing he loved.

He placed a kiss on her forehead. "Now, are you ready to go?"

"Yes."

She smiled at him, her smile warm enough to melt butter, seductive enough to make him uncomfortably hard. "Then we'd best leave before I conjure up a reason to go back upstairs."

She laughed. "I would not mind. We could be fashionably late."

"Being late is only fashionable when attending balls. Arriving late to the opera is not fashionable at all. And we would probably miss the whole first act."

He held out his arm then dropped it when Converse entered carrying a small silver tray.

"This just arrived for you. The messenger boy said it was urgent."

He took the note from the tray and turned it over. "It's from Chardwell." He tore it open then stepped closer to the light to read it better.

*Montfort,*
*It's imperative that I speak with you right away. Alone.*
*I'm on my way.*
                                        *Chardwell*

"Allison, something important has come up. You go to the opera without me. I'll be there as quickly as I can. It won't take long. I promise."

She hesitated as if she wanted to argue, then gave in. "Very well."

He saw the worry on her face and felt a pang of guilt. "Don't worry. It's probably nothing."

"If it's not? If it's something important?"

"I'll let you know." He pressed a kiss to her forehead.

He escorted her to the front door and helped her on with her cloak. He made arrangements for two footmen to accompany her, then escorted her beneath the portico and down the steps. "I'll be there before the end of the first act." He helped her into the waiting carriage. "I promise."

He kissed her hand then stepped back while the footman closed the door. He stared after her long enough to watch the carriage rumble down the street.

"I'm expecting someone," he informed Converse as he walked into his townhouse to await Chardwell's arrival.

His heart raced in his chest. He'd known there would

be repercussions because of the actions he took to help his father. But bloody hell! He didn't think they'd start already. It hadn't even been one whole day.

He walked to his study and paced the room while he waited for Chardwell to arrive. It didn't take long.

He breathed a heavy sigh when he heard a carriage stop at the curb outside his townhouse. He went to the small liquor table and poured two drinks, knowing they would probably both need one before this discussion was over.

The outside door opened and closed, then Converse knocked before opening his study door.

"The Countess of Paxton, my lord."

He turned in surprise.

"You look shocked, Montfort."

He set the two glasses in his hand back on the table and watched Lady Paxton glide into the room. Her every movement was as graceful as anyone he'd ever seen. She exhibited a natural confidence that made her seem perfectly at ease in any situation. Even alone and uninvited in a married man's home.

"What are you doing here?"

"I've come to make peace."

"Consider it done, my lady." He moved to open the door and escort her out.

"Oh, please, Joshua. Surely you aren't so angry with me from the other night that you'd eject me from your home?"

"I'm expecting a visitor and would like you gone before he arrives."

"Very well. I'll leave the minute your guest arrives. I promise."

He dropped his hands to his sides and stepped back

into the room. He left the door open wide. "What do you want?"

"Just a few moments of your time."

She walked to the table where he'd set down the two glasses and ran one long, graceful finger over the rim until it rang a tiny, high pitch.

"You'll have to excuse me," she said, turning away so he only saw her back. "This is not ease for me."

"What is not easy?" he asked when she kept her back to him so long.

"Apologizing. Saying good-bye. Like I said, I want to make amends for the other night. I misunderstood your devotion to your new bride and overstepped my bounds."

"Consider your apology accepted. Now, if you will excuse me—"

She turned around to face him with the two glasses in her hands. "It's a shame to waste the two drinks you already poured. Would you have just one last drink with me before I leave?"

He felt uncomfortable. He didn't want her here. The sooner she was gone the better he'd like it.

"I'd prefer you left right now, Lady Paxton. We have nothing to discuss and I hardly want to remember anything we might have shared in the past."

She held up one of the glasses. "If you will share but one last drink with me, I promise I will leave and never bother you again."

She stepped closer to him, yet not so close as to make him wary. "Just one drink." She held out a glass.

He looked at the glass then at her. He'd known Lady Paxton far too long to trust her. He was also well acquainted with her determination. She would get no encouragement from him.

"Please, Joshua."

"Very well." He took the glass from her hand. Without the slightest hesitation, he threw the contents to the back of his throat and swallowed. "Now..." He lifted the glass so she could see it was empty. "I've finished my drink. Please, leave."

She stared at him. Was that a flash of concern he saw in her eyes? Surely not.

"Joshua," she said, her voice soft, almost muted. "I have something to tell you."

"I'm not interested in anything you have to say. I'd like you to leave now."

She set her glass down on the corner of the table and turned to face him. The expression on her face seemed unfamiliarly sincere. Almost apologetic.

"We are often forced to make choices we'd rather not make if we could avoid them. Some choices are simple, with few or no consequences. Other choices are earth shattering and affect not only our own lives, but those of everyone we touch."

"What does that have to do with…" He paused to wipe his forehead. The room was suddenly terribly warm and even though Serena still stood in front of him, she now seemed very far away. He reached out to anchor his hand against the back of the settee.

"I want you to know I had no choice."

"No choice about what?" He suddenly felt strangely weak. He had to hang onto something for support. His knees would not hold him up.

"Let me help you, Joshua. It'll be easiest if you sit down."

He tried to digest her words but he couldn't think. What was wrong with him?

She came toward him and placed his arm about her shoulder, then led him to the settee and helped him sit.

He wanted to fight her, to at least resist, but he didn't have the strength. It was all he could do to let his body sink down onto the cushions.

"What have you done to me?" His words were slurred and his tongue barely able to form the words in his mouth.

"I'm terribly sorry, Joshua. Please believe me. I didn't have a choice."

"God…damn…you! What…have you…done!"

He brushed his hand across his eyes, desperate to wipe away the blur. He couldn't see. Couldn't stay awake.

"Don't fight it, Joshua. It will do no good."

He tried to struggle to his feet but her small hand held him down. He shook his head, trying to clear it. He couldn't.

"No!" He struggled to stay awake. To remain conscious. He couldn't.

"Allison," he cried out weakly as the world around him went black.

❧

Allison was never so relieved to hear anything in her life as she was the final round of applause at the conclusion of Verdi's *Rigoletto*. Something was wrong. She could feel it in her bones. Knew it to the very core of her. He'd promised to be here by the end of the first act. He still hadn't arrived.

"Montfort will be sorry he missed tonight's performance," Phoebe said as they walked together down the long corridor to the winding staircase. "I thought you said he was coming."

"He was." Allison led the group that included her three sisters and their husbands, and the Lords and Ladies Etonbury and Questry, and the Duke and Duchess of Bingham to the stairs. "Something must have happened. He is probably waiting for us at home."

She walked down the steps, keeping her gloved hand on the railing to support herself. She wished she had asked what was in the message he'd received from Chardwell. What if something had happened to him?

She focused her gaze on the crush of people in the foyer at the bottom of the stairs. Perhaps he'd been so late he decided to wait for them down here. Instead, her gaze rested on the Marquess of Chardwell. A wave of relief surged through her. And panic. He'd sent the message to Joshua. Why was he here without him?

"Good evening, Lady Montfort. Don't tell me your husband has deserted you."

"Didn't he come with you?" A wave of unease washed over her. He'd said the note had come from Chardwell.

The confused look on Chardwell's face told her he had no idea to what she was referring.

"I must have misunderstood. I thought he was with you."

She fixed an exuberant smile on her face and struggled to give the impression that nothing was wrong. "Never mind." She broadened her smile until it hurt. "Did you enjoy the opera?"

*Chardwell hadn't sent Joshua the message. Why had he lied to her?*

The look on Chardwell's face darkened. "I did." He cast his gaze to where her guests stood behind her. "Oh, I forgot," he said with a look of surprise on his face. "Montfort mentioned that you were entertaining. He invited me to join you. I'm not too late, am I?"

Relief flooded her. "No, of course not."

Chardwell was a pathetic liar but she was glad he'd invited himself. He was Joshua's best friend. She was suddenly desperate to have him with her.

If there was trouble, she knew her husband would want him there. If there wasn't trouble... Well, she'd cross that bridge when she reached it.

"I'd be delighted to have you join us."

"Wonderful."

They walked to the entrance and waited as the long line of carriages came forward.

If anyone noticed her unease, they concealed it well. Everyone was in the highest of spirits, their mood enlivened by the performance. She vowed to make Joshua take her again so she could enjoy the performance. His absence had certainly caused her mind to be occupied elsewhere.

She looked down the street and said a small thank you because her carriage was the first to arrive. Another because Chardwell's carriage was next in line. If something were amiss, he would be there to help her.

The ride home seemed interminable, but finally they pulled in front of Montfort House. The niggling fear she'd felt earlier erupted into full force worry. And yet ...

Nothing seemed amiss. Lights shone from every window, and Converse opened the front door the minute she alighted from her carriage.

Chardwell was at her side and held out his arm for her. "Is everything all right?" he asked as they walked up the steps.

"I hope so. I just can't imagine what detained Joshua. He promised he would meet us at the opera."

Together they walked through the open door, the rest of the group following close behind her.

"Montfort is going to receive the first harsh scolding of his marriage," one of the men bantered. The rest of the group laughed at his teasing, but just within earshot she heard Lady Etonbury comment that it would be hard for any woman to stay angry with any husband who possessed such inordinate charm.

Allison ignored their teasing remarks and walked past Converse. Her stride faltered when she saw the serious expression on their butler's face.

"Is Lord Montfort here?" She prayed he was.

"In his study, my lady. He has a guest."

"Still?"

"Yes."

The relief she felt was overwhelming.

"Perhaps your guests would like to go directly in to dinner, my lady," Converse suggested.

She knew his words were a warning, but his suggestion was met with immediate refusals from all the men who wanted a drink before they ate. And from the women, who wanted to hear Montfort's explanation as to what had been so important that he'd missed escorting his wife to the opera.

She took one step toward the closed door, but halted when she saw the desperate look Converse exchanged with the Marquess of Chardwell.

Chardwell stepped forward. "Perhaps you *should* take your guests in to dinner and I will see what has occupied—"

She didn't let him finish his sentence but surged past him toward the closed study door.

Her hand shook as she reached out. Every warning signal in her body screamed for her to turn back, that with a simple turn of the knob she could unleash horrors more devastating than she could bear to face.

Clasping her hand around the knob was difficult. Flinging the door open was even harder. But she turned the knob and pushed open the door. And forced herself to step inside the room.

Her knees buckled beneath her.

Chardwell's hands reach for her but she shrugged them away. She fought the deafening roar in her ears that accompanied the loud gasps of shock from the guests crowding into the room behind her.

Her husband's relaxed body stretched out on the settee. His chest was bare and the top buttons of his breeches were unfastened. His jacket, shirt, and waistcoat, along with his shoes, lay scattered on the floor beside him.

He was asleep, so deep in slumber he obviously didn't hear them enter. Lady Paxton did, however.

With a startled look of surprise, she rolled off Joshua and stood. Her expression was one of innocent nonchalance as she stared without blinking at some of the most influential members of the *ton.*

Strands of her disheveled hair fell over her face. Her flushed cheeks blushed slightly. With a delicate gasp of alarm, she snatched a pale pink petticoat and held it in front of her naked breasts.

An eternity of uncomfortable silence besieged the onlookers. Their gazes shifted from Joshua's prone body, to Lady Paxton's scantily covered breasts, to the mortification chiseled on Allison's face.

Lady Paxton was the first to recover. "I gather it would hardly be worth the effort to deny that anything happened." She looked down at Joshua, still sleeping soundly.

Allison felt herself sway.

Chardwell grasped her by the elbow. "My lady, why don't you—"

Allison jerked her arm away from him and reminded herself to breathe. She didn't think she could. The hurt was too unbearable. She wanted to order Lady Paxton out of her home. But she couldn't do that either. She didn't have the fortitude. She no longer had the will. She could do nothing but flee—because she couldn't bear to look at him any longer.

On legs that trembled beneath her, she walked out of the room. Past her three sisters, each with tears streaming down their faces.

Past her three brothers-in-law, who stood with their arms around their wives' shoulders, as if their comfort could make what they'd just witnessed go away.

Past the Earl and Countess of Etonbury, the countess one of the biggest gossips in all of London.

Past the newly married Marquess and Marchioness of

Questry, who undoubtedly welcomed the diversion from the marquess's indiscretion with Lady Paxton just a week ago.

Past the Duke and Duchess of Bingham, two of the most well respected and influential people in all of Society.

Without a glance back, she made her way across the foyer and to the stairs. Her soft slippers made hardly a sound on the marble flooring, yet each footfall echoed in her ears. When she reached the stairs she clutched her fingers around the wooden railing and steadied herself.

"Oh," she said, suddenly remembering they'd invited guests for a late supper. She turned. "Converse, would you please show our guests to the dining room?"

She turned back and slowly climbed the stairs. "You'll have to excuse me," she said to no one in particular. "I'm not hungry."

# Chapter 18

BLOODY HELL! HE WANTED TO DIE.

Joshua struggled to open his eyes but the second he tried, a sharp pain exploded in his head like a cannon shot. He sucked in a harsh moan, then closed his eyes again. The agony was so intense he thought he'd be ill.

"Lay still, Montfort" a gentle, yet familiar voice ordered. When he tried to move, a strong hand pushed him back against the mattress.

He wanted to drift back into the deep, dark abyss of unconsciousness to avoid the pain, but a gnawing fear told him he didn't dare. He struggled to pull himself out of the pit of terror into which he'd fallen.

"Don't move," Chardwell warned again.

He lay still until everything around him stopped spinning, then opened his eyes a crack. That small effort alone split his aching skull in two. He fell back against the pillow and didn't move. Bloody hell! It even hurt to breathe.

"What happened to me?"

He heard the scraping of a chair over the wooden floor and knew Chardwell had taken a seat next to his bed.

"We can talk about that later. When you're better."

He felt a wave of panic pulse through him. "No," he gasped, trying to force the words into the open. "I need to know what happened to me. I can't remember. I can't… remember."

The room was deathly quiet. Something was wrong. Terribly wrong. He forced his eyes to open. Thankfully, the draperies were pulled and the room was cloaked in darkness.

"What time is it?"

"Eleven. You've been unconscious for nearly twenty-four hours." Chardwell leaned closer. "Do you remember anything from last night?"

"No."

It wasn't easy for him to see Chardwell's face, but even from this angle he could read the worry in his expression. "I was supposed to go to the opera but I received your note."

Chardwell released a heavy sigh. "I didn't send you a note."

He digested Chardwell's words. "Lady Paxton came to see me."

Waves of panic washed over him like tidal waves crashing onto the shore. Each assault building with greater ferocity. Creating more havoc. Causing more destruction.

"What happened to me last night? Where's Allison?"

When Chardwell didn't answer immediately, he swung his feet to the edge of the bed and struggled to get up.

"Lay still, Montfort."

"Help me up, damn it!"

Chardwell helped him to sit on the side of the bed. His head throbbed like there was a meat cleaver embedded in his skull and his stomach rolled until he thought he would be sick. Eventually, the pain eased.

"Would you like something to drink?" Chardwell offered. "Some tea?"

"Serena put something in the drink she gave me." He clutched his hands to his throbbing head. His hands trembled violently, whether from the drug he'd been given or the terror raging through him, he didn't know. "Tell me what happened last night. Everything."

He sat in stoic disbelief as Chardwell related what had happened. What Allison and their guests discovered when they walked in on them.

He'd known it would not be good, but he had no idea it would be this devastating. He thought of Allison and the only promise she'd exacted from him before they married. An unbearable pain pressed against his chest.

"What I don't understand," Chardwell pondered after he'd related every gruesome detail, "is why Lady Paxton did it? Surely she doesn't envision herself so in love with you she wants to ruin your marriage?"

He shook his head. "This wasn't Lady Paxton's doing."

"Then who—" Chardwell's expression turned to shock. "Why? What could your father possibly hope to accomplish by discrediting you in front of the *ton*?"

"Not the *ton*. Allison. He knows about the stipulations included in my marriage contract. He knows the only demand my wife made of me was that I would never embarrass her in front of the *ton*. That if I did, she would get it all. Even Graystone."

He buried his head in his hands. "How my father must hate me."

Several moments of agonizing silence passed before Chardwell spoke. "I left you for awhile this afternoon and went to Lady Paxton's townhouse. I don't know what I thought to accomplish, but… The butler who answered the door informed me Lady Paxton left early this morning for an extended holiday to the continent. He said he didn't know when she'd be back."

"Thereby, making it impossible to corroborate my claim that I'd been drugged and was not awake during our liaison." He wiped the perspiration gathered on his forehead. "Bloody hell, Chardwell. How could I have been so stupid? Why didn't I see it coming?"

He knew there was nothing Chardwell could say. Nothing that would make what had happened any better. The little strength he had left drained from his body. "It doesn't look good, does it?"

"It will seem better when you're rested and the drug she gave you is out of your system. Why don't you get some sleep now?"

"I can't sleep. I've got to talk to Allison. I've got to explain."

"You're in no shape to go anywhere. Just rest. There'll be plenty of time in the morning to face your problem."

A cold shill stole down Joshua's spine. He suddenly realized that Allison wasn't here. "Where is she?"

Chardwell turned his gaze away.

"Where is she!"

Chardwell didn't answer him for a long time, and when he did, he said the only word Gray never wanted to hear.

"Gone."

❧

He took the steps to the Earl of Hartley's townhouse two at a time, then pounded the knocker against the door with enough force to wake the dead. His search for her since rising had been an effort in frustration and a bitter waste of time. He'd spent half the morning going from one of her sisters' homes to the other. Phoebe had at least allowed him to cross her threshold. Although after the dressing-down he received, he almost wished she hadn't. Mary had refused to see him. And Tess met him at the door, but the chilly reception he received was nothing short of blatant rudeness.

Unfortunately, they all disavowed any knowledge of Allison's whereabouts. He didn't believe them.

He stomped his foot on the red brick portico, listening impatiently for sound from within. He raked his fingers through his hair and rubbed his temples to ease the pain that pounded against his head.

He was desperate to see her. Desperate to talk to her, to explain. He knew she was angry with him, hurt by what had happened. He didn't blame her. But if he could only explain, surely she'd understand. Surely she'd believe him.

He reached out his hand again to slam the knocker but stopped when the door opened. The Earl of Hartley stood on the other side of the door.

"Where's Allison?" He stepped past the earl and walked to the middle of the foyer.

"I suppose it would do no good to ask you to leave?"

"None. Now, where is she?"

"In the morning room, but I'm not sure she wants to see you."

"Well, I want to see her." He stepped past Hartley and walked across the foyer.

"Wait!"

He spun around to face the earl. He would fight him if he had to. "You'll not stop me from seeing her. She's my wife and I need to talk to her."

Hartley hesitated as if he wasn't sure what to do. Then, in a visible act of frustration, he slapped his fist against his thigh and took one step toward Joshua.

"Damn you, Montfort. Did you have to embarrass her so publicly? Did you have to bring your whore into your own home, beneath the very roof you shared with your wife? Did you have to let her wait here alone for two days before you came to offer an apology?"

He felt his knees weaken. Is that what it seemed to the world? That he had such little regard for his wife that he'd flaunted his lover in front of her, then abandoned her as if her feelings meant so little to him?

His breath caught. Yes, that's what it seemed. And why should anyone expect anything different? That's how he'd lived his whole life, wild and carefree, as a rogue and womanizer with never a serious thought in the world. No one knew how much he'd changed since he'd married Allison. Even her family.

He opened his mouth to explain himself, but knew any excuse he made would sound hollow and weak. Especially if Serena was no longer in London to corroborate his story. Instead, he clenched his teeth and walked away.

"Montfort, now's not a good time."

He ignored him.

"She has a guest."

He halted for a fraction of a second, then stalked to the morning room and flung open the door.

Allison sat on the settee, her hands clasped in her lap, a look of surprise on her pale face. Her eyes were red and puffy as if it had not been that long ago since she'd shed her last tear. Although she'd always had a hale and hearty complexion, today her cheeks were wan and pale. The large dark circles beneath her eyes appeared even blacker.

His heart ached when he saw her, the pain he'd caused her plain to see. He wanted to go to her and take her in his arms. Wanted to hold her and love her and erase everything that had happened in the last two days. But it was too late to undo the damage that had been done. And from the expression on her face, impossible to take her in his arms. The look in her eyes told him she didn't even want him in the same room with her.

"Please, go away, Joshua."

"We need to talk."

She shook her head. "I can't. I'm not ready."

Frustration got the best of him. "I don't care. You have to hear me out."

"No!" She rose to her feet and stepped away from him. "You've done enough. Just leave me alone."

He closed the gap between them. He couldn't let her shut him out. "Avoiding me won't solve anything, Allison."

"Well, I can't pretend nothing happened."

"Just hear me out." He reached for her, then froze when he heard movement behind him.

The Earl of Archbite stepped into the open. "The lady

doesn't want to talk to you." The tone of his voice was clearly threatening.

Joshua glared at Archbite. "The *lady* you are talking about happens to be my wife."

"That, Lord Montfort, is a regrettable fact. But hopefully one that can be rectified."

"Get out." Joshua's temper teetered on the verge of exploding.

"I believe you were the one Lady Montfort asked to leave. Not I."

He fisted his hands at his side, trying to keep from striking the pompous fool. Archbite's leg was still bandaged, meaning his recovery from their duel had been slow, a thought he didn't find disturbing. "I would not object to finishing the discussion we started near Miller's Pond, Archbite. If that's your intent."

"No!"

Allison's voice sliced through their argument, but neither man paid attention to her.

"Obviously that's the only method you know when it comes to settling a dispute," Archbite said. His shoulders lifted in a paltry show of bravery. "Perhaps if you would have had a little more consideration where your wife is concerned you would not be here begging her to take you back."

He saw red. "You are hardly the person who should be concerned with my wife."

"Someone has to be. Obviously, you're not! The whole of London is abuzz with the scandal you and your paramour have created."

"And of course, you consider it your duty to rush to my

wife's side to comfort her."

"As a friend. Yes."

"How convenient you now have an excuse to seduce another man's wife."

"Joshua! That's enough." The tone of her voice held a hint of desperation. Her words an entreaty.

"I am hardly here to seduce, Montfort. Simply to offer comfort. You are the expert in seduction, the one who inflicted such grievous injury."

He would have struck Archbite except he made the mistake of glancing at Allison. Of watching the pained expression on her face deepen, the hurt in her eyes darken.

"My regret is that I was not successful in stopping you from marrying her in the first place," Archbite continued. "That I was not able to keep you from sullying her good name and reputation."

He wanted to kill him. It was all he could do to keep from wrapping his hands around Archbite's neck and squeezing.

"Get out!" He took a step toward him. "Get out before I kill you!"

"I have no intention of—"

"Hartley!" Gray bellowed. "Get this pompous ass out of here."

Allison's brother wisely stepped through the doorway and stationed himself in front of Archbite. "I think it best if you brought your visit to an end, Lord Archbite. From now on, I will see to my sister's welfare."

Archbite gave Hartley a hostile glare, then turned to Allison. "If you will excuse me, my lady. I will call again tomorrow. If there is anything I can do in the meantime to ease your distress, please do not hesitate to call on me."

Luckily, Allison didn't give him an answer. All it would have taken was one kind word from her and Joshua would have bashed his fist into the bastard's face. Especially when he couldn't get his wife to even look at him.

Archbite stomped from the room, the uneven sound of his boots on the carpet thudding as he left. Hartley followed but stopped at the doorway. "Call if you need anything, Allie." He left the door open.

For an agonizing eternity neither of them moved. They both stood a few feet from each other, yet to Joshua it seemed the distance could have been measured in miles. He kept his gaze on her, at the erratic rise and fall of her breasts, as if she had to remind herself to breathe. At the whitening of her knuckles clenched at her sides. At her pursed lips, her flushed cheeks, the worrisome frown that etched her forehead. But most of all, what disturbed him most was that she refused to look at him. She averted her gaze, looked around him, past him, through him to some obscure object on the other side of the room.

"Allie—"

She held up her fingers to silence him.

Her hand trembled. He closed the distance between them, aching to take her in his arms and comfort her. She stopped him by stepping away.

He raised his hands and lifted his palms outward in surrender then stepped back. She hurt too much to add to her misery. He held his ground, silently waiting for her to make the first move. Utter the first words.

It took a long time, but finally she did. And her words cut him to the quick.

"All I asked was that you not embarrass me in front of the *ton*. That you be content with me as your wife. As your…lover."

"I am. You are all I want, Allison. The only woman I will ever—"

"No! Don't say it. Don't add more lies to your list of transgressions. It was obvious to me as well as everyone who saw you lying nearly naked on the settee that you were not content with me as either your wife. Or your lover."

Her words stopped him short. For a long time he couldn't breathe, let alone speak. When he did, his words seemed painfully inadequate.

"If I told you nothing happened?"

She glared at him with an icy stare then turned her back to him.

"In other words, you wouldn't believe me if I told you that what you saw was not what it seemed?"

"Oh, Joshua! I'm not a fool! What is there to misunderstand about walking in on my husband passed out on the sofa and his lover lying on top of him?"

She clamped her hand over her mouth to stifle a choked sob. "If there was any doubt as to what had happened between the two of you, it was erased when Lady Paxton rolled off your body with her breasts bared for the world to see."

She swiped her fingers across her damp cheeks then spun around and glared at him.

"Dear God! How could you do this to me? To us? All I wanted was…" She stopped as if unable to go on.

"I know, Allison. A husband whose reputation was

beyond reproach."

"Yes! And I was a fool to think you could give it to me. That you were no longer the rake you'd been before we married and could be satisfied with just me. That you would not make me the object of ridicule."

Allison clasped her hands around her middle and turned away from him. "I should have known when I saw the two of you together on the patio that night. I should have known I could not make you want me like you wanted her. I should have known…"

He struggled against the painful pressure that gripped his heart, the ache in his chest that hurt more with every word she said.

"I've already told you. It wasn't like that. Lady Paxton means nothing to me. Nothing!" He stopped, ice water flowing through his veins. "But you aren't going to believe me, are you? You're going to choose to believe the worst."

She swiped her fingers against her cheek again and he knew she'd lost the battle to hold back her tears.

"All I wanted was for you to want me. For me to be enough. I would have done anything, Joshua. Anything."

"You were enough for me, Allie. You are. I never wanted more."

"You must have."

"Allison." He reached out to her. He clasped her shoulders and held her tight. She swung her arms, trying to slap his hands away, but he wouldn't let her go. He didn't want to lose her.

With a cry of frustration, she raised her fists and pounded them against his chest. "Why, Joshua? Oh, why?"

He wanted to hold her to him, but this time she shoved

him hard. Fire shot from her eyes and she glared at him with as much anger as he'd ever seen from her.

"Don't touch me! I don't ever want you to touch me again!"

He dropped his hands and stepped back. The heavy weight squeezed tighter inside his chest. "You don't mean that. If you do, there is no hope for us. I will have lost everything."

She looked at him, her eyes filled with the pain of struggling to understand the nightmare in which he'd forced her to live. And then her gaze cleared. "What is it you're afraid you've lost, Joshua?"

Her voice held more bitterness than he thought she was capable of.

"Me?" she laughed. "Or your precious Graystone?"

He backed up, stunned. Surely she didn't mean that. She couldn't. "Graystone is not worth having if you're not there to share it with me."

He heard the small catch in her voice, the hurt and indecision. "A few days ago I would have given my life to hear you say that. Now, your promises are just words. Empty and false."

Her words punched him in the gut with the force of a doubled fist. He evaluated what she truly meant, then forced himself to admit for the first time that he'd lost her.

"What if I told you that Lady Paxton drugged me to make it appear that we'd had an affair? That I believe my father devised the scheme to destroy me, and Lady Paxton helped him?"

She looked at him as if he'd just spoken blasphemy. "I would think you quite desperate if you had to make up such a preposterous story. And me quite a fool if you expect me to believe it."

He felt the faint flicker of hope die. No matter what excuse he gave her, she wouldn't believe him. Not after she'd seen Serena with him in the garden. And especially after the performance Serena had given the other night.

"Trust me. Please. Just long enough for me to prove I'm worthy of you."

She shook her head.

"I love you, Allie."

She turned on him. "Love! You don't know the meaning of the word. If you did, you would have honored the vows we gave each other. You would have cared enough for me that you wouldn't have made a mockery of our marriage. You would have given us a chance."

"I have given us a chance, damn it! I didn't do what you're accusing me of. Just trust me enough to know that what you saw wasn't my fault."

She looked at him, the expression on her face, the longing in her eyes told him she wanted to. The tears rolling down her cheeks told him she couldn't.

"I have to go now," she said and walked past him to the door.

He wanted to reach out and stop her but he couldn't. What more was there to say? How could he make her believe something he couldn't prove? How could he hope to make their marriage work when her doubts were so plain to see? How could he ask her to trust him when in her eyes it had taken less than two months for him to be unfaithful to her?

"You aren't going to give our marriage a chance, are

you?" he asked when she reached the door.

She straightened. "I already did. You are the one who destroyed it."

# Chapter 19

SHE SAT ON THE CUSHIONED WINDOW SEAT staring out at the garden below but didn't notice the blooming flowers or perfectly manicured bushes. How could she notice anything of beauty when her whole world had fallen apart? She'd managed each hour since she'd walked in on her husband and his lover as if in a fog, every part of her numb and unfeeling. If only she could release the flood of tears dammed behind her eyes until the pain inside her chest washed away. If only she could drown the hurt that at times had the power to take her to her knees. But she couldn't.

There were no more tears to shed. Instead, she sat dry-eyed and emotionless, with her legs tucked beneath her and feigning interest in what was going on around her.

She had an open book in her lap but so far hadn't read a word or even turned a page. Reading held as little interest as talking, or eating, or breathing. Or living.

A part of her died three nights ago and she doubted she could go on if her life contained this much pain. There was a void inside her chest, a gaping emptiness that took every ounce of her willpower to take another breath.

How could a heart that was dead keep on beating? Another painful ache knotted inside her and she pressed her hands against her chest, praying the hurt would go away. Knowing it wouldn't.

She forced herself to focus on the garden outside. Birds still chirped, the sun still shone, and flowers still bloomed in riotous abundance, as if nothing disastrous had happened. As if this were a day as perfect as the days had been before he destroyed everything.

Oh, dear Lord, she wished she could cry. Wished she could scream and rant and rave at this cruel trick of fate. Wished she could strike out at him, yell at him. Make him hurt as much as she hurt. Break his heart as he'd broken hers.

She wished she had such power over him, but knew she didn't. Doubted he even cared.

She leaned her head against the wall and closed her eyes. Her sister's words came back to haunt her. Her warnings that a man would make all kinds of promises when he was in dire need of the money you could give him. Promises he had no intention of keeping once your dowry was his.

How could she have been such a fool?

The door opened, but she didn't have the energy to look to see who was there, nor did she care.

"I've brought you a tray with something to eat," Lynette said, setting a pot of tea and some small sandwiches on the corner of the writing desk.

"Thank you, Lynette. I'll eat something later."

"Like you ate what I left you yesterday? And the day before?"

Allison ignored her concern.

"You have to eat something, Allison. You'll become ill if you don't."

"I know you're concerned, but there's no need. I'm fine."

"At least have a cup of tea."

She tried to smile. "I will later. I'd like to be alone now. I have some letters to write and am nearly finished with this book. Perhaps when I'm—"

"David wants to see you. He wants you to join him downstairs."

"I'm terribly tired. Tell him I'll be down later."

There was a long pause before Lynette said, "It's important, Allison. Joshua's solicitor is here to see you."

The air left her body. "Tell him I'm not receiving guests. Ask him to come back later."

"I can't. David sent me with instructions to have you come down. They're waiting for you in the study. Now, drink some tea and eat a little before you have to meet with them."

Her world shrank around her. The air grew thinner until she couldn't breathe. She tightened her fists around the rose floral cushion beneath her and hung on to keep from losing her balance.

"Here, Allison." Lynette held out a cup of tea and refused to move until she took it.

She took one sip then handed it back, her hands too unsteady to hold it in her lap.

"Is Joshua there too?"

"No."

She braced her shoulders with a bravado she far from felt, then set the book on the cushion and stood. Her legs wanted to crumble beneath her but she took a fortifying breath and forced herself to move.

One by one she made her way to the bottom of the steps, determined to mask her emotions so they wouldn't see how Joshua had hurt her. More determined to hide her breaking heart.

There was only one reason Joshua would send his solicitor.

Her heart thundered in her breast as she made her way across the marble foyer and stood at the study door. Heaven help her. She couldn't face this yet.

The door stood open and she took a deep breath of resolve, praying she could survive this next step. When she entered the room, both men rose. David walked over to her and held out his hand.

"Allison, this is Mr. Graham, Joshua's solicitor." He gave her hand a reassuring squeeze.

"Lady Montfort." Mr. Graham bowed politely. "It is a pleasure to meet you."

She looked at him, vaguely recalling seeing him at Graystone Manor. He was very distinguished-looking, tall and broad-shouldered, his hair tinged with silver, his eyes brimming with intelligence. But what struck her first was his air of confidence. He was an impressive man, a man she could not imagine hesitant on any point.

"How do you do, Mr. Graham. It is a pleasure to meet you, too. I recall you came to see my husband… Lord Montfort at Graystone Manor, but we were not introduced."

"No, Lady Montfort. An omission I'm glad has been rectified. I only wish we were meeting under more pleasant circumstances."

The air caught in Allison's throat and she wiped her damp palms on her checkered muslin skirt. The worry that sat like an anvil on her chest suddenly seemed more burdensome.

"Come in and sit down, Allison." David ushered her to a chair. "Mr. Graham has some business to discuss with you. Would you like me to leave or would you prefer that I stay."

"No, David. Please, stay."

David nodded. "Can I offer you some tea, Mr. Graham? Allison?"

Mr. Graham declined the offer, and Allison shook her head, too.

"Then perhaps we should begin."

Mr. Graham nodded, then opened the dark leather folder he had with him. "As I'm sure you are aware, Lady Montfort, I am your husband's solicitor. Because of recent…events, there are a number of items that need to be discussed."

She swallowed hard, the ache in her chest becoming more painful. The first signs of disaster stared her in the face and seemed to suck her under as if she'd stepped into a quagmire of sinking sand. "This is not a good time, Mr. Graham." She tried to keep her voice steady. "I am quite busy."

"Then I will be as direct as possible. I am here because of the terms of your marriage contract, my lady. Lord Montfort realizes you see the…events that happened as a breach of the promises he made, and intends to see that each stipulation he agreed to before your marriage is met."

It was too soon. She didn't want to face this now. Every demand she'd insisted be a part of their marriage contract flashed before her. The paper she'd forced him to sign as well as the vow he'd given her on their wedding day— that if she ever found him unfaithful he would lose it all. A desperate voice screamed in denial. She didn't want it to come to this.

She lifted her head, jutting out her chin in a show of defiance. "I don't want to discuss this, Mr. Graham. I have not asked my husband to meet the terms of our contract."

"That may be, Lady Montfort. But your husband was quite insistent it be handled today."

Her eyes focused intently on Mr. Graham, trying to interpret his thoughts. He skillfully kept his emotions well concealed.

"This," he said, handing her a paper, "is the deed to your husband's London townhouse. Along with the keys. As you can see, it is deeded in your name."

She stared at the paper as if it was a snake that could bite her. Then she looked at the keys as if they would burn her when she touched them.

"Please, take them, Lady Montfort. They are yours."

She stared at them, wishing them to disappear. Knowing what Joshua was telling her by giving them to her.

Her chest hurt as if he'd plunged a knife into it, but she was left with no choice. With trembling fingers she reached for the paper and the keys, then placed them in her lap.

"And this," he said, handing her a thicker packet of

papers, "is a complete listing of all Lord Montfort's financial assets and accounts. There is an itemized, detailed listing of how every pound of your dowry was spent and the amount still remaining. The balance of your dowry will now, of course, revert back to you, as was stipulated in the original contract, along with other accounts held in the marquess's name. You now have complete control of all the marquess's money."

She hesitated, then numbly reached for the papers Mr. Graham held out to her. This was the bargain they'd struck, the terms she'd insisted upon. This was what she'd agreed she'd get, and he'd agreed to give up. And she knew taking them would change the rest of her life. Would make their separation more irreversible.

"These," he said, lifting a third set of papers, "are the deeds to all other Ashbury properties and estates not entailed. Lord Montfort freed them from debt with the money from your dowry and therefore considers them rightfully yours. The only assets not covered by your agreement are the entailed Ashbury holdings. Those will, when the present Duke of Ashbury dies, pass on to the Ashbury heir."

She was past feeling. She numbly placed these papers on her lap along with the rest. This was Joshua's legacy. This was what he'd sacrificed his freedom to save. What he'd married her to gain. What he'd battled his father to protect. Her heart ached with a pain she didn't know how to ease.

"And this..." He held out a single piece of yellowed parchment paper. "...is the deed to Graystone Manor. It is now yours."

Her heart shattered inside her. He'd given her Graystone Manor. He'd given up the home that meant more to him than everything he would have gained as the next Duke of Ashbury. The only place he'd ever been happy. The place where his mother rested in her grave.

She looked at the growing pile of papers on her lap. At the mounting wealth she'd acquired, and felt physically ill.

"There is one more item to cover, Lady Montfort. This is not a part of the marriage contract but is a special request made by the Marquess of Montfort. First, he agrees in writing that he will not contest your filing for divorce and will agree to whatever reasons you choose to give the courts. He does ask, however, that you wait to proceed with the divorce until you are certain you are not carrying a child."

She couldn't stop the gasp that sucked the air from her. A babe. Joshua's babe. Her hand trembled when she moved it to her stomach. What would she do if she were pregnant with his child?

"If you do find yourself with child, Lord Montfort asks that you wait until the babe is born before you proceed with the divorce. To eliminate any question that the child is Lord Montfort's rightful heir, as well as the future Duke of Ashbury."

She couldn't listen to any more. On legs she prayed would support her, she stood. The papers fluttered to the floor. She left them lay. "I'm quite tired now and would like to retire."

"One more detail, Lady Montfort," Mr. Graham said before she'd reached the door. "Lord Montfort said to remind you that he signed his name to the contract knowing full well the ramifications. He realizes therefore, that there is no choice for either of you."

She remained motionless, trying to stop the panic building inside her from suffocating her. She only had to hold out until she could be alone. "Thank you, Mr. Graham." She took another step toward the door.

"I'm sorry, my lady, but there was nothing I could do once Lord Montfort demanded the terms of the marriage contract be met."

Another surge of pain attacked her. With a nod she made her way to the door. She stopped when she reached the other side of the room and turned.

Her gaze focused on the papers scattered on the floor. Papers that mattered more to Joshua than anything. Estates she'd never seen, money left from a dowry that was more a curse than a blessing, the townhouse where they'd made love the first time.

She stared at the keys the solicitor had given her. "Do you know where he's staying?"

"I'm sorry, my lady. Lord Montfort did not disclose his place of residency."

"What income does he have to live on?"

"I'm not aware of that either, my lady. All I know is that he signed everything over to you. As for any other source of income, I'm not aware that he has one."

She swallowed the lump lodged in her throat and walked out of the room, leaving behind the pile of papers that was the sum and substance of her life. Deeds to homes and estates that were to replace her husband. An astronomical wealth that was to be her substitute for a love she wasn't sure she could live without.

He'd given her everything. Even Graystone Manor. There was nothing more she could take from him.

❦

A week had gone by since Mr. Graham had been to visit her. Or perhaps it had been a month. She wasn't sure. There were no days, or nights, or morning, or evenings. Only never-ending hours filled with pain and longing. And an emptiness that stole from her a will to live.

That was why she was here. She couldn't go on like this any longer. She had to find him.

She stepped out of the carriage in front of the Marquess of Chardwell's townhouse and stared at the imposing front entrance. She wasn't exactly sure why she'd come here. Other than perhaps he knew where Joshua stayed. Could tell her if he was all right.

She'd already been to Joshua's townhouse, the house she'd taken from him by default. She'd pounded on the door, doing nothing but rousing Converse from his bed in the early, predawn hours.

Joshua wasn't there, but then she knew he wouldn't be. He'd made an exit from her life. The keys his solicitor had given her were proof.

*"What if I told you that Lady Paxton drugged me to make it appear that we'd had an affair?"*

His words echoed in her mind. Night after night she'd paced the floor, sifting through what was true and what was a lie. What if he'd told her the truth? What if nothing had happened between them? What if that ugly scene had been a terrible ruse to make it look like they were having an affair? To discredit him? Ruin him? Take everything away from him?

*What if it hadn't been?*

What if what she saw had actually happened? What if he was having an affair and she'd walked in on them? What if he didn't care for her enough to give their marriage even two months before he took a lover?

A fresh wave of hurt and anger raged within her. Hadn't she already seen the two of them locked in a lover's embrace with their arms twined around each other and Lady Paxton's lips reaching for his? Hadn't her sisters reminded her over and over not to believe their lies? That they'd promise you anything—until they got your money?

*Trust me. Please.*

She brushed her hand over her face and nearly turned back to her waiting carriage. There was no mistaking what she'd seen. Joshua and Lady Paxton lying nearly naked on the settee.

But perhaps, just perhaps, it wasn't what it had seemed. If there was any chance he was telling the truth she had to find it. She didn't want to spend the rest of her life without him if he hadn't lied to her.

*"You aren't going to give our marriage a chance, are you?"*

At that moment, she knew she couldn't stop until she'd made every effort to discover the truth.

She walked up the steps and pounded on Chardwell's door until a very grumpy, very surprised, butler opened the door. It was still far too early for any respectable member of the *ton* to receive visitors.

"I need to speak with the Marquess of Chardwell." She didn't give the man a choice as to whether or not he intended to let her enter but stepped through the doorway. She stopped in the center of the foyer.

"Lord Chardwell is not receiving yet," the butler answered in his most haughty demeanor.

"I'll wait."

His eyes narrowed. "Very well. Who shall I say is calling?"

"The Marchioness of Montfort."

His jaw dropped slightly, then he nodded his head. "If you'll follow me."

He led her to a small masculine study that had obviously never seen a feminine hand, and offered her a seat in one of the dark leather chairs flanking the cold fireplace.

"I'll send in tea," he said, his tone a little warmer than before. "Lord Chardwell will be down momentarily."

"Thank you." She leaned back against the chair and hugged herself. She was so very, very tired; so very worried and confused. How would she know what to believe?

The tea arrived along with a footman to light a fire in the fireplace. She welcomed its warmth.

Not long after, the door opened and Joshua's friend stepped into the room.

He'd obviously dressed in a hurry. His sandy blond hair was still slightly mussed, his handsome face still etched in sleep. There was also a faint shadow of stubble on his face that told her he had not taken time to shave. She remembered the feel of Joshua's face when he first woke up. The raspy feel of him against her naked flesh when they made love in the early pre-dawn hours.

Her heart suffered with a lurch.

"Lady Montfort, I wasn't expecting guests so early.

Especially you."

She noticed a sharp edge in his tone but she didn't have the time or the patience to let it deter her. "Is Joshua here?"

"Are you searching for him?"

"Yes."

"I'm surprised."

She lifted her chin and leveled a defiant look in his direction. "Have you seen him?"

He stared at her for a moment, then turned away and walked past her. When he reached the glowing fireplace he turned to face her. "Not since yesterday."

"Do you know where he's staying?"

"You care?"

She lifted her shoulders and glared at him. "Of course I care. He's my husband."

"I seem to recall Montfort saying you no longer wished for him to remain your husband."

She took a deep breath, a painful breath that quivered when she released it. "I'd like to find him, Lord Chardwell. It's important."

He studied her a long time then shook his head. "I'll not let you hurt him again, Lady Montfort. I'm not sure he can survive more."

"You think he's the only one who's been hurt?"

His dark eyes narrowed in anger. "No, you have both been hurt."

She stopped short. A multitude of doubts raced through her mind.

"Did he tell you he'd been drugged?"

"Yes."

"But of course you didn't believe him."

"Why would anyone do such a thing?"

"Montfort thinks his father was behind what happened."

She shook her head, unable to believe any father could hate his son enough to cause such a scandal. Hate him enough to want to ruin him and take everything away that should be his.

But then she remembered the vile scene when Joshua's father had come to see them shortly after they'd returned to London.

Chardwell walked to the long, velvet-covered window and pulled back one panel of the heavy drapery. For a long time he stood with his back to her, his silence an ominous warning. Finally, he dropped the edge of the curtain and turned. "He was not unfaithful to you, my lady. He cares for you too much."

She shook her head, the doubts not willing to go away. Not yet. "You saw them, Lord Chardwell. Did you see something different than the rest of us?"

"No. I saw the same as you. A scene carefully orchestrated to convince us all that he and Lady Paxton were having an affair."

Chardwell poured himself a cup of tea, then leaned back in his chair. "Except, I remained with your husband after the guests left. After you abandoned him. I sat in his room for the fourteen hours it took until he woke.

"And I stayed with him when he became violently ill from the affects of the drug." He took another swallow of tea, then leaned forward and placed his cup and saucer on the table. "And I furnished the two bottles of whiskey it took until he passed out after he'd been to see you and he realized that you'd never believe what Lady Paxton had done to him."

She clutched her fingers around the cushions of her chair until they ached. "What possible reason can there be for Lady Paxton to involve herself in such a scandal?"

"I don't know. And neither does your husband."

"But you're sure nothing happened between Joshua and Lady Paxton."

He shrugged his shoulders. "I am. But you can believe what you want. The choice is yours."

She couldn't fight her way through the turmoil flooding her mind. She felt as if her heart was being pulled from her chest. But Chardwell was right. The choice was hers. And whatever decision she made, it would affect the rest of her life.

She could either take Joshua at his word and trust that he'd kept his vow to be faithful to her. Or she could make the break clean and final, and never have to live with the doubts and fears and mistrust again. Never have to risk that her husband would be unfaithful and live with the humiliation when Society discovered his indiscretions.

It was all a matter of choice. Her choice.

She slowly lifted her head. "I need your help, Lord Chardwell."

The frown on his face deepened.

"I am going to host a ball on Wednesday night. I need you to make certain my husband is there."

His brows arched high. "Why?"

"The reasons are my own."

Chardwell hesitated a long time as if evaluating his decision. Finally he took a deep breath that lifted his broad shoulders.

"I'll try. That's all I can promise."

# Chapter 20

ALLISON STOOD at the bottom of the ballroom stairs and greeted one curious guest after another. There didn't seem to be an end to the steady stream of nobility who'd accepted her impromptu invitation. Joshua's London townhouse was filled to overflowing, which was exactly what she intended.

Every room was packed, from the card room to the dining room to the long gallery. Even the terrace leading from the ballroom was crowded with as many people as could squeeze out there. Not one of the *ton* wanted to miss a single moment of anything that might occur tonight.

All eyes focused on her, watching, just in case the rumors that circulated throughout the room were true and the Marquess of Montfort did arrive. No one wanted to miss her reaction. Miss what promised to be an explosive situation.

The anticipation was nearly palpable, the prevailing mood of the guests growing to a fever-pitched frenzy.

There was a carnival atmosphere in the house. As if all

in attendance knew something was about to happen. Why would the Marchioness of Montfort host a ball when she was embroiled in such a devastating scandal? What would make her so brave as to face the public a few weeks after her husband humiliated her so soundly? What could she hope to accomplish by inviting such a crowd?

*The answer: Revenge.*

The opinion was unanimous. She wanted to humiliate Lord Montfort in return for what he'd done. And she wanted the entire *ton* to witness her husband's debasement.

Those were the whispered comments circulating the room. Consequently, not one of the guests took the chance to venture too far from where she stood. None of them wanted to miss even one second of the spectacle they all knew would fill the gossip mills for weeks to come.

She tried to slow her pounding heart, but as each minute passed without Joshua making an appearance, her nerves raced out of control.

*What if he didn't come?*

She greeted her next guests, the Earl and Countess of Fillmore, with a fixed smile on her face and a false show of bravado. She reached out a trembling hand and said the correct words, even though her legs felt weak beneath her. The roar from the growing crowd was deafening, thundering in her head, threatening to suffocate her. She'd made her choice and she needed all of Society to know what she'd decided.

*What if he didn't come?*

She forced another smile to her face and looked around the room.

As if in answer to her prayer, she heard a collective gasp,

then saw the looks of shock on everyone's face as they lifted their gaze to the top of the stairs. As if on cue, the deafening roar from the crowd quieted.

*He was here.*

She said a silent thank you, then slowly turned—slowly lifted her gaze upward.

He stood there. Every bit as handsome and breathtaking as he'd been the first time she'd seen him. No wonder he'd earned such a scandalous reputation. What woman could resist his inordinate charm?

He'd pulled his dark hair back from his face, portraying every noble feature with stark boldness. His high cheekbones, the severe cut of his jaw, the straight line of his dark, hooded brows—every one of his distinguishing features as perfect as any God had ever created.

But there was a wariness in his gaze, a confusion. A resignation. As if he, too, had come to the conclusion that her reason for wanting him here tonight was because she intended to publicly humiliate him.

He raised his shoulders and lifted his chin.

She knew by looking at him that he would allow it. She could see his willingness to accept his punishment in front of the *ton*.

Then, his gaze narrowed and his intense expression focused on her in warning. She read his mind. Knew his thoughts.

She could do as she willed this once. Because he understood how important Society's opinion was to her. But this would be the final concession he would allow her.

She locked her gaze with his and watched for any reaction. She saw nothing.

His face remained impassive, his long, muscular legs braced wide, his back rigid and straight, his broad shoulders set.

She concentrated on any expression she might see in his eyes, but knew he would reveal nothing.

She would have to make the first move.

With stoic determination, she lifted the hem of her skirts and took the first step.

∽

Joshua watched her make her way toward him, slowly, cautiously, step by step. There were nine steps in all and his heart pounded harder with each step she climbed. He'd never seen her look more beautiful. Never wanted to reach out his arms and hold her like he did right now. Yet, the closed look on her face warned him that his worst fears were about to be realized. He'd known she insisted he attend only because she wanted to publicly humiliate him like he'd publicly humiliated her.

He'd concede to her tonight. But never again. He wasn't sure he could survive the degradation this one time. Let alone again.

All eyes focused on her as she neared him, the looks of anticipation obvious. As if everyone knew what she was going to do. As if everyone expected to see the culmination of one of the biggest scandals in years. The retribution of a woman scorned.

The total humiliation of one of London's most renowned rakes.

Having an unfaithful husband had been her greatest fear. Taking the chance that Society would find out she could not satisfy her husband either in bed or out had been the reason she'd avoided marriage as desperately as she had. And he'd turned her greatest fear into a reality. He'd been the kind of husband she was most terrified of having.

She was almost to him. Two more steps and she would be level with him, standing so close he could reach out his hand and touch her. Oh, how he ached to. How he wanted to place his palm against her soft cheek and have her lean into him. How he wanted to run his fingers through her hair and let its silky weight sift through his fingers. How he wanted to gather her in his arms and hold her because that was where she belonged.

He didn't move. He stood with his hands at his side while all of London remained transfixed on the two of them.

She took the last step and stopped. Her gaze lifted to meet his.

Not a sound could be heard. Not a whisper or a sigh or the clearing of a throat. Not the clink of a glass or the plunk of a violin string or the swish of satin rubbing on silk. Not one sound. No one wanted to miss one word of the exchange between the two.

He waited.

She stepped up to him, standing so close the hem of her gown wrapped around his ankles. He tried to read her face, tried to see through the closed, hooded expression she wore. But couldn't.

"I was afraid you wouldn't come."

Her voice was steady and clear. Loud enough so that no one standing below could miss one word.

"I wasn't given a choice."

"I thought it might come to that. But I had faith Lord Chardwell could convince you."

"I'm not sure I should have let him."

Her brows lifted upward. "Then why did you?"

He tried to smile but wasn't sure how convincing he was. "I don't know. Perhaps because I had to know for sure."

"I see."

She stared at him as if she were searching past the facade that had been such a part of him when they'd first met. Beyond the hurt he was determined to conceal. To the very core of him, where the slightest glimmer of hope stared back at her.

He couldn't stand the torture of waiting to hear her verdict any longer. He sucked in a deep breath and said, "Perhaps you should get this over."

"Very well. But surely you know the reason it must be so public. The reason none of this could be handled in private."

"Yes. I think I do."

She nodded. "I want not only you, but everyone here to know what a tragic mistake I made."

*Mistake. She wanted everyone to know what a mistake marrying him had been.*

Joshua lifted his chin while he stoically waited for the blow he knew was coming.

"I want everyone to know I had a choice to make and chose wrongly."

A weight dropped to the pit of his stomach. Oh, please, he prayed. Just don't let her say she didn't love him. That she never had.

"I want everyone to know the fault is—"

A loud crash interrupted her words. She spun around, her gaze darting to the commotion behind her.

He froze.

A terror unlike anything he'd known before gripped every muscle in his body as his father stumbled toward them. He reached out and pulled Allison safely out of his father's reach.

There was a wild look in the Duke of Ashbury's eyes, his clothing askew, his hair disheveled and uncombed, his face contorted with fury. He staggered near them as if drunk, yet not from liquor, but from a bitter hatred that had left him unstable.

The deep frown on his father's forehead pulled his thick, dark brows together in a menacing threat. There was no sign of kindness or rational thought, but only a murderous look in his eyes.

And a pistol clutched in his hand.

The crowd below gasped. The gathering of women shrieked in alarm.

When Joshua looked into his father's eyes, the duke's intent was obvious.

He saw the hatred. Realized his murderous intent. And knew his father intended to kill him.

The duke slowly raised his arm and pointed the barrel at the middle of Joshua's chest.

Joshua pushed Allison further behind him.

A malevolent smile crossed his face as he moved his finger against the trigger.

"No!" Allison cried out.

Her scream cut through the murmurs from below.

Joshua tried to keep her where she'd be safe, but before he could get a firm grip on her, she bolted from behind him and stood midway between him and his father. Directly in the path of his father's bullet.

"Allison!"

Fear gripped him with an iron fist.

A look of shocked surprise paled the duke's face and Joshua reached to push her away. His father's roar stopped him.

"Stay away from her!"

Another round of sharp cries and loud gasps echoed as the terrified crowd reacted to the scene playing out before them.

His father looked confused, disoriented. His hand wavered as his gaze darted from one side of the room to the other. An angry expression covered his face, a furious look because his plan to kill Joshua had been thwarted by a mere woman.

"Get out of the way!" the duke bellowed, motioning for Allison to step to the side.

Her face lost more of its color but she held her ground. "No."

He swung his pistol through the air. "Move, damn you! Or I'll kill you, too."

Joshua's heart thundered in his chest. "Move, Allison. Go down with the rest of your family. Now."

She ignored him and took a step closer to the duke. "Please, Your Grace. Perhaps we could talk privately." She took another step. "If you'll just come with—"

"Fool!" Ashbury roared. "He's not worth risking your

life to save."

She stopped. "Oh, but he is, Your Grace. He is."

Joshua's heart skipped a beat. The crowd gasped in disbelief.

"Do you think I won't shoot you?" Ashbury waved his gun in the air. "This is your fault, you know."

Joshua struggled against the panic. Against the terror that told him how close he was to losing her. "None of this is Allison's fault. It's mine. Mine alone."

"No! It was her dowry that saved you."

From the corner of his eye, Joshua watched Chardwell make his way toward them. If he could keep his father talking, perhaps Chardwell would have a chance to disarm him.

"I couldn't save it, Father. Haven't you heard? I lost it all."

The demented sound of his father's laughter echoed throughout the ballroom. "You fool! Don't you realize why you're here?"

His father steadied the gun, leveling it to the middle of Allison's chest.

"No, Father. Why am I here?"

"She's taking you back! And she's invited half of London to witness it so there's no mistaking her feelings for you."

The crowd below them murmured in hushed tones.

"Allison has no feelings for me. She—"

"She *loves* you! Anyone can see that. And you love her!"

Joshua turned his gaze to Allison.

*She loved him.*

He saw it in her eyes. He'd known it, of course, but it had never been more obvious than now.

A lifetime of emotion flickered in her gaze as she stared at him, then she took another dangerous step toward his father.

"Allison, no!"

She didn't heed his warning.

"Yes, Your Grace. I love him, and I won't let you kill him."

A fear unlike any Joshua had ever known consumed him. "Allison, step away."

His father ignored Joshua's efforts and waved his pistol, aiming it again at Allison.

"You think you can protect him?" he slurred. "You think I don't have the courage to kill you, too?"

"You are the Duke of Ashbury. I think you are far too noble to harm a woman."

Ashbury shook his head from side to side, then roared a pathetic cry of dismay. "You weren't supposed to take him back."

"I almost didn't," she interrupted. "Until I realized that your son would never break the promise he made me." She looked out over the awe-struck crowd. "The scene I walked in on was a sham," she said loudly. "Lady Paxton drugged my husband to make it look as if the two of them were having an affair." She turned again to face Ashbury. "I'd simply like to know how you forced Lady Paxton to participate in your plan."

A sinister grin lifted the corners of the duke's mouth. "Everyone has at least one secret they'll do anything to keep the world from discovering."

"You blackmailed her?"

"I did what I had to do so *he* wouldn't get everything.

It's Philip's! Philip was supposed to have it!"

The duke pointed his gun again, but his grip was as unsteady as a flag flopping in a windstorm. "You weren't supposed to take him back! He was supposed to lose everything!"

"He'll never lose it. Because I love him. And he loves me."

The gasp from the crowd sucked the air from the room.

She turned. "I was wrong, Joshua. You told me you loved me and I doubted you. I never should have."

She turned again to face his father. "I invited everyone tonight because I wanted the world to know that I love your son."

"Fool!"

His father's composure slipped and Joshua struggled with the riot of emotions that erupted inside him. "Allison, step back."

"I won't let him kill you." She stood firmly in front of the duke.

A look of demented terror filled his father's gaze.

"Why couldn't it have been you? Why did Philip have to die? He was to have it all. Not you."

His father's gun hand lifted and Joshua stepped to the side. Away from Allison.

The gun in his father's hand followed him, and without hesitation, his father fired.

"No!" Allison screamed as she lunged forward.

Joshua tried to shield her but before he could push her out of harm's way, the bullet struck. She staggered backward.

Joshua gathered her in his arms while the room burst

into pandemonium. Wild screams of terror erupted all around him, the roar inside his head adding to the din of confusion. The scene before him turned to a picture of madness. And there was nothing he could do to undo what had happened. He'd failed to keep Allison safe.

"Allison!"

At first she stared at him with a surprised look on her face, as if she didn't understand what had happened.

He pulled her close and held her tight as the color drained from her face. He lifted his hand from her back. His fingers came away dark and wet.

"Why, Allie? It was supposed to be me."

A faint smile lifted the corners of her lips. "It was...my... choice."

She stiffened in his arms as if struck by a stabbing of pain. "Joshua—"

"Shh, don't talk. You're going to be fine. I'll take care of you."

He looked to where his father stood, restrained by Chardwell and Hartley. The duke's wild, demented look appeared more like what he really was; a weak, disgusting picture of insanity.

"What have you done?" Joshua demanded as he lifted Allison in his arms and carried her toward the door.

His father shook his head. "It was supposed to be you. You! Your life for his."

"You fool! Killing me won't bring Philip back!"

Joshua carried his wife past his father. There was no other way to leave the room. Was it possible for hatred to be so strong, so corrosive? He looked at Allison's pale, limp body in his arms and knew it was.

"It should have been you," the duke hissed again with even more bitterness than before.

"I wish to God it had been," he answered, his eyes blurring as tears burned his eyes. He didn't stop but hurried to get Allison away from this madness.

"She wasn't supposed to take you back. You were supposed to lose it all."

"Don't worry, old man," he said to no one in particular. "If she dies, I will."

Joshua carried her up the stairs, his father's voice echoing behind him, the loud demented bellows of a man consumed by insanity.

"You aren't mine!" his father yelled. "You never were. Only hers."

"Only hers!"

# Chapter 21

JOSHUA PACED THE FLOOR OF THE LIBRARY, trying to avoid the worried expressions on Allison's family's faces. They were all there, as well as Chardwell, waiting for the doctor to tell them how seriously she'd been injured.

"Do you require anything, my lord?" Jenkins asked from the door. "More tea?"

He nodded, even though the thought of eating anything turned his stomach. But maybe someone else did.

"It won't be long now, Montfort," Chardwell said, clamping his fingers atop Joshua's shoulders. "She'll be fine. She's a fighter."

"I can't lose her," he said, needing to say the words. Needing someone to know how frightened he was.

"You won't lose her," Lady Fortiner said with confidence. Allison's other sisters agreed.

"I never wanted to hurt her."

"We know you didn't," Hartley said. He had his arm around his wife's waist and held her close.

Each of Allison's sisters stood next to their husbands.

If nothing more had come from tonight's tragedy, the attentive show of concern each husband felt for his wife was evident. Each couple stood with their arms around each other, as if to offer each other support.

Allison would have been happy to see the gestures. She would have tried to use the opportunity to point out to her brothers-in-law how important fidelity was. He suddenly wanted to make the effort for her.

"All Allison wanted was a husband who was faithful to her. Who was satisfied with the love she had to offer and didn't seek his pleasures elsewhere." He paused to look at each of his brothers-in-law. "I think that is all any woman wants of her husband. For the man she married to honor the vows he made before God. For her to be able to wear her husband's name with pride. I know that is what Allison would tell you if she were here."

Tears ran down her three sisters' cheeks. Looks of shame and embarrassment covered his brothers-in-law's faces as they gathered their wives closer to them.

His heart tugged inside his chest. Allison would feel good about what he'd said to her family. She'd feel good to know someone had pointed out indiscretions her sisters were too weak to face.

He turned away and swiped at an errant tear that ran down his cheek. He didn't regret what he'd said. He only wished she were here to hear it. And she would be if she hadn't stepped in front of him to protect him from his father's bullet.

Joshua thought of his father. "Where is Ashbury?" he asked. Not that he cared. Not that it mattered to him one way or the other any more. He simply wanted to make sure he couldn't hurt Allison more than he already had.

"Several men escorted him home," Chardwell answered. "He's been confined to his house with guards posted at every entrance to make sure he doesn't leave."

"Good."

He braced his hands against the fireplace mantle and dropped his head between his outstretched arms.

Chardwell's supportive fingers clasped his shoulder. "Why didn't I see this coming?" Joshua whispered to his friend. "I should have known he'd lost his grip on sanity when he tried to bankrupt the estates rather than allow me to inherit them. I should have—"

Chardwell tightened his grip on Joshua's shoulder. "It does no good to live in the world of 'should haves', friend. You reacted as any son would have. No one wants to believe the worst of their father. No one wants to take that final step until they are forced to."

Joshua stood straight and raked his fingers through his hair. "Well, I don't have a choice now, do I?"

Chardwell shook his head. "After what happened tonight, no one will question what you have to do."

Joshua knew that was true, but it didn't make what was to come easier. "I only wish—"

He turned when the door opened and Jenkins led the doctor in.

"How is she?" he said, crossing the room in long, anxious strides.

"She'll be fine," Doctor Maddox said, straightening his jacket. "Make sure she gets plenty of rest."

"Oh, we will," one of Allison's sisters said through her tears. "We'll take turns keeping her to her bed."

When Joshua turned around, there were tears on everyone's faces, including the men's in the room. "Is she awake?" he asked, already making his way to the door.

Doctor Maddox smiled. "She's waiting for you."

That was all the permission Joshua needed. He raced across the room and took the stairs two at a time. He needed to see her. Needed to make sure she was all right.

He'd come so close to losing her. He wasn't sure how he would have survived if he had. He wasn't sure *if* he could have survived.

He raced to her room and opened the door without knocking. "Allison." He rushed to her bedside. "Oh, Allison."

He knelt at her bedside and gathered her small hand in his larger one. "Why, Allie? Why did you do it?"

She smiled, her grin a feeble attempt to try to convince him she wasn't in pain. Her eyes, though, gave her away.

"I had to. Your father intended to kill you. I couldn't have survived a lifetime without you."

"Oh, sweetheart. You've never been more wrong. I'm the one who couldn't have survived."

She tried to lift her hand to touch his cheek, but she gasped in pain, then lowered her arm. "I should have believed you when you told me you'd been drugged," she said when she recovered her breath.

"My father contrived a very convincing plan. Even I didn't believe he could hate me that much."

"Why? What reason could he have to want to destroy you?"

"He doesn't believe that I am his."

"Surely he doesn't—"

"Doubt my parentage? Yes, I think he does."

He stood to straighten the covers then walked to the window and looked outside. The sun was just rising, beautiful shades of purples and pinks lightening the sky.

"I remember when I was small," he said, bracing his palm against the window frame, "my mother sat me down one day and asked me who my parents were. I was quite young, perhaps seven or eight, but old enough that I'd been taught my ancestry. I was also old enough to remember the tears that streamed down her face.

"I answered I was Joshua Camden, the second son of the Duke of Ashbury. She made me repeat it twice more, telling me before she left not to ever doubt that I was the Duke of Ashbury's son."

"But you don't think your father believes you are his?"

He shook his head. "I think he believes my mother cuckolded him. That would explain everything. Why he never accepted me. Why mother had to escape from him so often and took me with her to Graystone Manor. Why Philip was taught everything and I excluded from even the basic knowledge concerning the Ashbury holdings. Why my father couldn't tolerate the thought of me inheriting everything upon his death."

He pounded his fist against the wall. "Bloody hell, but he must have made her life miserable. And neither Philip nor I were old enough or perceptive enough to realize it."

"You can't blame yourself, Joshua. You were so very young. How were you to know?"

He breathed a heavy sigh. "I don't know. But I wish I had. Maybe I could have done something to make her life a little more bearable."

He walked back to the bed. "Can you imagine how

furious he must be, thinking that all his Ashbury holdings are going to a bastard son?"

"Where is your father?"

"They took him home. He's being watched. You don't have to fear him any longer."

"I'm not afraid," she said, "I'm..." She closed her eyes and took a deep breath.

"You're tired. You need to rest. I'm going to let your family see you for exactly one minute, then I'm leaving orders that you are not to be disturbed."

He leaned down and kissed her, then opened the door to let her family in. They surrounded her bed and made her reassure them several times that she was all right. Just when he was ready to tell them their time was up, Chardwell stepped up beside him.

"You're needed at Ashbury House."

"What happened?"

"They found your father a few minutes ago. The doctor thinks he doesn't have long to live."

Joshua reached out to steady himself. He needed to go to him. He didn't want his last memory of the two of them to be filled with angry words.

"Joshua? What's wrong?"

He looked at the worried expression on Allison's face then rushed to her bedside. "I have to leave you for a little while, but I'll be right back."

The furrows above her eyes showed her worry. "What's wrong?"

"It's Father. Chardwell will explain."

He kissed her tenderly. "Make sure she rests," he ordered over his shoulder, then rushed from the room.

"Joshua?"

He stopped at the sound of her voice and turned back. "Take care."

He smiled. "I love you, Allie."

"And I love you," she whispered.

He took one final look at her resting on the bed, then rushed from the room.

How could he be so lucky to have found her?

His heart thundered in his chest. Someday, if he were fortunate enough to have a son or daughter, he swore they would be surrounded by love. How could it be any different with Allie as their mother?

❧

The sun was beginning its descent below the horizon, turning the sky a beautiful mixture of pinks and blues and brilliant oranges. She'd fallen asleep several times since Joshua left to see his father, but each time she woke with a start. She relived last night's nightmare, only this time she wasn't the one who the Duke of Ashbury shot. It was Joshua. And he didn't survive.

She focused her gaze on the door and waited for the knob to turn. Eventually, it did, and Joshua entered.

His face was drawn and pale, his eyes lacking their usual luster. The forlorn look etched on his face tore at her heart.

"Joshua?" He looked as if the ordeal with his father sapped the strength from his body.

His eyes closed. When he opened them a tear fell from his lashes. "He's dead, Allie."

She extended her uninjured arm and reached out to him.

He closed the gap between them in two long, weary

strides, then grasped her hand and sat beside her on the edge of the bed. "He took his own life. He thought I'd be pleased."

He rose from the bed and walked to the window. The last rays of dying sunlight filtered through the window panes now, the dimness covering the room in a peaceful calmness.

"He thought I would be pleased because I'd have it all, even though he died believing I didn't deserve it."

He turned to face her. "He thought Mother had foisted another man's brat on him. He took his life because he couldn't bear to think of me as the next Duke of Ashbury."

"Oh, Joshua." Her heart ached for him. Her arms were desperate to hold him.

"And yet he loved her. He told me he did. But he refused to believe that she loved him. Instead, he chose to believe some vicious Society gossip."

She couldn't stand to watch him hurt without trying to comfort him. "Come here." She held her arm out to him.

He came to her bedside.

"Remove your shoes. And your coat."

He placed his jacket and his waistcoat over the chair near the bed. Then untied his cravat. When he finished, he sat on the side of the bed next to her and removed his shoes.

"Now, lay beside me."

He shook his head. "I won't chance hurting you."

"I need you, Joshua. I need you and you need me."

He sighed in resignation, then cautiously lay down next to her. He took care not to touch her, but she would have none of it. "Hold me."

He shook his head.

"Hold me," she whispered again, and he gently wrapped her in his arms and held her next to him. There was a little pain when she tucked herself close to him, but not more than she could stand. She leaned closer and kissed the crook of his neck. "Each of us has a choice in the decisions we make."

"I know we do, but how could he choose to believe the gossip of strangers over the denials of the person he loved?"

"It happens all the time. I nearly made that same mistake. I nearly lost you."

"That wasn't the same. You saw us with your own eyes."

"Yes, but I *chose* not to believe you when you told me what really happened."

He hesitated for several moments, then asked the question she knew he eventually would.

"What changed your mind?"

"I was forced to make another choice: I could either believe what I thought I saw and live the rest of my life without you. Or I could choose to believe that you would never break the promise you made me before we married and spend the rest of my life with the man I love."

He lifted his head and looked down at her. "I love you, Allie."

"I know you do. And I love you. We both chose to love each other a long time ago. I just forgot for a little while. But I'll never forget again."

"I know you won't. Because I'm going to spend every day for the rest of my life showing you how important you are to me."

She turned her gaze to the flickering candles lighting the room.

"Tomorrow will be a new day, my love," she said, drawing his lips close to hers. "Perhaps you should begin tonight by reminding me how much you love me."

"It will be my pleasure," he whispered against her lips. "Loving you will always be my first choice of important tasks I need to accomplish each morning when I wake and each night before I fall asleep."

And he kissed her.

*The End*

# *About the author*

Laura Landon enjoyed ten years as a high school teacher and nine years making sundaes and malts in her very own ice cream shop, but once she penned her first novel, she closed up shop to spend every free minute writing. She has written more than a dozen Victorian historicals.

Laura loves to hear from her readers. You can write to her by visiting her web site at www.lauralandon.com.

ALSO BY LAURA LANDON

MORE THAN WILLING
SHATTERED DREAMS
WHEN LOVE IS ENOUGH
coming August 2011
WHERE LOYALTY LIES

CPSIA information can be obtained at www.ICGtesting.com
Printed in the USA
BVOW07s0955270415

397857BV00001B/13/P

9 781937 216092